Enemies In

Enemies In Love

Muriel Mae

The Pentland Press Limited
Edinburgh • Cambridge • Durham

First published in 1994 by
The Pentland Press Ltd.
1 Hutton Close
South Church
Bishop Auckland
Durham

ISBN 1 85821 102 6

In some instances,
the names of characters
have been changed to
protect the family.

Acknowledgement is made to Prisca Furlong
for her contribution to the book.

Typeset by CBS, Felixstowe, Suffolk
Printed and bound by Antony Rowe Ltd., Chippenham

To Stephen Beaumont
whose guidance
has been excellent

CHAPTER 1

It was 1945. The war had been over a few months. For me it was just another routine workday – or so I thought. How could I have known, as I left the house on that autumn morning, that this was the day my world would turn suddenly from dullness into excitement, adventure and ... utter turmoil.

As the door banged shut behind me I hardly noticed the trees in the arboretum opposite our house. I hardly ever did. They were just there. Just as Rosehill Street was just there, to walk down every workday to the main road and the bus stop.

The same old routine. The same old faces and places. Nothing very momentous ever happened around me in Derby. Even the bomb that dropped near us one night didn't bother to explode.

I suppose I had never thought very much about the war at all really. It was a fact of life. Something we lived with. I was a giddy young girl of nineteen and didn't dwell on the unsavoury aspects of life.

No, to me life was for living. Not to be taken too seriously. Life was for laughing with my mates, dancing with anyone, but no-one in particular, and singing ... I was a good singer; always being requested to trill 'A Nightingale Sang in Berkley Square' at our Friday lunchtime concerts in the works canteen.

Yeah, life was definitely for living. Definitely not to be taken seriously. I remember the army trucks that used to turn round our corner, taking all the new conscripts off to war. And seeing the wives. Some of them would be standing there crying as they watched their husbands wave goodbye. I used to think, 'Whatever's Mrs. Whatsit crying for, Mr. Whatsit's a real miserable bugger anyway.'

We got used to rationing and coupons, sharing and swapping. It was a way of life.

When the war was over, we still had rationing, still had coupons. Still feared the Germans. Still had German prisoners of war. There were some in a camp just near us up at Alvaston. We actually had a couple of people everyone said were Germans living in a house near us. There was a lot of talk about how they should have been interned. No-one knew why they hadn't been. I never actually saw them but I used to peer into their windows as I walked past in the hope of catching a glimpse of them. I didn't know what Germans looked like. But I'd heard. I'd heard all the unspeakable words under the sun used to describe them.

If I walked past that house with one of my mates when the war was on, she'd say, 'I bet they're on that transmitter, bloody Jerry buggers.' But, as I say, I never even saw them.

We had a big four-bedroomed house on Rosehill Street where I lived with Mum and my elder sister, Peggy, who was twenty-two. My brother Pete was away in the army and Dad had died back in 1939.

I really loved Dad. He was kind and full of fun, always teasing us kids. He'd been an architect. But, in the First World War, he'd had his right arm shot off and afterwards couldn't get architectural work. He'd got a disability pension and later found work as a nightwatchman. Naturally we lived in pretty reduced circumstances but Dad had a wonderful way of dealing with it. If ever we wanted something he couldn't afford, he'd draw the object and say, 'So you want a bicycle. Here you are, here it is.' And he'd shove the paper into our hands. We'd get so annoyed with him but really laugh at the way he went on, 'You said you wanted a bicycle. Well, there it is. That's the finest bicycle you'll ever see. Just think, it'll never go rusty.' And, do you know, it really did make us think. He was a clever, lovely man.

Ours was a nice house with a good-sized garden. It used to have a fine intricate ironwork fence and gate at the front but, of course, that was requisitioned as soon as the war started. I remember watching through the front window as they dismantled it. Maybe that was the saddest thing about the war that actually struck home to me. As a kid of fourteen I knew our home would never look the same again. But, there again, that thought might have come from deeper down and had more to do with Dad dying that year.

But then life just went on and I slipped from one routine to the next. Always embalmed by strictness and certain moral codes, which I suppose I viewed not so much as major constrictions but rather as annoyances of varying degree to be side-stepped somehow.

First there was the moral discipline from the nuns at the Catholic Convent school I'd attended, with the constant reminder of the four or so places I might end up in – heaven, hell, purgatory or limbo. Always there was Mum's strictness – 'Don't forget you must be in by half past nine. Don't do anything wrong or anything that'll make me ashamed of you. If you ever do that I'll banish you from this house.' She really was terribly strict and watchful over us. I suppose after Dad's death she must have felt doubly responsible for us. I became adept at side-stepping and wriggling out of tight corners, but not without suffering terrible pangs of guilt.

After working in a chemist's shop for a while, I got my papers to go and work at the Royal Army Ordnance Depot in Sinfin Lane.

There I was, year in year out, clocking on and off. And that was where I was bound on that fateful autumn morning in 1945.

Joan was just climbing aboard the trolley bus as I strolled up.

'Come on, Muriel! Not like you to cut it so fine.'

She was right. I was always in good time for the bus.

'It must be early,' I shouted, jumping on behind her and thinking what a good thing it was that Peggy was on the late shift at the depot that day, as it was her who always had to run for the bus. Today she would never have made it.

The bus was crowded as usual. Joan and I stood together near the back. Joan was my best mate. She was three years older than me and worked at the depot too, on the stencilling machine. My main job was hand-stencilling the huge wooden boxes, but I did other things too, like tarring the linings of the boxes. The boxes were filled with spare parts for all the army vehicles abroad.

3

'I heard a rumour that some of the P.O.W.s, up at Alvaston, are coming to work at the depot,' Joan said.

Her words hardly sank in as I felt the trolley bus slowing and a sinking feeling inside me. This was not a scheduled bus stop.

'Blo-ody hell,' Joan groaned for all to hear. The trolley bus stopped. All the traffic behind us stopped.

'Not again. That's the second time this week,' I moaned as the conductor and the driver disembarked and together withdrew the pole from the side of the bus to put back the trolley-wire that had come off. It took them over ten minutes to do this, to the accompaniment of distant honking horns from drivers who couldn't see what was causing the hold-up. They might have guessed it was a trolley bus. It usually was.

But I think none suffered as much as us depot workers aboard. It meant we would be late clocking on. We'd be hauled in front of the charge hand and dressed down for being late. They wouldn't take any excuses, not even genuine ones. They'd had too many in the past to be able to cope. Worst of all, our wages would be docked.

By the time the trolley bus dropped us at the depot gates it was twenty to eight and we were a good ten minutes late.

Joan and I flew past the guard at the gate and towards J shed, almost breaking our necks on the way as we tottered wildly in our six-inch heels. We'd been planning to go out for a fish and chip lunch and were dressed up to the nines under our shapeless heavy denim overalls.

Whoever designed those overalls never had the cat-walk in mind, more likely Madame Tussaud's Chamber of Horrors. We called them our convict overalls. They were navy-blue, had ridiculous small collars, two pockets and a belt with two buttons at the front. And, as I say, they were shapeless.

Yes, shapeless was the word. Even us girls with trim pretty figures felt like drab nonentities dressed in them, hardly to be distinguished from the poor shapeless lumps who looked the same in or out of overalls...or so I thought...

Me, I was only four foot, eleven inches tall. Really tiny. My hair was long and thick, light brown with highlights. Actually it was wonderful hair. I could do anything with it, style it any way I liked and it always looked good.

J shed was enormous. After clocking on I made my way through one of the doorways behind a lorry that was just driving in. That's how big it was. There were two other doors like that with lorries coming and going all the time and conveyor belts with boxes constantly passing along, after coming down chutes from above. I worked by one of the chutes, stencilling all the boxes that came past me on the conveyor belt.

I took off my jacket and shoved it in the bench where I kept my tools. 'Music while you work' was coming over the tannoy. Some of the girls were singing along to 'In the mood'. I soon forgot about the annoyance of clocking on late and joined in too – at the top of my voice. We were a jolly lot. Nothing ever got us down for very long. When you're in a drab place like the depot, doing boring routine jobs, you'd go crazy if you let things get you down. Well, actually we did go crazy, but in a positive sort of way – laughing, joking, composing notes to pack in the boxes for some poor sod abroad to discover ... 'If you are lonely and feeling blue, write to me and I'll write to you', with our names and addresses added.

A few of us had got pen pals that way. I'd had several replies but only wrote to one bloke, called Norman. I don't know why I bothered to write back. Just for something to do, I suppose, and because most of the other girls had these pen pals.

And then of course we'd jitterbug, not in the work area but in the loos where the tannoy was just as loud. The 'ladies washroom' was very large, with about ten loos down one side in separate cubicles, a wide aisle and a row of basins on the other side. We'd often be in there jitterbugging away when the female charge hand came in.

Four Eyes we called her. Not just because she wore glasses but also because she had a knack of finding us if ever we left our work posts for more than a few minutes.

She was only about thirty but really matronly and old-fashioned. She never wore any make-up and her hair was scraped back without style to accentuate her ugliness. The best that could be said about her was that she'd make a good prison warder.

5

Just as I was really getting into the swing of singing along with the music, the tannoy suddenly went off. This happened from time to time and usually meant that an announcement was to be made.

We all looked up and there, through one of the shed doors, a group of about twenty German P.O.W.s were being marched in. There was a guard in front and a guard behind them. Once inside they stood to attention. I stopped work and watched agog. I was so surprised. Not one of them was a seven-foot gorilla-type man wearing jackboots, as I had been led to believe all Germans were.

One of them stood out. I noticed him straight away. He was tall, about six foot, with the most gorgeous thick, black hair. His features were very good, though I wouldn't describe him as handsome, and he had a very nice figure. But there was something more about him. Something beyond his physical appearance; it's difficult to describe. There was this wonderful aura about him which immediately drew me to him. It had something to do with his personality, to do with happiness, jollity, kindness, gentleness and a touch of daredevil, all rolled into one.

They all wore maroon battle shirts and trousers. The shirts had round yellow patches on the backs and there were yellow patches on the trousers too. The one who stood out was also, I noticed, the smartest. The creases in his trousers were razor sharp. He wore his P.O.W. uniform with such dignity it could just as easily have been a formal evening suit.

And then I noticed something else, just as he stepped out of the group to stand beside the guard. He wore a black armband with white letters spelling 'Interpreter'. The guard started giving instructions as to where the men were to work and the interpreter translated. From where I was I could just hear what he was saying. He spoke in absolutely perfect English without a trace of an accent, when he spoke to the guard.

Then the tannoy squeaked into service again and his words were lost to me as an announcement was made over the system. We were told that the P.O.W.s would be working here in J shed and that any fraternization whatsoever with them was strictly forbidden by law. Anyone caught fraternizing would be in serious trouble.

The music started up again and I got on with my work but kept glancing over to the Germans. Once the interpreter caught my glance and smiled so warmly at me that my stomach churned and I immediately looked down, petrified at being caught even smiling at him.

A little later I went over to Joan on the stencilling machine and tapped her on the shoulder.

'Don't look now but those Germans are looking at us. I hope you get one on your machine so that we can have a few laughs.'

'Well, we could do with a few laughs. It's getting worse in here.'

'I like the look of that interpreter one.'

'You'd better stop that thought right there before you get into trouble.' Joan started singing along with the music again and I went back to work. But I didn't sing anymore that day. Or for several days after. I was too busy watching the interpreter as he moved around the shed with a guard. Often he came past me and each time he smiled at me, but I always looked away, scared to death that the guards might see me if I smiled back.

I began looking forward to going to work each morning so that I could see the interpreter. Then one day I decided, what the hell. I would smile back. You couldn't be shot for smiling at someone.

The next time he passed by and smiled at me I did smile back. His eyes lit up and I felt him holding me so tenderly with his look. I was like jelly inside. I had never felt so caressed in my life and that was without any physical touching.

I'd been out with blokes before but had never had a serious boyfriend, never been really attracted to any of them. This German was awakening something in me I had never known existed. I was frightened. Very, very frightened.

That all happened about nine o'clock in the morning. A little later on an announcement was made over the tannoy that us girls could go home at half past ten and finish work for the day, as we would be needed back at nine in the evening to work a late shift. My heart dropped. After today I had four days' leave coming. That meant that after this morning I wouldn't be seeing the interpreter again for an intolerably long time.

'Quick, Muriel! Meet me in the loos. I have to talk to you.'

Joan seemed terribly flustered and I wondered what on earth was the matter with her as I watched her head off to the loos. I waited a couple of minutes, noticed Four Eyes was right down the other end of the shed, and went to join Joan.

She was sitting on the sinks – our favourite and only safe conference place.

'Muriel, what am I going to do? I'm supposed to be meeting my Yank at half past seven tonight. He's coming over from Hilton camp. And now I have to be back here at nine o'clock. Not bloody likely.'

There she was in terrible turmoil and I was in turmoil too. I sat down on the sink beside her. My own emotions were a mixture of thrilled excitement and doom and gloom about my impending temporary loss. I really felt for Joan. I could identify with her plight and the emotions she must be feeling.

'Look, don't worry, love. I'll clock you in at nine. You just get here as soon as you can. You'll have plenty of time to think of an excuse for the guard on the gate.'

'Oh thanks, Muriel. You're a little clinker. I'd do the same for you anytime. You know I would.'

I knew she would. It was great to see the look of relief on her face. I wished my own problem could be so easily solved.

Mum met me at the kitchen door.

'Why are you home so early?'

'Got to work the late shift.'

'Well now, have I got a surprise for you?'

I didn't think I could take any surprises. I'd had enough excitement for one day already.

'Guess who I've got in the front room waiting to meet you?'

I couldn't possibly imagine. I knew who I'd like it to be but I was well aware of the impossibility of that.

'It's Norman. He's just got back to England and been demobbed. Ooh, he's ever such a nice lad, Muriel.'

'Oh no, Mother. I don't want to meet him. You'll have to send him away. He was only a pen pal. I never expected to have to meet him.'

'Don't be ridiculous, Muriel. He's brought you presents and, as I say, he's such a nice lad. Come on now.'

Mum left the kitchen and headed down the hall. There was nothing I could do but follow her.

Norman was nondescript. Nothing about him caught my attention or fancy in the slightest. He was a very unwelcome inconvenience. Poor bloke. I daresay if he had arrived one week before I just might have looked at him twice. But, then again, I doubt it. You see, he really was just nondescript.

He gave me the presents. I thanked him and put them on one side without even looking at them and wondered how I could get rid of him quickly.

'I've told Norman you've got four days' leave due. He'd like to take you to the West Country on the train to meet his parents.'

I just couldn't believe what I was hearing and had to think very quickly. I looked daggers at Mum and then smiled sweetly at Norman.

'Oh, I don't think I'm having that leave after all. They've got a lot of extra work on just now.'

'Yes, it's quite all right love. Peggy phoned the office and they confirmed it.'

What could I do? What could I say? What on earth could Mum see in nondescript Norman that I couldn't?

I was numb. I just sat there and let them arrange for me to go to the West Country with Norman the following afternoon.

I clocked myself and Joan in at nine o'clock that night. The P.O.W.s weren't there. The dull routine work rankled and all the time I dreaded the coming of the following day. I kept looking up, hoping Joan would arrive before she was missed and it was noticed that she had been clocked in. And every time I looked up I wished the interpreter was there. I felt that somehow his very presence would have eased my anxious state.

At half past ten I went to the canteen for my break and a cup of tea.

9

I haven't told you about the canteen yet, have I? What a sorry story. The tea was always so weak it had a struggle to get out of the pot. The coffee was even worse. Nothing there was, strictly speaking, edible. We only ate because we did get very hungry. Joan was always complaining about the food and getting into trouble for it. She had guts. She wasn't afraid to say exactly what she thought to anyone. Me, I was quieter. Always afraid of getting into trouble.

Just as I finished the tea Joan came marching in. I was so relieved to see her.

'I told the guard on the gate I'd overslept. Everything's O.K.'

'Am I pleased to see you. I thought you weren't going to show up at all.'

'Cheer up, I'm here now.'

'Oh Joan, I'm in such a state. That pen pal of mine, Norman's, turned up.'

'Hmm. Judging by the look on your face, that's bad news. What's the matter with him?'

'Well, I suppose he's a nice enough bloke but not my sort. And Mum's only gone and fixed it that I spend my leave with him and his family in the West Country.'

'Great. You might get to like him. You go and enjoy yourself.'

'Well, I've got to go. But I won't enjoy myself. You see, I fancy someone else.'

'Oh no, it's not who I think it is, is it?'

I nodded.

'Blo-ody hell.'

It was time to get back to work. We couldn't chat there any longer. But later, on the trolley bus home, Joan gave me all the sympathy and moral support I so desperately needed.

'Maybe it's a good thing for you to go away for a few days. It'll help you get things in perspective. Treat it as a holiday, never mind the poor bloke.'

'That'll be very difficult, Joan. I just want to be near that interpreter.'

'Umm. Well, at least you've got something to come back for. To look

10

forward to. Think of it that way. But if you'll take my advice you'll be bloody careful.'

'I can't tell you how he makes me feel, Joan.'

'But you've never even spoken to him.'

'No, but we've got some kind of communication. There's something really special there. I just know it.'

'You frighten me, Muriel. It's dangerous talk, that. But look, you know I'll always stand by you, whatever you do. We're mates.'

'Thanks, Joan. You're a real clinker.'

As it turned out I only spent three days away with Norman, not four.

I hardly had a dozen words to say to him on the train journey down to the West Country. He put my quietness down to me being shy about meeting his parents. I was quite happy to let him think that.

Really, all the time I was thinking about the German interpreter. Thinking about the way he had looked at me when I had smiled back at him. That thought made me feel so warm inside. It kept me going and gave me some sort of strength to cope with the predicament facing me in the opposite seat.

Joan was right. Going away was helping me to get things in perspective. But not, I'm sure, in the way she thought. Distancing myself from the interpreter made me suddenly realise something. Something there could be no doubt about. I was falling in love with him.

Those three days with Norman were really just a blur. I met his Mum and Dad. They were nice enough people. Even his brother drove over from the next town to meet me. Who on earth did he think I was, for goodness sake? Norman's girlfriend? I felt as if I was in a false world and, worst of all, I felt false myself. I wasn't really there at all. Norman surely must have sensed it.

On the second morning I bought a post card. In the privacy of my bedroom I scribbled a few words to Joan: 'It's really awful. I don't know what Norman expects but, as you know, my heart is somewhere else. I can't wait to get back.'

Norman and I walked up to the post box together.

'Give it to me. I'll post it,' he said, as we approached the box.

'It's O.K.' I didn't want him to see what I had written and I dived for the box to post it myself.

'Oh no! I forgot to put the stamp on.' It was too late - the card had already slipped from my hand. In my desperate hurry I had made a fatal mistake.

'Never mind. We can come back in half an hour when the postman collects.' He said it in such a cheery way but I was just full of dread.

To kill time we went for a walk and all the while I was so anxious. I knew I had to stop Norman from seeing what I had written on the card. If only I hadn't got so flustered and had remembered about the stamp.

The postman arrived about five minutes after we got back to the box.

'Hello, Norman. You're back in England then!'

'Yep. Good to see you again, George.' He told the postman about my card. I watched the box being opened. There wasn't much in there and I could clearly see my card lying on the side. I pointed.

'That's it.'

To my horror, the postman handed it to Norman, not me.

'Give me the stamp then and I'll stick it on.'

I prayed he wouldn't read it as he stuck the stamp on. He didn't seem to. And then he handed the card back to the postman.

On the walk back to the house Norman seemed the same as ever. I was convinced he hadn't read anything.

'Come on, Muriel. I'm going to take you to the best fruit shop in town,' Norman said to me the next morning.

To me that seemed rather an odd place for him to want to take me. But we went. There he bought me two beautiful pears and two of the best apples. He put the bags in my hands.

'There you are,' he said, 'these are for your train journey home this afternoon. And now I'll take you back to the house and help you pack.' There was no change in his voice or manner, or expression, or anything. It was only the third day. The day before I was due to return home.

I felt awful. And yet I was so relieved.

And then I had to face Mum. No sooner was I in the door than the questions, demanding tricky explanations, began. Oh, I was clever. I'd become quite a conniving little so-and-so. It was the only defence against Mum's barrages. The practice certainly stood me in good stead for future months.

'What on earth are you doing back a day early?'

I just looked at Mum standing there so nice and neat in her good costume and good pearls. She never wore anything that wasn't real. She didn't have a lot of jewellery but what she had was genuine. Her hair always looked nice too. She was an honest, straight person all the way through. So I looked at her and thought, how can I lie to her? But I did. And I felt terrible about it. I certainly didn't feel clever, or like deceiving her, poor Mum.

'Ooh, it was awful, Mum. You know that Norman's actually got a girlfriend down there?'

'No. I don't believe it!'

'Yes, really he has. It's all over between us, Mum.'

'But he seemed such a nice young man. And very keen on you. Are you sure he's got a girlfriend?'

'Oh yes. These things go on, Mother. Shame really, he was quite a nice lad.'

I went upstairs to unpack, leaving Mum in the hallway looking quite mystified. Norman was never mentioned again.

I was so keen to get back to work I got to the bus stop about quarter of an hour earlier than usual. I was in a dream with the image of the interpreter and his smile so clear in my mind. I knew I would smile back at him again today and longed to feel his tender look on me. Inside I was all fluttery in excited anticipation and yet, at the back of my mind, an unwelcome little voice was telling me, 'Be careful, Muriel. This isn't right. It's dangerous.'

Joan wasn't at the bus stop but Grace was. She was an older woman who worked at the depot. Always talking she was. About the war. About 'them Jerry buggers'. The sort of talk that usually wafted over me. It was

13

like a kind of background mumble I heard from so many people who wanted to let off steam.

Today I didn't want to have to listen to her. I wanted to concentrate on my dream. Then, suddenly, her words were no longer a mumble in the background. They began striking hard into the core of my soul.

'Them Jerry P.O.W.s want putting up against a wall and, do you know, Muriel, I'd shoot every one of the bastards.' She was looking at me so intently. There was real hate and determination in her eyes.

'Umm, I know,' I said innocently. But I thought, 'My God, does she know about me? Has she heard somehow that I fancy the interpreter?'

These and more terrifying thoughts swept through my mind in a flash. Suddenly I was consumed by panic and guilt. Maybe she did know, maybe she didn't, I started reasoning, but knowing there were millions more like her around with such hatred for the Germans just made me painfully aware of how I must keep absolutely secret this love growing inside me. I knew there were few people I could trust. Then I saw Joan approaching and my anxiety eased a little. I could trust Joan.

To my delight the interpreter was practically the first person I saw in J shed that morning. He was standing not far from my chute with his guard, Doug.

Our eyes met only for a moment but I felt as if we were holding each other in an embrace for all the world to see and looked away quickly.

Funny. Doug was smiling at me, I noticed. Something told me Doug knew the German and I fancied each other and, what's more, he seemed to approve. Most of the guards hated the Germans and treated them brusquely but Doug was different. He was actually a very nice bloke. He'd often have a joke and a laugh with us girls when the other guards weren't about.

Doug and the interpreter moved off to another part of the shed and I began singing along with the tannoy music. I felt really happy. Really special. If you'd asked me two weeks before I'd never have put J shed down as the best place on earth to be. More like the worst. But today it was definitely the best. The only place I wanted to be.

The interpreter and I smiled at each other once or twice more that morning, whenever he happened to pass me.

'That Doug keeps looking over at you,' Joan said in the canteen at coffee break. 'When you were away he asked me, "Where's that little one?" I said you were on leave for a few days. Then he asked if you had a boyfriend. I told him you were one who courts 'em all and doesn't bother with any of 'em. Do you think he fancies you?'

'No. He's married, isn't he?'

'Maybe, but he's certainly showing a lot of interest.'

'I think he knows I fancy the interpreter.'

'Oh Muriel, for God's sake be careful. You really are playing with fire. I've warned you.'

'I know. But I can't help it. I think I'm falling in love with him, Joan.'

'But it's impossible. You can't go with him. He's a prisoner, for God's sake, always under guard.'

'All I know is how I feel. And I can't do anything about it.'

Joan looked at me pityingly. We both knew it was an impossible situation. And yet I wasn't in any way depressed about it. I was just full of excitement and that special warm feeling you have when you really fancy someone you are in close proximity to.

As soon as I got back to my chute Doug came over to me on his own. 'Hello. You're back then.'

'Yes.'

'I think your mates have missed you.'

'Who, Joan?'

'No. One of my mates ... that interpreter, Werner.'

It was as if I had been struck by lightning. Suddenly everything became so real. My feelings were real, not just a silly dream and the interpreter had 'missed me'. He really did have feelings for me. And he had a name – Werner. No longer was he the interpreter. He was Werner.

'Here you are. There's a letter for you.' Doug slipped something in the box I was stencilling and went on his way.

I pulled a small sheet of Izal toilet paper out of the box. It was covered in tiny, immaculate handwriting. Shaking like a leaf I read it.

'I've been watching you. I'd like to be friends. Would you

15

meet me near the bridge at Raynesway at 8.00 p.m. tonight? If you are agreeable please nod twice when I pass. Please destroy this note, you know you must be very careful and I don't want to get you into trouble.'

A million thoughts rushed through my mind, and I was in an emotional turmoil. Should I meet him or shouldn't I? I desperately wanted to be with him and yet ... the consequences ... and, anyway, how could he get out of the prison camp? ... What if we were caught? ... What should I do? ... Should I nod?

I needed time to think. I needed to talk it out with someone. I went over to Joan and asked her to meet me in the loos.

Five minutes later we were sitting on the sinks and Joan had read the letter.

'What should I do, Joan?'

'Well, flush this down the loo for a start.'

'Oh no, I want to keep it.'

'Don't be daft. You might get searched by the gate guard when you leave here tonight.'

I hadn't thought of that. The guards often did spot checks when we left the depot to make sure no-one got away with anything. Some of the blokes tended to pilfer spare parts and some of the girls took light bulbs. You could virtually guarantee if you were in a hurry when you were leaving you'd be hauled up to be frisked by an A.T. S. woman. There was one guard who particularly enjoyed hauling in as many workers as he could. We called him 'Misguts' and he really was the worst, one of those miserable people for whom authority goes to their heads.

'No, I really want to keep it. I know, I'll roll it up in my hair.'

I had curled my long hair in big rolls round my head that morning. Now I let one of the rolls down and carefully rolled it up again with the letter inserted safely.

'I still think you should flush it down the loo, you're taking an awful risk.' Joan jumped off the sink, 'Quick! Get in the loo, I can hear someone coming.'

I rushed into a loo and stood on the seat so that my feet couldn't be

16

seen underneath the door.

'Have you seen Muriel?' I heard Four Eyes ask Joan, who was washing her hands.

'She was heading down to the store shed a few minutes ago.'

I heard them both leave the washroom and a few seconds later I went over to the Main shed store and got a new stencilling roller. Then I went back to work. We hadn't had time to discuss what I should do. But I thought, if Werner comes past now I will nod, I really want to be with him.

Unfortunately Werner didn't come past for over an hour and by then I was all jittery and indecisive again and I didn't even dare look up at him.

Then it was time for lunch. Joan and I puzzled over the contents of the note in a quiet corner of the canteen. Mainly we wondered how Werner could possibly get out of his prison camp to meet me.

'I shouldn't worry about his side of the problem. Obviously he can get out or he wouldn't be arranging it.'

I could see the sense of that. But it still left me with the problem of whether to go or not.

'Look, if you want to go, go. Whatever happens I'll stand by you. Just don't expect me to go with you!'

About half past four that afternoon Werner came past me for the umpteenth time. It wasn't long until home time. I had to decide now. Suddenly I looked up at him, smiled and nodded twice. His face lit up and I looked quickly away. I was a bundle of nerves. What had I done? There was no turning back now. A little later Joan came over to me.

'You've nodded, haven't you?'

'Yes.'

'I can tell. Just look at him, he's all smiles now. You want to watch out he doesn't take advantage of you.'

That thought hadn't even occurred to me. I didn't let it penetrate too deeply now.

'Can you come to the loos and do my stockings for me please, Joan?'

17

It was a very effective trick us girls had, to cover our legs with gravy salt and then draw a crayon line right up the back of the legs so that it looked as if we were wearing seamed stockings. If I was going out tonight I'd better start getting prepared. I went over to my tool box for my packet of gravy salt and a dark wax crayon. Joan laughed and we went off to the loos.

Four Eyes must have been watching us like a hawk because she came into the loos for a second time that day. Of course we heard her coming. We knew her elephant-type walk very well. Unfortunately Joan had only completed one of my legs. I dived for the loo and she started washing the brown off her hands. In came Four Eyes.

'Yuck, whatever's that you've got on your hands?'

'Oh, it's the ink from that damn stencilling machine again.'

'Can you get it off all right?'

'Yeah. Won't be long.'

Four Eyes left and I emerged from the loo. Very quickly Joan did the other leg for me.

At home time I was one of the first to leave. I had a lot to do if I was going to be ready in time to meet Werner at eight. I rushed past the gate guard, seeing the trolley bus already waiting.

'Not so fast, Miss. Not so fast.'

I stopped dead in my tracks and turned round to see Misguts crooking a horrible fat finger at me. My stomach turned and I thought, 'Oh no, this is it. Now I'm in trouble.'

An A.T.S. girl frisked me quickly. She didn't even touch my hair. I thanked God and jumped on the trolley bus just as it was pulling away.

I sat right at the back and carefully withdrew the letter from my hair and read it again. Suddenly it occurred to me that it would be nice to get a little present for Werner. So I got off the bus a few stops further on and went to the chemist's. The chemist, Mr. Wallace, was a cheery soul. He'd just finished serving an old lady as I came in.

'Have you got any Brilliantine?'

'Yes, my ducks.' He had a wicked twinkle in his eye.

'It's for my brother.'

'Oh, I see. I've got two kinds. Which would you like?' He let me smell both and I chose the one I thought was the nicest. I had no idea which Werner would prefer.

'That'll do.'

'That's nine-pence then.'

Next I went to a sweet shop and used my coupons to get some caramels. I never ate sweets myself but I guessed Werner would be pleased with them.

When I got home I rushed up to my room and hid my letter in the left-hand side of the chimney breast. Then I quickly wrapped up the presents and slipped the little parcel into my coat pocket.

Mum had the tea waiting as usual and called me down to come and have it. It was boiled potatoes, carrots and spam, gourmet food compared to what our canteen served up, but I couldn't eat a bite.

'Whatever's the matter with you, are you ill?' Mum asked as I picked at the food and pushed it round my plate.

'No, I'm just not really hungry. Joan brought a cake into work and I ate quite a lot,' I lied.

She seemed satisfied with this explanation but if she had known the turmoil I was really in she'd have had something to say about it all right. I left the table to go upstairs and wash my hair.

'I'll have hers,' Peggy said. 'Not like her to be off her food.'

Getting ready to go out didn't have the calming effect on me that I thought it might. I was still a jittery bag of nerves, petrified about what I was doing.

After I'd washed my hair I got a little sugar from the kitchen and dissolved it in hot water to make a setting lotion to comb through the hair before curling it. You only needed a tiny bit of sugar or your hair became too stiff and sticky.

'You've just about wasted all your sugar ration doing that, you daft girl,' Mum said. She was reading the paper and only half noticing what I was doing. I didn't answer her back. I wasn't in the mood for any kind of conversation or possible argument. I just went upstairs again, combed the solution through my hair and put in the dinkie curlers and pipe

19

cleaners.

I was already dressed in my navy-blue pin-striped costume and white blouse, with tie-bow and a nice pair of six-inch heeled shoes. But I had some time to wait while my hair set. I lay on my bed and tried to read a book. I saw the words but I couldn't take them in. All I could think about was Werner. The way he smiled at me that made me feel so good ... and the danger I might be getting into with him.

I got up and looked around for the 4711 eau de cologne. I found the empty bottle in Peggy's room. I'd heard her leave the house a few minutes earlier. She was going out with her Army boyfriend tonight. She wasn't there to ask but I guessed she wouldn't mind if I searched her drawers for some kind of scent. We always shared things together. With coupons we'd both bought a couple of nice outfits each, which meant we had four to share between us.

All I could find in her drawers was a bottle of lavender water. That would have to do. I put some behind my ears and on my wrists.

I wanted to be in good time to meet Werner so I planned to leave the house at half past seven. Glancing at the clock I saw that it was that time now. I quickly brushed my hair and put on my coat. Then I rushed down the stairs. In doing so I felt my right heel give way underneath me.

'More haste less speed' was one of Mum's favourite quotes. How right she was. The heel had come right off the shoe and in a near frenzy I rushed back to my room, routed out several pairs of shoes and finally settled on a pair of square-toed black patent leather ones with five-inch heels.

Down in the hall Mum gave me her usual interrogation and lecture.

'Where are you going?'

'Just over to see Joan.'

'What, dressed up like that?'

'We might go out for an hour or two.'

'Well, you know to be back by half past nine or ten. No later than ten.'

'I know. I will be, Mum. Bye.'

'Try and make it half past nine. I like to lock the door at half past nine. Don't do anything to make me ashamed of you.'

And then I was on the bus. I was longing to be with Werner and still that longing was mixed with the most awful trepidation. What was it Joan had said? 'You want to watch out he doesn't take advantage of you.' I thought about that now and knew why I hadn't been too worried about it when Joan had said it. Even though I hadn't even spoken to Werner yet, I knew I could trust him. It was that 'something' about him which I can't describe but which I had noticed the first time I had seen him. I was sure I was right. Yes, I was certain he was a good, decent man whom I could trust.

So why was I so jittery, literally trembling as the bus dropped me off at Raynesway? I walked slowly along towards the bridge.

The chill air didn't make me hurry, as it normally would have done. Here, with the open fields either side of me and the stars far away in the night sky, I felt completely alone, at the mercy of whatever fate had in store for me. And I had no idea what that was.

Then I saw a tall man in a pale-coloured, shiny raincoat that shone in iridescent patterns as he walked towards me. I had expected to see Werner in his P.O.W. uniform but suddenly I realised this man in the raincoat was him. I caught my breath. Stopped. And waited for him to get to me.

CHAPTER 2

And then he was standing in front of me, smiling down at me as I trembled inside. He had a fresh clean smell. That was just one of the things I took in about him in those first seconds. That, and his wonderful warm smile which told me everything about the way he felt about me. He took my hands in his and held them, still smiling so tenderly.

'Hello, Muriel.'

I couldn't speak. I just held him in my eyes. He must have known how nervous I was. My hands were like ice because of the chill night and because I'm sure the blood had stopped pumping inside me. Gently he stroked my hands with his thumbs, just for a few seconds as he held them. His fingers were long and soft and by the way they touched me I knew he was a sensitive man.

Just having him say my name thrilled me. It had the same effect on me as Doug telling me his name was Werner. Somehow it suddenly made everything so real.

'Shall we walk?' he asked, gently letting go of my hands. I was sorry to lose this physical contact so quickly and yet relieved to be released, because those moments had been so intense. I needed time to think, to sort out my emotions. Maybe he felt the same and that's why he let go and we started walking. Then I found my tongue.

'Let's walk down to the London Road and along there. Do you know these roads at all?'

'Oh yes. I know everywhere around here. I have studied the area from the back of the army truck they cart us around in.'

'I see. Well if we walk that way it'll be walking towards my home. I have to be in by half past nine, Mum's very strict about what time I get in.' He turned and smiled down at me then, in an almost fatherly way.

'Mothers are like that!' The way he said it was rather as if he had some sympathy with mothers. He seemed so tolerant and understanding.

'So how did you manage to get out of the camp then?'

'Ah! I have a very good friend in Doug, my guard. He has a German girlfriend. A young fraulein. I write his letters from him to her in German and in return he helps me. He gave me this mac. Also he conveniently left some wire clippers in my bed which one day I used to cut the camp fence. Just a small section so that I could crawl underneath and then replace the wire netting so that no-one would notice.'

'But what if you get caught?'

'For myself I am not afraid. What could be worse than being a prisoner of war? ... Well, I could be put in solitary confinement. That would not be very pleasant. But it is worth the risk. To be with you it is definitely worth the risk!' He looked down at me again with that wonderful tender smile that made me feel so special. Then he went on, 'Of course, I am very careful. I don't want to get Doug into trouble.'

Werner wasn't nervous about talking to me at all. But I was still trembling and glad that he seemed to like talking. There was so much I wanted to know about him.

'Whereabouts in Germany do you live?'

'In Kriftel. It is a village near Frankfurt, not far from the beautiful Hoffein forests. Have you heard of the Hoffein forests?'

'No.' I wasn't even exactly sure where Frankfurt was.

'Ah, they are truly beautiful. We have many cure houses there. I think, in England, you call them convalescent homes. My father works for I.C.I. Chemicals and I was training to be a teacher before I was conscripted into the Germany army. I didn't see much of the German army. I became a prisoner within the first six months of war.'

'And you've been in camps ever since?'

'And I've been in camps ever since. First I was in Belgium. I tell you, Muriel, it was terrible there. Do you know, I was wearing the same clothes I was caught in for three months and unable to wash at all. And the food. Ach, it was terrible, what little there was. You know I was really glad to come to England. If you have to be a prisoner of war nowhere is good but England is much better than the camps I was in in Belgium.'

I suppose it was hearing about the dreadful conditions he'd had to suffer that made me suddenly remember about the presents I'd bought for him. I took the little parcel out of my pocket and pressed it into his hand.

'Here, there's a little present for you.' We stopped walking and he turned to face me. There was such a soft expression on his face.

'Shall I open it now or later?'

'Later, back at the camp.'

'Thank you, Muriel.' Now he took my hand in his and squeezed it. We continued walking along, holding hands and with him talking mostly and me listening, until we got to the pub at the bottom of Bateman Street which was about a five-minute walk from my house.

Several people were coming out of the pub as we stood under the lamp with him holding my hands in the same way that he had done when we first met that evening. We must have looked like an ordinary courting couple to anyone else. For a moment I forgot he was a prisoner of war and that this was an illicit liaison. Certainly Werner was totally unconcerned about the fact and perfectly relaxed as he asked me:

'Do you have a boyfriend?'

'No.'

'That's good. Do you think we could meet again then?'

'Oh yes! when?'

'Well, on Saturday Doug is on duty and I can get out until about eleven in the evening.'

'Where shall we meet?'

'Here, if you like. Shall we say two in the afternoon?'

'Yes, fine.'

'Goodbye then, Muriel, take care.' He turned to go.

'Werner?'

'Yes?'

'How will I know you got back safely?'

24

'If I'm in another shed in the morning I'll send Doug with a message.'

'Thanks ... be very careful, Werner.'

'Of course.' There was that lovely smile again, this time tinged with a sparkle of daredevil. And then he was gone.

I felt so happy, so full of expectation as I walked back to the house. Werner was such a kind, gentle person. Again I thought of Joan's warning, 'You want to watch he doesn't take advantage of you.' He hadn't even kissed me. But his eyes, his smile, his looks had caressed me so much, just as they had done in J shed. It was thrilling to take things slowly like this, thrilling and tantalizing.

The next morning I caught the trolley bus to work as usual. Joan wasn't there but hers was the first face I saw in J shed, beaming away wickedly at me.

'Hi! I got the petrol bus this morning, missed you. I hope you remembered what the date was last night!'

We all used that phrase on girls after they'd had a date with someone. It meant you should remember the date for nine months hence. Joan came over and joined me at my chute.

'How did it go then? Bet you had a bit of snogging.'

'No, we just held hands and that was it.'

'Oh blimey, there must be something wrong with him.'

'No, I think he saw that I was ever so shy.'

'You! Shy! What, singing at the top of your voice with the tannoy the way you do when he's not around? Shy? That'll be the day.'

Four Eyes was advancing then and so Joan went back to her stencilling machine. Werner was nowhere to be seen and I began to feel anxious about him. By eight o'clock I was imagining the worst and then, to my relief, Doug came in. After talking to one of the women at the other end of the shed he came over towards me. When he said, 'All's well', I felt as if a ton weight had been lifted from me.

By half past ten I still hadn't seen Werner. I guessed he must be working in Main shed. Peggy worked in there so I decided that, after my coffee break, I'd come back through Main shed and have a word with her

25

in the hope of seeing Werner.

Sure enough Werner was there. But he was standing with two guards and a group of P.O.W.s interpreting something, so I daren't look directly at him. I went over to Peggy.

'Hey, what do you think of that interpreter, Werner, over there?'

Peggy glanced at him quickly, 'Just like all the rest of them Jerry buggers, he wants shooting.'

'No, he doesn't. He's ever so nice. You don't know him.'

'And I don't want to, thank you very much. Ever so nice? Bloody hell, Muriel, have you gone stupid? Go and get back to your work.'

I felt it was Peggy who was stupid, and all the other people who tarred all the Germans with the same brush, condemning them without even knowing what they were like. They were human beings, just like us. And Werner was quite definitely the loveliest male human being I had ever met.

'By the way, you took the last of the 4711 last night and left none for me.'

'Well, what did you want it for?'

'I had a date too...with Werner.'

She looked at me then. Straight in the eyes. 'I don't want to hear about this, Muriel. It's disgusting. You'd better drop him now or I'll make it my business to tell Mum.'

'If you do I'll never speak to you again.' I gave her the same penetrating look she had given me and then I went back to J shed. I wasn't afraid of Peggy's threats. I knew how to handle her. We had one thing in common: Mum's strictness. Peggy was just as much in need of an ally in the house as I was when the barrages started.

Later that day, I was just leaving the canteen and returning to my chute past some stacked boxes when Werner suddenly appeared beside me. For just a second he squeezed my hand and said, 'Thank you very much for my present.' I looked up at him quickly and there was that same soft expression I had seen when I first placed the parcel in his hand. And then in a panic I looked around. Fortunately there was no-one about who could have seen us.

On the Saturday I met Werner at the bottom of Bateman Street. He had his mac on again and was there waiting as I rushed up. That morning I'd seen that there was a good Betty Grable film on at the Gaumont cinema.

'Would you like to go to the pictures?'

'Well, yes, but I haven't any money and I don't want you to pay for me.'

'Don't be daft, its only ninepence. Come on.'

I gave Werner the money and he bought the tickets. We sat up in the circle and the first thing I did when we sat down was kick off my shoes. The heels were so high they were making my feet ache.

I really enjoyed the film and I know Werner did too because I was watching the expression on his face a lot of the time. And then, every so often, he'd whisper to me. Like the time when the film was showing a luxury banquet in a big house where champagne and caviar were being served.

'One day, when I am no longer a prisoner, I will take you to something like that,' Werner whispered. And somehow I knew it wasn't just an idle comment. I knew he meant it, that, one day, he really would take me away from Derby and show me the kind of life I had never even imagined before.

When the film was over I felt around with my feet for my shoes. I found one but the other had vanished. Werner helped me to look for it and he finally found it in the front row, where it must have been kicked down. He was laughing.

'Is this something all English girls do in the cinema - kick off their shoes, I mean?'

'Oh no. It's just that my feet were aching.'

'O.K. Just as long as I know it isn't a custom I must get used to - searching for shoes after films!'

I laughed too then and wondered if English girls were really so very different from the German girls. Maybe we were just the same, with the same hopes and feelings. And yet I'd always been led to believe ...

Oh well, the war was over now, anyway. Here I was with Werner and we were laughing and having a wonderful time. It was so good to be together.

After the film we walked up the street and I asked Werner if he was hungry. I thought he must have been, because I was starving.

'A little.'

'Come on then, let's go in this café.'

'But I don't want you to spend your money on me, Muriel. Look, you go in and I'll wait outside for you.'

'Don't be so daft. You're coming in. Come on. What would you like to drink? Beer? It's not too strong. I think you have to have about thirty glasses to feel any effect.'

'Anything then.'

I bought a beer for Werner, a coffee for myself and two spam sandwiches. Then we went and sat at a table where Werner had his back to the door and I could see everyone who came in. To my horror, a group of squaddies came in and I must have looked visibly nervous because Werner picked this up and looked round casually at them and then back at me.

'Muriel, don't worry. You have to act naturally. If you are nervous they will sense it and wonder why.'

I was amazed at his own calmness and as he talked and laughed I began to forget about the danger too.

He ate his sandwich quite quickly and I knew he must be very hungry.

'Here, have this one too. I'm not a bit hungry,' I lied.

'No, you eat it.'

'No, really, I couldn't eat a thing. It'll only be wasted.'

'Well, in that case ...' It was good to see him enjoying himself.

Much later he walked me up to my house. It was about nine o'clock and I asked him to come in for a cup of tea, knowing Mum would be out at my aunt's for the evening until about eleven o'clock and only Peggy would be in. Deep down, I wanted Peggy to meet him so that she could see how nice he was.

'No, I won't come in. It might cause you some trouble.'

'It's only my sister, Peggy, in there. It'll be O.K. Mum's out 'til late.'

'I'd better not. I really don't want to get you girls into trouble.'

'Come on. You're coming!' I practically dragged him into the house and parked him in the front room while I went to check who was in.

I found Peggy in the kitchen, making a pot of tea.

'Want a cup?'

'Yes, please. And could you pour one for Werner too?'

Peggy almost dropped the kettle. 'You haven't brought that Jerry here?'

'Yes. He's in the front room.'

'You bloody little fool. Well, he can have a cup of tea and then you get him out of this house. I shan't tell Mum this time. But let me catch him in here again and I will.'

'Shut up. He might hear you.'

'I don't care if he does or not. He's only a Jerry bastard, isn't he?'

'Oh please, Peggy.'

She softened a little and went quiet. And then she carried the tea-tray through to the hall and poked her head round the door of the front reception room.

'Come on, Werner. Come and sit with us in the lounge for a few minutes and have a cup of tea.'

I was so surprised, she actually sounded as nice as pie.

'Look, I don't want to get you girls into any trouble.'

'It's all right,' Peggy said as she led the way into the lounge. 'Mum won't be back until eleven.'

We all sat and drank our tea without talking much. Then I had an idea of how to lighten the atmosphere.

'Would you like a tinkle on the piano, Werner?'

'No, I think I'll give it a miss. I only play the violin a little. My parents insisted I had lessons but I was never very good.'

'I'll play then.' I sat down and gave a quick rendition of 'A Nightingale Sang in Berkley Square' with two fingers.

Afterwards Werner smiled at me and stood up. 'That was nice, Muriel. But I think I had better go now.'

Clearly he couldn't relax. Maybe he had heard what Peggy had said about him in the kitchen. I had never seen him looking so uncomfortable and decided it really was time for him to leave. Together we walked back down to the bottom of Bateman Street and stood under the lamp, talking for a while.

'I won't be able to get out tomorrow because Doug isn't on duty.'

'Oh, that's a shame. When can we meet again then?'

'Thursday night?'

'That's a long time.' For a split second I wondered if Werner wasn't as keen as I was for us to be together again soon. What happened next cast that doubt out of my mind immediately. He pulled me towards him, smiled down at me in that beautiful, tender way of his that I loved so much, and with equal tenderness he kissed me. Then, quickly, he let go of me and walked away, almost as if he thought he had done something terribly wrong. For another anxious second my heart sank. But he stopped and looked back at me. There was such love in that look he gave me as he waved goodbye and I knew there was a bond between us that was so strong it could surely never be broken ...

On the Thursday at work Joan mentioned that she and her Yank, Tex, were going to a dance at the Assembly Rooms that evening. I really envied her being able to carry on a normal courtship, doing the things all young couples liked to do, without having that nagging fear at the back of the mind which I always had when I was out with Werner. It would be so wonderful to be able to go dancing with him. As I've said, to me, one of the best things about life was dancing. I just loved it. And I'd won medals for my ballroom dancing.

Then, when I opened my tool-box, I got a real surprise and my heart leapt. There, staring up at me, was a little hand-made, heart-shaped brooch. It was made out of some kind of thin metal and was engraved with the words, 'No can do' and was attached to a card with kisses printed all over it.

I didn't have to guess who it was from. 'No can do' was a popular song that was always coming over the tannoy - 'No can do, no can do, my

Mamma and my Pappa say I no can do, but the moon, she say come out, come out tonight, I want to hold you tight'. Werner had given it to me, knowing we were going to go out that night.

That little brooch and all the love that I knew came with it just thrilled me. I suddenly thought, 'What does it matter that our courtship isn't exactly normal, that we have to be so careful all the time? What does it matter when the love between us is so strong? Nothing else in the world can possibly matter so long as Werner and I love each other and can be together sometimes.'

A little later Doug came past me. I was still looking at the brooch.

'You got your brooch then?'

I felt myself blushing to the roots of my hair.

'If you're at Raynesway at eight thirty Werner'll be there,' With that Doug headed out of the shed.

'Blimey, you don't half blush, you know.' Joan had been standing nearby and watching.

'Meet me in the loos, Joan.' A daring scheme was just hatching in my head and I needed to discuss it.

We sat on the sinks and Joan had a look at the brooch.

'They're clever, those Germans, aren't they? There's no telling what they can do. And they're hard workers, I'll say that for them. You know how they make these things, Mu? Doug saves all his toothpaste tubes for them to use. He was telling me about it the other day.'

'Joan, I want to take Werner to the Assembly Rooms dance tonight. Where do you think I could get him some civvies?'

'Where do you think? Your Pete's got a wardrobe full of clothes, hasn't he? He's about the same size as Werner I'd say ...'

'But how can I get 'em out of the house, with Mum always watching me like a hawk?'

'Wear 'em, love. Wear 'em over your dress and under your coat. Hey, it'll be great we can go as a foursome. We can trust Tex. I've already told him about you and Werner and he's very sympathetic. Look, Werner can change in the loos at the Assembly Rooms. Loads of people go there straight from work and change into their dancing gear when they get there. He can put his P.O.W. uniform in a bag and I'll give it to Mary, my neighbour who serves the teas there.'

'Do you really think it'll be all right then?'

'It'll be great, Mu. We'll have a really good laugh.'

I was walking on air for the rest of the day. In the afternoon I went over to have a chat with Doug, who was standing on his own by the door, and I told him I was going to take Werner to the dance.

'Bloody hell, don't take him there! There'll be bloody Army blokes galore there!'

'No, it'll be all right, Doug. They're all from Normanton barracks that go there. They won't know him.'

'Hmm. Well, it's up to you, but if he doesn't arrive back in the camp I'll know what's happened.'

'Oh, it'll be all right.'

After tea at home I went into Pete's bedroom and had a look in the wardrobe. Mum must have heard the characteristic creak of the wardrobe door because the next thing I knew she was shouting up the stairs, 'Muriel, what are you doing in Pete's wardrobe?'

I'll swear she had eyes and ears in the back of her head. I had to think quickly now.

'I'm looking for a pair of thick socks. My feet were that cold in the shed today.'

'Well, why are you looking in the wardrobe? You know he keeps his socks in the chest of drawers. Mind you don't take his best pair.'

I quickly grabbed a shirt and a pair of grey flannels from the wardrobe, shut the door noisily and then went to the chest of drawers and opened that noisily to get out a pair of socks.

Back in the bedroom I put on the shirt over my dress and then looked at the trousers. I knew there was no way I could wear those. Holding them up against me they came well over my shoulders. So much for the plans of the utmost simplicity! There was nothing for it. I would have to wrap them and the shirt in a parcel and carry them. But how to get a parcel past Mum? I would have to throw it out of my window and pick it up off the lawn after I left the house. So that's what I did. I took off the shirt and wrapped it in a parcel with the trousers and threw it out of the window.

I heard the soft thud. And then I heard the footsteps coming towards my room.

To my relief it was Peggy who came in.

'Something's just landed on the lawn. Has it got anything to do with you? I heard you in Pete's room. I don't want you supplying any Jerry P.O.W. with my brother's clothes.'

'What you don't know, you don't have to worry about, Peggy. Look, I'm going out and I won't be back 'til after half past eleven. Will you help me by putting the ladder up to my window?'

'Putting the ladder up to your window? I've never heard anything so daft. Anyone could come up that ladder, burglars or anyone!'

'Come on, Peggy. When have you ever heard of burglars round here? In London maybe, but not round here. Oh, go on. Please help me or you know what it'll be like if Mum catches me coming home late.'

No-one's life was worth living when Mum was in a fury, as Peggy knew only too well.

'Oh all right ... I'll do it this time. But never again.'

I caught the petrol bus up to Raynesway. It fairly sped along and in no time at all I was with Werner. The first thing I did after he kissed me was look at his feet.

'What sort of shoes have you got on?'

'These black ones Doug got for me.'

'Lovely, they'll do fine. We're going dancing tonight, Werner.'

'Dancing? That's good. But maybe I don't dance the same way you English dance. I might be noticed.'

'Don't worry about it. Just follow me. I'll tell you which steps to make.'

'All right then, *mein klein liebling*, I'll follow you.' He was looking down at me with a teasing sparkle in his eyes. I could see he was as excited about the evening as I was. He really was game for anything, another one like me believing that life was for living.

33

We caught the trolley bus for the twopenny ride back into town. At the Assembly Rooms I packed him off to the Gents to get changed. When he came out I looked at him, really stunned. He looked so good in those civvies. It was as if they had been made for him and I knew he'd fit in anywhere. We sat and had a cup of tea while we waited for Joan and Tex to arrive. I couldn't take my eyes off Werner.

'You look smashing in those clothes, you know.'

'Now I pass as an Englishman, yes?'

'Yes, definitely. Or a Dutchman. A lot of Dutch come here dancing...and Americans.'

Soon Joan and Tex arrived. Joan took the parcel and gave it to her friend at the tea bar and Tex shook hands with Werner. He was a stocky, red-faced, very jolly man, always laughing and making jokes.

'Good to meet you, pal. We'll have a darn good night tonight. God-darn it's thrilling what you two are doing.'

For once Werner seemed lost for words but he laughed along with Tex and I could tell he liked him. We found a table and sat down to talk for a little while before dancing.

'It's fantastic, it really is, what you two are doing,' Tex went on, as if he couldn't get over it. 'Anyway, you didn't cause the war, pal, did you? And neither did I. I can tell you I didn't want to have to come over here to war. No way ...' and then he looked at Joan and put his arm round her. 'But I'm glad I did now, or I wouldn't have met Joan.'

'Yes, and because of the war I met Muriel.' Werner looked at me with that special smile.

I felt so happy. Things were going so well. I wished there were more people around like Tex, who had accepted Werner right away. Then we started dancing. We danced for hours and it was wonderful. Werner quickly picked up the English style. I had forgotten all about him being a P.O.W. Then Joan called over to me.

'Tex and I are going to have a cup of tea. Do you two want one?'

'No thanks, we had one earlier.'

Werner and I carried on dancing and I could see Joan and Tex over at the tea bar, but because of the distraction I hadn't noticed that this dance was an 'excuse me'. Suddenly a Navy bloke came and tapped Werner on the shoulder, wanting to dance with me.

'Excuse me.'

Werner didn't understand what was going on. Didn't know what to do. He just stood there. I couldn't explain to him or the Navy bloke would have been suspicious. Thank heavens Joan was watching all this. She caught Werner's eye and beckoned to him to go over and join them, which he did.

In those seconds all my fears and anxieties came flooding over me again and I found I could hardly lift my arm up to place my hand on the Navy bloke's shoulder.

'Whatever's the matter with you? Lift your arm up a bit.'

'Oh, I'm sorry. I'm not a very good dancer.'

'You seemed to be doing all right with that civilian. Has he been in the forces?'

'No.' I began to panic. This was becoming like an interrogation. 'Do you know why?' I asked, playing for time so that I could think up a convincing excuse for him.

'No. Why?'

'He's got a medical. He's medically unfit.'

'Hm. He doesn't look unfit.'

'Oh he is, love.'

I almost charged for our table as the dance ended. I wanted to get out of that place and quickly. Werner, Joan and Tex must have seen the panic in my eyes.

'Sit down,' Joan said, 'Just relax.'

'No, I think we'd better leave.'

'If we leave now he'll know there's something suspicious going on. Don't look now, but he is watching us.'

'Werner's right,' Tex said. 'Carry on having fun and you'll be fine.'

So we had a few more dances but I was still a little uneasy and after about an hour Werner and I left.

He was singing a song in German, just very softly to me, as we walked to the bottom of Bateman Street. And he said such beautiful things to me that night as he kissed me under the lamplight.

'It was a wonderful evening, Muriel. Thank you. You know you mean everything to me now. Nothing else in the world is important to me. I'd do anything for you and I will guard you with my life, *mein klein liebling.*'

I felt so safe, so protected and loved, being held there in his arms. I wished he could always be by my side and that there wasn't that awful barrier between us caused by that stupid war. And yet I knew that no barrier could really stand between us, not when our love was so strong and we were so determined to be together. Then he was talking again.

'You know I fell in love with you the first moment I saw you?'

'What, with me dressed in that dreadful overall?'

'It wasn't the overall I fell in love with. It was the girl underneath it.'

We laughed and he kissed me again then. After a long time I broke away from the kiss and looked up at him.

'I wish you were a free man, Werner.'

'You know, I used to think about escaping to Ireland and getting back to Germany that way.'

'Oh, don't do that. That's too dangerous.'

'There is no point now. Now I have you. I couldn't leave you behind, *ein suss, mein klein liebling. Du biest mean klein liebling.*'

'What does that mean?'

'It means you are my sweet one. My little darling.'

'And what was that song you were singing as we walked down here?'

'That was from an opera, it is called *Oh Dona Clara*. Roughly translated, the words are "Oh, Dona Clara, I have seen you dancing this night. Your fascination stole my heart away ..." You are my Dona Clara, Muriel.'

I didn't want to leave him that night but it was getting near the time he had to return to his camp.

'Won't your mother be angry you are so late back?'

'No. Peggy'll let me in. She'll have told Mum I'm in bed. Mum never bothers to look.' That last bit was true but I daren't tell Werner I had to climb a ladder to get in. I didn't want him worrying. I was worried enough about it myself, being petrified of heights.

36

I'd left the back gate unlocked so that I could get in easily but, when I got there, I found it had been locked again, which meant I had to climb over it. I could have done without that. It was about five foot high and no easy task to climb for someone of my short stature. First I had to throw the clothes parcel over. As I jumped down the other side I jarred my foot quite badly and was really worried in case I couldn't climb the ladder. But somehow, miraculously, I managed it. I just didn't look down and was so relieved when I crept in through the window.

I flung my coat on the bed and started getting undressed. Then one of the floorboards creaked underneath me. Would you believe it! That was like an alarm bell to Mum.

'Is that you, Muriel? What are you doing out of bed?'

'I've just been to the bathroom, Mum.' I dived into bed in case she was just about to come in and, as I did so, I felt something soft and furry under my hand. I screamed. It was my aunt's cat. She and the cat were staying with us that week and if there was one thing I hated it was cats. That did it. All the lights went on and in came Mum.

'Whatever's the matter with you?'

'It's that damn cat in here again.'

Mum came over to the bed and picked up the cat. All the time I had my eye on my coat, petrified Mum would see it on the bed and more questions would start. But for once she didn't even notice it. She was more interested in the cat. She just took it outside, whispering consolingly to it.

'What's that silly girl been doing to you then?'

About an hour later I suddenly remembered I'd left the clothes parcel on the lawn where I'd thrown it over the gate and for the rest of the night I hardly slept a wink, knowing I'd have to be up really early to remove it and put the ladder away before Mum got up. Mum was an early riser!

At half past five I crept downstairs and outside. Everything was fine until I came back in again. With the parcel in my hand I carefully avoided the third stair - the one that always creaked - only to step on the fourth and to my horror discover that that one had also developed a

37

creak.

'Who's that? Is that you, Muriel?'

'Yes, Mum. I've just been to get an aspirin. I woke up with a headache.' I rushed up the stairs and into the bathroom before Mum could materialize on the landing and see me with the parcel. But she didn't bother to come out of her room so, a little later, I crept into Pete's room, took about five minutes carefully opening the wardrobe door so that it wouldn't creak and replaced the clothes.

CHAPTER 3

That Friday wasn't a good day for me. After such a wonderful evening with Werner, with all the fun and love we'd shared, the things that happened that day seemed sent to jolt me, to wake me up to the reality of the really nasty side of human nature - and the potential danger for Werner and me.

It started off all right. I saw Werner early in the morning, soon after clocking on. He must have been waiting for me because when I walked past the high-stacked boxes there he was. No-one else was about so he gently touched my hand and whispered, 'It was wonderful last night, Muriel,' and then he was gone, back to Main shed, where he remained for the rest of the day.

I was in good spirits, naturally enough, as I started work, singing along with the tannoy happily. Joan kept glancing round at me and I knew she wanted to hear what had happened after we'd left the dance. I thought I'd leave her guessing for a while, especially as Four Eyes was hovering. But after half an hour I went over to the stencilling machine. I was bursting to tell her how much in love we were, how gorgeous Werner had been.

'You don't have to say anything. It's written all over your face. I just hope you remembered the date last night!'

'Don't be daft, Joan. Yes, he was really lovely and he said the most beautiful things to me. He told me how I mean everything to him and that he'll guard me with his life ... but I'll tell you now, Joan, if and when I get married it'll be in white.'

'Pull the other one!'

'No, really it will.'

She looked at me sideways then and laughed in her good-natured way.
'Well, knowing you I can believe that. Yes, I do believe it.'
'Ouch. What was that?'
'What?'
'Something hit me on the face. Probably something off your machine.'
My cheek was smarting a bit but I didn't take too much notice of it.
'Tex and me ... ouch ... bloody hell, Muriel!'
Joan held her hand to her face and looked up to the gangway above where several P.O.W.s were loading boxes onto the chutes. I followed her glance. There was one German standing there, smiling all over his face and holding a pea-shooter in his hand. He was a huge, bulky, thick-set man with brown curly hair. The expression on his large square face made him into just about the ugliest man I had ever seen, as it changed from a smirk into a sneer full of malicious spite. That look struck me with the very fear of God. Then, what he did next made my legs go like jelly. He held up a large piece of card with 'MURIEL' printed in large letters on it. He walked up and down for what seemed like an eternity with that damn card, probably it was only thirty seconds, then he turned away and got on with loading the boxes.
'That bugger wants reporting. I'm going over to the office.'
'No, wait, Joan. I think he must know about Werner and me – why else would he hold up that card like that? If we report him I have an awful feeling he'll make trouble for us.'
'I think you're right, but you'd better watch him. Did you see that mean look on his face?'
'Don't remind me. It just about scared the living daylights out of me.'
I went back to my chute, still trembling. The music on the tannoy was just a hazy sound to me now as I worried about how the German might have found out about Werner and me. But I wasn't so preoccupied as not to notice that uncharacteristic crashing sound. I jumped backwards in the nick of time as one of the heavy wooden boxes came hurtling down towards me, having missed the chute altogether. Joan came rushing over.
'Are you O.K.?'
'Oh, Joan ... it could have killed me!'

'It must have been that mean-looking German again. Look, you'll have to report it, Muriel. It's got beyond a joke now. You really could have been killed.'

'I know. But I just can't ... what if ...?' I was shaking like a leaf. I couldn't even think straight.

'Look, the best thing we can do is tell Doug about it. He might be able to handle it without causing any trouble for you and Werner.'

'I don't know.'

'Next time I see Doug, I'll tell him.'

At coffee break Joan and I sat talking about whether we should tell Doug or not. I was still trembling and Joan kept telling me I looked as white as a sheet. But in the end I managed to persuade her not to tell anyone. I was more frightened about it being found out about Werner and me than I was about any possible danger to myself. Werner meant everything to me and I honestly felt that I'd rather lose my life than lose him. Joan, I'm sure, understood me, perhaps better than anyone else could have done. There can be few mates people have in the world who would support them the way Joan supported me. Against her better judgement she went along with my wish that we should keep quiet about the incident. Until lunchtime ...

After the coffee break two or three of us girls were standing with Joan at the stencilling machine. Joan was being really funny. She had so much personality and could dissolve people into fits of laughter just with a word. I'm sure she'd engineered this little gathering to help get me out of my state of shock. She'd almost succeeded and then Sid came over.

Sid had been a merchant seaman until he'd become partially disabled and had to take a job at the depot. I don't know if he'd always had a nasty character or if it was his disability that had given him some kind of complex which resulted in him being really insolent and unkind to everyone he spoke to – especially women. But then I think of my father, and how gentle and kind he always was, despite losing his right arm. No, I think Sid was just born nasty. He gave us his usual mouthful when he came over.

'Where's them bloody stencils I've been waiting for? If you bloody bitches'd stop gassing you might bloody get some work done around here. You know what's wrong with you frustrated old maids, don't you? You'd rather have a bloody Jerry in the bed than under the bed, wouldn't you? Wouldn't you?' He leered at us with all his bad teeth showing.

'You've got an evil little mind, you have,' Joan told him. 'You have to make up these things because ...'

She stopped there, not able to quite bring herself down to his level of unkindness. Madge, an older woman, thought the sentence deserved to be finished, though. She'd taken more obscenities from Sid than most.

'... Because you're jealous because no-one would look at you twice.'

They all continued bantering but I'd had quite enough. Again a spasm of panic had hit me. Did Sid know too? Was that what his snide remark about the Jerry in the bed had been all about? For God's sake, did everyone know about Werner and me? I was probably over-reacting. At the back of my mind I was aware of that. And yet I went back to my work very uneasy. I couldn't take much more of this. But there was more ...

At lunchtime Joan suggested that we went over to the Main shed canteen so that we could see the Friday concert. I went over to my tool-box to get my jacket. Opening it I nearly died of fright and screamed as a kitten jumped out with two rattling cocoa tins tied to its tail.

'Oh my God, the buggers!' Joan was looking directly at a group of P.O.W.s who were leaning over the gangway laughing at me. 'That's so cruel. Now that's what you call rotten, dirty, Gestapo swines. They're the ones you can't trust.'

She grabbed me by the arm and led me out of J shed. I'll never forget the look on the ringleader's face. It was the same man with the pea-shooter, who had thrown down the box. That cold sneer, so full of malice and hatred, just filled me with fear and haunted me for several weeks after.

Nasty little incidents like that continued for a couple of weeks but none were ever as serious as the falling box and we never again thought of reporting the German. It was not pleasant to find an empty poison bottle with the skull and cross-bones on it in a box, and other such things, calculated to un-nerve me. The German had made it quite plain what he thought about me. I just hoped that one day he would tire of reminding me or else move on to another shed to work. As it happened the latter occurred first. They never let a group of prisoners work in one shed for long – moving them around lowered the risk of liaisons and fraternization taking place.

That Friday concert wasn't very good. Most of the entertainers were booed off before they even got going. There was a really horrible atmosphere everywhere at work that day and I was glad to go home in the evening. At home I could look forward to the following day, Saturday, when Werner and I would be together.

We met at the bottom of Bateman Street as usual and decided to go to the museum. But first we went into the Wardwick Café for a cup of tea. I didn't tell Werner about the horrible German. I didn't want him worrying and, anyway, just being with him took away all the fear I had experienced the previous day. It was like being in a different world, being with Werner. Here, everything was good and happy and healthy.

We left the café just as a group of squaddies were coming in. I thought I recognised some of them from somewhere and, with utter horror, I suddenly realised they were from the depot. Werner and I had previously arranged that, if ever he was in danger of being caught, we would act as if we weren't together so that I wouldn't be incriminated. Now I just carried on walking and crossed over the street, hoping against hope that Werner hadn't been recognised and would follow me. When I was a safe distance away I looked back and my heart sank. The squaddies were talking to Werner. I knew that was it then. He'd been caught and he'd be sent away to another camp where I wouldn't be able to see him again.

Not really knowing what to do with myself, I went into the museum. I looked at some fish in a tank. The only thing I remember thinking was that they were like Werner, poor things, always kept in captivity. Then I went over to look at some pictures and photographs. I haven't a clue what they were of. I haven't a clue what I was thinking about. I just felt so alone and I felt the rest of the world didn't give a damn. And then ... I felt two hands placed on my shoulders from behind. At first, just for a split second, I thought I was going to be arrested. And then I felt the electric charge of love that was transmitted to me from that touch. I turned with tears in my eyes to see Werner.

'It's all right, Muriel. They're some mates of mine.'

'Mates? But they're from the depot!'

'Yes. They just told me to behave myself and get back to camp in good time! I tell you, Muriel, I could never have got away with that in Germany. I know what the expression "True Brit" means now.'

Later in the week I met Werner in the evening, up at Alvaston. It was a very dark, cloudy night with no stars. We decided we'd just go for a walk. I didn't have to be back by half past nine because Peggy had agreed to put up the ladder for me.

It was lovely walking along in the quiet darkness. All there was in the world was Werner and I. Or so it seemed ...

Suddenly I saw a flashlight in the distance and could just discern that it was a policeman holding it. In a panic I grabbed Werner's arm.

'Wern, Wern!'

The next thing I knew he had picked me up and thrown me over the four-foot privet hedge that we were standing beside. I landed with a thud but wasn't hurt. It had happened so quickly and with such surprise I hadn't had time to tense my body. Then Werner jumped over after me. He pushed me right underneath the hedge and wedged himself under it too. I had a nice, light-coloured camel coat on and it crossed my mind that it must be filthy now. But that was the least of my worries. The flashlight was getting closer and I could literally hear the policeman breathing in the cold night air as he flashed it along the hedge and at the exact spot where we were lying. How he didn't see us I'll never know. I'm sure God must have been on our side. When he'd gone by, I made to move but Werner whispered, 'Stay still.' So I did. A little later the policeman came back again, flashing the light all along the hedge. Again he didn't spot us. We continued to lie there for a good quarter of an hour, until we were sure he had gone, and then we ran across the back gardens of some houses until we came out near the railway line. At one of the houses a wretched dog started barking.

'Oh God. Do you think that policeman'll hear that dog, Werner?'

'No. We are far away now. We are safe.' He bent down and kissed me.

We walked through the graveyard nearby and past a big old house with boarded-up windows.

'When we were kids we were told this house was haunted by a grey lady. We always used to peep through the boarded windows to see if we could catch a glimpse of her.'

'Have a look then. Perhaps you will see her tonight. Or is one scare enough for you for one night?'

We laughed and I went over to look in a window. Just as I did so an owl swooped over me screeching. Well, that was enough to frighten me out of my wits and I screeched too. The next thing I knew Werner had his arms round me and was holding me tight against him, kissing my hair.

'*Mein klein liebling*, you are a bag of nerves. I am so sorry I am leading you into danger all the time.'

'As long as I'm with you, Werner, you can lead me wherever you like.'

I didn't get home until half past eleven. I went straight to the back of the house and couldn't believe my eyes. No ladder!

There was nothing for it, I would have to ring the bell and face Mum.

I needn't have bothered to have rung the bell. She must have been waiting just inside the door because, as soon as my finger pressed the buzzer, that door was flung open and there stood Mum.

'Where have you been until this unearthly hour?'

'What time is it?'

'What time is it? Its half past eleven. That's what time it is. And that's no time for a decent young girl to be out. Get to bed at once and tomorrow morning I want a full explanation.'

I started going up the stairs.

'What on earth have you done to your coat?'

I looked down at the back of my coat. Sure enough it was covered in mud, as I had feared when I was underneath the hedge.

'Oh damn! I slipped up on Reginald Street. Went a terrible wallop.

But I didn't realise I'd got my coat so dirty.'

I didn't sleep much that night. The next day I gave Mum a cock and bull story about going to a dance with my mates and afterwards missing the bus and us all waiting an hour for another that never arrived. I don't know if she believed me or not but, apart from making some comment about us all being simple to wait an hour for a bus that never arrived, she said no more on the subject, thank goodness. It transpired Peggy had gone to stay with a friend for the night. I certainly had something to say to her when I saw her.

'Thanks for letting me down last night.'

'Quite honestly I'm getting fed up with it, Muriel. You're making me into a regular little fibber, covering up for you, and I don't like it.'

'But they're only white lies, Peggy. The nuns always taught us that white lies are sometimes necessary.'

'Well, I don't like doing it. Don't expect me to help you with that ladder again.'

Everyone and everything seemed to be conspiring against me. Why should being in love have so many drawbacks? One minute I was on top of the world, the next I was in the depths of despair or frightened to death. But still Werner was the only important, the only real thing in my life. When it came right down to it, he was definitely worth the emotional agony.

That week I had my first unofficial lesson in fork-lift truck driving. An A.T.S. girl who usually drove it around J shed asked me if I'd like a go. I loved it and went whizzing up and down the shed. Once I passed Werner and wanted to stop to get off and say hello to him. But of course I couldn't, because the A.T.S. girl was sitting on the back of the truck. However, I caught the sparkle in his eye as he watched me. I just wondered what it was he was thinking. The next time I went out with him he told me.

'If the German army had had you as a driver, we would have won the war!' He had a lovely sense of humour. That was one of the things about him, I later realised, that made him so popular with everyone he met, not only his fellow prisoners, but his guards as well, and not least with me, of course.

I'd been asked to perform at the next Friday lunchtime concert. I was quite happy about it because it meant I'd have a couple of hours off work beforehand to prepare for it.

There was a bloke on before me, called Bert, who worked in Main shed. He was supposed to be doing a comedy act but he wasn't getting any laughs at all and finally he was booed off.

I dreaded going on next, seeing the unfriendly mood the audience seemed to be in. But with a bit of encouragement from Mabel, the organiser, the next thing I knew I was up there on the stage. I started off with my favourite, 'A Nightingale Sang ...' and I got such a loud cheer and wolf whistles and deafening applause that I was suddenly really at ease and launched into my next number with real enjoyment. It was a song by the Andrews Sisters, 'Three Little Fishes'. Well, they went really wild about that and I felt really chuffed with myself as I left the stage with the applause ringing in my ears.

Later that afternoon, back in J shed, Doug came over to speak to me.

'Werner tells me you did really well and got a great applause at the concert today!'

'How did he know?'

P.O.W.s were not allowed in the canteen, they ate their lunch in a separate shed, away from everyone else.

'Oh, he walked past the open door and saw you on his way back to work after lunch. But I'll tell you something. He doesn't like you performing at these concerts.'

Doug was off before I could question him any further. I couldn't understand why Werner didn't like me performing. I went over to chat with Joan and told her what Doug had said.

'Well, he must be jealous.'

'What do you mean, jealous?'

'He probably doesn't like all those other men admiring you and whistling at you.'

'No, I don't believe that. I don't think he's like that at all.'

'Well, if I'm right, it shows how much he must love you.'

I never asked Werner why he didn't like me performing and he never mentioned it to me. I think it was more of a cultural thing than jealousy. Werner didn't have a jealous streak in him but I did know, from things he said, that the customs he was used to in Germany were often very different to the English customs I was used to. As time went on, I came to realise this more and more.

CHAPTER 4

Winter turned into spring and our love was growing all the time. Well, right from the start it was incredibly strong but I think we got used to the dangers that were attached to it. Jumping over hedges at night, climbing ladders to my room and fobbing Mum off became second nature. Once I'd got over my initial fears and panics, they were easier to face on the numerous occasions they occurred. And maybe the longer evenings, the warmer days, the sunshine ... maybe all that made life outside and around Werner and me all the more pleasant.

In those months we got to know each other well. I learnt a lot about Germany from Werner and he learnt a lot about England from me.

Often we went to dances with Joan and Tex, or the pictures. Just about all the things normal courting couples do, we did. We talked and joked and laughed and danced. We lived. And in living we discovered we loved being in each other's company.

There were just a very few people who knew about our relationship. Each one of them was a real gem. They were people without any kind of prejudice, people we could trust.

Two of them were Frank and Alice, a really lovely couple I had been friends with for many years. They lived over at Chaddeston, just outside Derby. Frank was a taxi-driver.

One Saturday afternoon Werner and I were just going for a walk when a car pulled up beside us and Frank leaned out of the window.

'Hello you two! What are you doing this afternoon?'

'Oh, we're just going for a walk.'

'Would you like to go to Tittlecot fair? I've got to go over to Little Eaton and could drop you off there for an hour if you like.'

'Oooh, that'd be smashing, Frank. Thanks.'

'Yes, that'd be smashing,' Werner said, winking at me. He'd adopted a lot of my Derby expressions.

We got in the taxi and first we drove over to Chaddeston to see Alice. She insisted Frank must bring us back there to tea after the fair.

'We'll have the chicken Frank killed for our Sunday lunch tomorrow.'

They kept a few fowls in their garden and occasionally killed one. To Werner and me chicken would be a rare luxury, but I was a bit concerned about eating their Sunday meal.

'But what will you have tomorrow then?'

'Oh don't worry, Muriel. We'll probably kill another one.'

'As long as we don't have Pantry Joint,' Frank said and he and Alice dissolved into fits of laughter at that.

'What is this Pantry Joint?' Werner asked. 'What is it about pantry joint that makes you laugh so much?'

'Don't ask,' Frank said, still splitting his sides.

'No? It sounds a good story to me. You must tell us, eh Muriel? Tell them they must share this joke.'

'You won't believe it, Wern. Really you won't.' Alice held onto Werner's arm, trying to steady herself, she was laughing so much. 'We'll never forget about Pantry Joint, I can tell you. I was going out one day, just as Frank was coming in. So I just shouted to him to find himself something to eat as I wouldn't be back for a couple of hours ...'

'So I went into the pantry,' Frank took up the story, 'and I saw the joint on the side there. Well, I carved myself a few slices and made a couple of sandwiches. Jolly tasty they were too.'

'When I came back that night I asked Frank what he'd had to eat, knowing there wasn't a lot in the house and thinking I'd better cook him some supper with what I'd bought that afternoon. I asked you, Frank, didn't I? I asked you if you'd like me to cook you something.'

'You did indeed, my love. And I said, no thanks, I'm all right, I've had some of that nice joint in the pantry. It was lovely.'

At that they both fell about laughing again. I just couldn't imagine what was so funny and I think Werner must have thought he'd missed the joke because he had a very puzzled expression on his face.

'Well, I could have died,' Alice went on, 'I said, oh no, Frank! That was the cat's dinner - the lights I'd cooked up this morning!'

Werner laughed his head off then. For a moment I felt a bit sick and then I saw the funny side. You couldn't help but laugh with them all rolling about there.

'I went straight off to the doctor, I can tell you. But he said I'd be fine. It wouldn't poison me.'

'Now I can see why you don't want to be stuck with Pantry Joint, Frank,' Werner told him, slapping him on the back.

'Never again, Wern. Never again.'

Werner and I had a smashing time at the fair. We even went on the roundabouts, something I'd never have done on my own, but with Werner I wasn't afraid. He held me tight all the time and I remembered what he'd said to me that evening after the first dance, that he'd guard me with his life. He really lived up to his promises.

They had some lovely brandysnaps there which we ate quite a lot of – and ginger biscuits which were so hot with ginger they made your tongue burn. But we didn't mind a bit, we were having such a good time. And all the while a steam organ was playing fairground music, very loudly. It was magical. It really was. We were like two little kids let out to play and we made the most of it.

Werner had a go on the coconut shy. He was a good shot and won a very pretty little Venetian glass bowl.

'I'd like to give this to you, *mein liebling*, but let's give it to Alice for having us to tea, shall we?'

'I think that's a lovely idea, Wern.'

'You know, Muriel, when I am no longer a prisoner and become a working civilian, I shall have to make over my entire salary to you for the first couple of years. I will owe you that much after all you have been spending on me these last months.'

'Don't be daft. It's really nothing at all. It's just so smashing being with you.'

We had a lovely chicken tea at Alice's with fresh vegetables, also from her garden. Then we played Monopoly and cards until about nine o'clock in the evening. Frank offered to drive us back into Derby as he had a late job on, but we said we'd like to walk.

We enjoyed our evening walks. I loved Werner holding me in the darkness and kissing me and saying beautiful romantic things. He never once attempted to make love to me, and I know why. He had respect for me. He knew I was Catholic. He was Catholic too. He knew all about my upbringing, all about my mother, and he really understood me. I couldn't help but love him all the more for his understanding.

And then in no time at all, or so it seemed, it was summer. By now I thought it was about time I introduced Werner to Mum. I had an idea I could get away with it if I told her he was Dutch. There were quite a lot of Dutch blokes in Derby then.

Werner said he'd be pleased to meet Mum now. And he too thought he could get away with pretending to be Dutch.

I thought I'd give it a few weeks to soften her up first. I'd start by coming home earlier at night. She'd caught me coming home late on several nights recently, either because Peggy had forgotten to put up the ladder or because I just hadn't bothered to ask her to, I was becoming so blasé about it all.

But Werner and I were still cautious when we were out together. We were always very well aware of the danger of him being caught. Occasionally, just very occasionally, Werner would shock me by taking what I thought was a terrible risk.

Once he came out of his camp in his P.O.W. jacket. As bold as brass, if you please.

'Come on, Muriel, let's go rowing. It's a beautiful day!'

'But your jacket?'

He took off his jacket and rolled it inside-out, then dragged me behind him, running down to the lake at Alvaston. He threw the jacket into the boat first and then helped me in. We rowed right over to the island where there were hundreds of ducks and got out to sit there for about an hour. Then he rowed me back to shore. The boat seemed to be rocking quite badly on the way back.

'I don't like this, Wern. What if we fall out?'

'If we fall out, Muriel, I have to tell you, I can't swim!'

But I knew Werner and I knew that daredevil sparkle in his eye. He was teasing me.

'Oh yes you can, you rotten tease. Don't forget I've seen you swim in the brook in Markeaton Park.'

We often went to the brook that summer and had some smashing times. We went there the day before I finally introduced him to Mum.

'Where are you going today, young lady?' Mum asked as I was going out of the door with a picnic basket.

'I'm going to the park for a picnic with my Dutch boyfriend, Werner.'

'Dutch boyfriend, Werner?' Mum had a pleasantly interested note in her voice.

'Yes. I've been out with him once or twice in the last few weeks. We've been dancing with Joan and Tex mostly. Oh, he's ever so nice, Mum. You'd like him.'

'Well, I'd certainly like to meet him. Why don't you ask him if he'd like to come here for his tea tomorrow?'

'Yes, I will. Thanks, Mum, that'd be smashing. I'm sure he'd love to come.'

'Have a nice picnic then. Don't be late back.'

Werner was already waiting for me at the bottom of Bateman Street. I rushed up and kissed him.

'Guess what?'

'What?'

'You're invited to tea tomorrow. I've told Mum about my Dutch boyfriend. She's dying to meet you and seems really pleased about it.'

'That's good. I will try to make a good impression on this Mum I've heard so much about.'

'Oh, you'll do that all right. She'll love you. I know she will.'

53

By the time we got to the park we were already quite hungry. There were a lot of people there sunbathing and swimming. Many had bottles of cold tea they were drinking. It was a lovely hot, balmy day with that kind of stillness that hangs in the memory for ever. We walked beside the brook to where the current runs fast and deep and then disappears underground.

Werner helped me to lay out the rug and we sat down to have a couple of jam sandwiches out of the basket and a drink of cold tea from the bottle I'd brought. We watched the kiddies playing. Little girls were running about in their knickers and splashing in the water, watched by their proud mums and dads. Everyone seemed very happy. But, then, when you are in love the whole world seems a happier place.

Later I went behind the bushes to change. I already had my swimming costume on under my dress so it only took a minute. When I came out Werner was in the water splashing about.

I stepped in gingerly. It was ever so cold. And then Werner started splashing me and laughing. We larked about and swam a little. And then we just sat in the water, watching a group of kiddies further downstream. They were caking themselves in muddy slime which they were fetching off the bank. One little lad said, 'Hey, my grandad says this is sailors' soap, makes you nice and clean.'

Werner and I just looked at each other and grimaced. Then we laughed. The children were having such fun. They were black from top to tail.

Then a mother shouted to them to get themselves clean 'that minute'. They swam like fishes into the middle of the brook where it ran deeper and disappeared under the water. When they came up again they were all pink and shiny, spotlessly clean. What a transformation. Werner and I were amazed. Obviously the little boy's grandad was right.

Later I went behind the bushes again and got dressed. It was the regular changing area for women. The men were not so modest and struggled with towels out in the open. I took my towel to Werner so that he could dry himself off and dress.

We sunbathed and talked for hours before I got out the real egg

54

sandwiches I'd made. Usually you could only get powdered eggs but a friend of mine, who kept chickens, had given me these and they were a real treat. We followed them up with jam tarts and more cold tea.

'This is the life, eh Muriel? This is how people should always be, happy and enjoying themselves. Not making wars!'

The next morning Mum called up to me.

'Are you coming down to breakfast, or are you staying in bed all day?'

I got up and went downstairs in my dressing gown. It was late. I must have slept like a log. I felt so fresh and happy.

Mum was in the kitchen, busy baking in preparation for Werner coming to tea. Peggy was out for the day. I had my breakfast and then did all the washing and drying up for Mum. When I was dressed I did the hoovering and dusting.

After washing up the lunch things I sat in the lounge, reading the paper. When I'd finished that there was still about an hour to kill until Werner was due. I tried doing some of my embroidery but my heart wasn't in it. I was getting anxious about how this first meeting would go.

Werner arrived punctually at four o'clock. When I opened the front door I was surprised to see him wearing a lovely new light jacket. He really looked smart.

'Doug got me this,' he whispered to me as I led him into the lounge to meet Mum.

He wasn't at all nervous. Not like me. I was so worried about whether he'd be able to pass himself off as a Dutchman.

'This is Werner, Mum.'

'Hello, Werner!' She was smiling warmly at him and I could tell, instantly, that she liked the look of him.

'I'm very pleased to meet you, Mrs. Webster. It is very kind of you to invite me to tea.'

'Not at all. Sit down and make yourself at home.'

'Thank you.'

We all sat down and I was still so nervous. Werner, I knew, sensed this because he kept smiling at me and winking.

'Muriel tells me you're Dutch, Werner.'

'Yes.'

'Do you live in Amsterdam?'

'No, my family come from a town further east. You have heard of Utrecht?'

'Oh yes. What's it like there?'

'Well, it is a beautiful city, Mrs. Webster. There are a few canals, like in Amsterdam, and a beautiful cathedral. I was training to be a teacher back home, before the war, of course.'

'Now that's interesting, isn't it, Muriel?'

'Yes, Mum. Werner intends to go back to teaching, don't you?'

'Yes, when I go home, I will go back to teaching.'

Soon Mum left us to go and get the tea ready. We could hear her in the dining-room. Within a few minutes she was calling us.

'Come on, you two. Tea's ready.'

She had laid on a magnificent spread. She'd really gone to a lot of trouble for Werner, and he showed his appreciation by his lovely manners and flattering Mum on her baking. She lapped it up. Really, it was all going very well indeed. My nerves disappeared. I had been really impressed with the way Werner had passed himself off as a Dutchman, without actually telling any lies.

After tea I washed up and Werner wiped. Mum was very impressed ... Werner could come again, it wasn't every young man that offered to help in the kitchen, in her experience.

In the early evening Werner and I decided to go for a walk. I went upstairs to change, leaving Mum talking to Werner in the lounge. I couldn't quite catch what she was saying but she seemed to be giving him the third degree on something.

They were in the hall waiting for me when I came down.

'Well, thank you again for a smashing tea, Mrs. Webster.'

'You must come again, Werner, any time.'

'Thank you very much.'

'Now mind you're back early, Muriel. Half past nine, ten at the latest.'

'Yes, I know, Mum. See you later.'

It was a beautiful warm summer evening so we decided to walk in the arboretum. To me it had never looked so beautiful before. The grass must have been cut that afternoon, because there was that lovely new-mown scent hanging in the air. Quite a few people were there and we sat on a bench for a while to listen to the brass band playing.

'Whatever was Mum talking to you about while I was changing?'

'Hah! She was telling me the facts of life, more or less.'

I studied his face and could see that he was embarrassed.

'Oh dear. That's what I get every day, so I know what it's like. It's not exactly with her full permission I climb up the ladder or shin up the drainpipe late at night!'

Once I'd got used to climbing the ladder and wasn't afraid of it anymore, I had told Werner that was often how I got in. Now he laughed.

'I know you have always told me what your Mum is like but now I have seen it for myself.'

'Yes, I'm afraid the Gestapo got to you.'

He looked at me quizzically then.

'Well, my Mum is the equivalent of the German Gestapo.'

'Ah yes, I see. But maybe not quite as bad.'

He kissed me lightly and we got up to walk some more. We watched the monkeys and the tropical birds and stopped every so often to hold each other and kiss under the enormous old trees. It was a lovely evening light, bathing everything in golden peacefulness. It was an English summer evening at its very best. Pure perfection. And it was the perfect ending to a perfect weekend.

Perhaps all this happiness was God's way of preparing me for the anguish of the following day – an intolerable anguish that was to last for weeks.

Werner and I parted at the bottom of Bateman Street at nine o'clock.

Back at home Mum was full of praise for him.

'What a nice boy he is, Muriel. Such lovely manners and so polite.'

'Yes, I thought you'd like him, Mum.'

'Mind, I told him there was to be no hanky-panky. I want you arriving home in the same state as you leave this house. He's not to put his arms round you or anything like that ...'

'Oh really, Mum, I hope you didn't embarrass him.'

'Well, as I say, he looks like a well brought up lad. What do his parents do?'

'I don't know, Mum. I really don't know much about him at all.'

I went to bed early so that I could go over and over the joys of the weekend in the peacefulness of my room. Funnily, after sleeping so well the previous night, I hardly slept at all. All night I tossed and turned. I'll swear my system knew what I was to discover the following day before I was made consciously aware of it ...

CHAPTER 5

That Monday morning I was up with the lark. Having hardly slept a wink all night it was quite a relief to see the light coming through the curtains and to hear the birds singing.

Mum was already in the kitchen when I went down to have my breakfast as six.

'Peggy's still dead to the world. I don't know how anyone can sleep on a beautiful morning like this.'

'It's still quite early, Mum.'

'Even so, I can't understand how some people prefer to burn the midnight oil than to get up early. This is the best time of day.'

'Well, it was a lovely evening last night too. That sun didn't seem to want to go down at all. Did Peggy get in late then?'

'About ten.'

I got off to work even earlier than usual and caught the petrol bus. I was longing to see Werner's face, which was quite sun tanned after our Saturday at the park. Having spent so much time together over the weekend, being apart for just those few short night hours was quite a wrench for me. Ideally, I would have liked to have been with Werner all the time. By now I had got over the excitement of being in love but was feeling the pain of every moment's separation. In those first months my daydreams, which helped me relive every word and every touch from Werner, time and time again, saw me through the days when we were not able to be together. But now the daydreams were not enough. I just wanted to be with him all the time.

Joan arrived at work soon after me and I told her what a good weekend we'd had and how well his introduction to Mum had gone. But we didn't have long to chat, things were busy in J shed that morning and Four Eyes was making sure everyone kept their noses to the grindstone.

By lunchtime I hadn't seen Werner at all. But that wasn't unusual. I guessed he must be working in Main shed.

When Joan and I arrived at the end of the queue in the canteen we could see there wasn't much of a selection of food left.

'Bloody hell, these greedy buggers take everything and just leave us with bloody jam sandwiches.'

'No. Look, Joan, there're a few sausages left.'

'Umm. But what kind of bloody sausages?'

We decided we'd chance them anyway and went over to our usual corner with our plates to sit down. Joan took her first bite.

'Good God!'

'What's the matter?'

She stood up and started shouting out for everyone in the canteen to hear.

'I knew the buggers did anything here but to fry these dead mice in that bloody chip pan is disgusting.'

At that the cook came marching down.

'Now what's the matter? You're always complaining, you are!'

'Well, you taste this then. This is never sausage. Not on your bloody life.'

Cook took the plate up to the counter where she dissected a sausage.

'It's full of meat!'

'Yes, bloody mouse meat,' Joan shouted back at her.

'Look, if you don't like the food here, don't bloody well eat here. I'm fed up with your complaints.'

There was no more to be said. No more to be done. Joan was forever complaining but the food never improved. I didn't eat my sausages either. Not because they were disgusting, which they were as I had discovered on the first bite, but because I just didn't have the stomach for them. We had to put up with so much at that damn place. But what I found worst of all was the injustice of a beautiful person like Werner being kept as a prisoner of war. When would he be free, so that we could

60

live and love like normal people? The whole world seemed so very unjust and somehow that silly sausage incident just brought it all home to me and made me feel so utterly helpless and sad.

Back at work there was still no sign of Werner. By half past two I was getting more than a bit anxious. I went over to Joan.

'I haven't seen Werner all day, Joan. I hope he's all right.'

'You often don't see him 'til late afternoon. Why don't you pop over to Main shed for a minute?'

'I can't, Four Eyes seems to have been watching me every second today.'

'Well, I've got to go over to the store in a minute. I'll have a look for you.'

'Oh, would you? Thanks, Joan.'

I went back to my work feeling a little better. But about half an hour later Joan came and told me she hadn't seen Werner anywhere in Main shed.

I'd never known him to work in any of the other sheds. But I thought it was just possible that he might. The whole depot seemed to be in overdrive that day. I hadn't known such a busy atmosphere there for a long time.

About half past three a guard from Main shed came in to talk to me. I didn't know him by name.

'Are you Muriel?'

'Yes.'

'Message from Doug. Says he'll be over about four to see you. He's been too busy to get away yet so he sent me.'

'But why? Is anything wrong?'

I didn't let the thought at the back of my mind come forward. I didn't want to even consider it. His next words put me at ease a little.

'No. It's all right. He just said to apologize because he can't get over 'til about four.'

'Oh, all right. Thanks.'

Many possibilities flashed through my mind in the next few minutes. Maybe Werner was ill. Perhaps he had a touch of sunstroke after the weekend. Somehow that didn't really seem likely, especially as I had had as much sun as him and I was all right. Finally I decided he must be working in another shed and Doug would be over to tell me which one. I wouldn't let myself consider my worst fear.

As Doug approached me my heart sank. I just didn't want him to tell me what I knew that look on his face meant. I wanted the earth to swallow me up. Somehow I had to escape this moment. It just must not be true.

'I'm sorry, Muriel. Werner was caught coming in last night.'

I didn't know what to do, what to say. I literally couldn't speak. But Doug went on:

'There were many guards about inside and he couldn't get through his usual hole. In the end he went to the gate because he thought the guard there was asleep. I don't know what he thought he was doing but he took the gun off the guard. The guard woke up and Werner told him he didn't want to hurt him but please would he open the gate so that he could get in. Well, the guard opened the gate and Werner gave him his gun back and walked in ... straight into the arms of two more guards. They were waiting for him, you see, Muriel. His mates had put clothes in his bed to make it look as if it was him in there for the night check, but it didn't work this time. The guard prodded the bed.'

'Oh, Doug, what's happened to him then?'

'Well, he's had his head shaved and he's been put in solitary where he'll stay for a couple of weeks. Then he'll be shipped off to another camp somewhere else.'

I must have looked really pathetic. That's how I felt. I couldn't take it in. Doug squeezed my arm.

'Look, don't worry, love. I'll get some paper in to him somehow so that he can write you a letter before he goes. He's a good bloke. One of the best. I'm so sorry this has happened. You know, they asked him where he'd got that nice jacket from but he didn't rat on me. He didn't rat on anyone, Muriel, and he's suffered the consequences.'

As soon as Doug left, Joan came over. She had guessed what had happened. What I hadn't wanted to believe had been obvious to her ever since she'd found out he wasn't working in Main shed. She told me this now and was full of commiseration.

It all meant nothing to me. I was stunned. I don't remember the bus ride home. I don't remember what excuse I made to Mum for not wanting any tea when I got in. I just remember collapsing on my bed and sobbing my heart out for hours on end. And when there were no tears left inside me, I got down and knelt beside the bed and prayed. I prayed that Werner wouldn't suffer too much, and I prayed that we could be together again.

Later, I got the little letters, and some love poems Werner had written me, from the chimney breast. I read them over and over and cried until I must have fallen asleep.

I woke the next morning with a slight feeling of hope. Of one thing I was certain and that was the strength of our love. I knew Werner would move heaven and earth for us to be together again and I had complete faith in him. And yet without him beside me I felt so desolate.

That day Doug gave me the letter from Werner. In it he told me he had had his head shaved. He begged me to wait for him and promised he would find a way for us to be together again.

This only served to confirm what I already knew but somehow, seeing it written there by Werner himself, it gave me even more hope.

And yet the weeks went by so slowly. I knew Werner had been moved away but I didn't know where to and I didn't hear anything from him. All I had was that glimmer of hope and the certain knowledge that when Werner could do something he would.

Not seeing him at work anymore made that depot seem like a morgue to me. I was never known to catch the early petrol bus, never, ever again.

Mum, of course, noticed how down I was. I told her it was because Werner had had to move away with his work. I was glad I'd started that new phase of coming home early at night before I'd introduced Werner to Mum or I'm sure she would have associated that fact that I was never out late now, with him.

One day, at breakfast, Mum said something that brought all those wonderful late nights back to me.

'I've got the man coming to put that bracket back on the drainpipe today. I still say that thing falling off the way it did was an omen.'

'An omen for what, Mum?'

'Who knows? You wait 'til something tragic happens and then we'll know.'

Unbeknown to Mum, something tragic had happened, of course. Now I relived that night when the bracket had come off the drainpipe. I had come home about half past eleven, after spending one of those lovely summer evenings with Werner, to discover Peggy had forgotten or refused to put up the ladder for me. My bedroom window was still open as I had left it. So I decided to try shinning up the drainpipe. All went well until that last stretch - from the drainpipe to the windowsill. The force of me pulling myself off the pipe onto the windowsill made the whole pipe draw away from the wall. The bracket came right out and clattered onto the paving stones below, making enough noise to wake the dead and certainly enough to wake Mum. I had dived into bed fully clothed, knowing what would happen next.

Sure enough, right on cue, in came Mum.

'Whatever was that dreadful noise? Did you hear it, Muriel?'

'Yes, Mum. It woke me up. What was it?'

Mum went downstairs and outside to investigate. Two minutes later she was back in my room again.

'Well, you'll never believe it. The bracket's come right off the drainpipe. That's what that noise was. I can't understand how it happened. It must be an omen!'

With that she had left the room. But she often mentioned the incident in the weeks after. She was convinced that such an unaccountable thing was an omen. And all the time I was thanking God that she hadn't fathomed the real cause of it ... but maybe Mum had been right all along ... maybe it had been an omen.

In those awful weeks after Werner had been caught, Joan and Tex often used to ask me to go to dances with them, but I never did. There didn't seem to be any point in doing anything without Werner.

The tannoy played music as loud as ever at work but I never felt like singing along with it anymore. And I certainly didn't have the heart to sing at the Friday lunchtime concerts. There was literally no joy left in my life.

Then one day I was just setting off for work when I met the postman.

'Do you want to take these?'

'Thanks.'

Most of the letters were for Mum so I just pushed them through the letterbox. But one was for me and I slipped that in my pocket, hardly looking at it. I had become that dull, really, that I just didn't take any interest in anything.

At work, when I took off my jacket to put it in my toolbox I remembered the letter and took it out of the pocket. Then I looked at it properly, recognised the writing and my heart started pounding.

'Oh Wern, Wern, you've written to me!'

I said it out loud but there was no-one around to hear. Then I rushed off to the lavs so that I could read it in peace.

'Dearest Muriel, *mein liebling* ...' it started. He went on to tell me he had been sent to Ollerton camp and that it might take him a few weeks but he would find a way to come and see me. He told me that I was the only one for him and begged me to wait for him. He also gave me his parents' address in Germany and said that, if I didn't hear from him within three months, I was to write to them. He finished up by telling me 'Where there is a will there is a way', and that gave me such hope.

But still the weeks dragged on and I heard no more. When I got really down I would think of what he had said – 'Where there is a will there is a way' – and that always restored my hope.

And then, about seven weeks later, I got another letter. It was brief and to the point.

'Muriel, I'm coming to you this weekend for a day. I'll meet you at Jo and Mary's in Carrington Street. Go and see them. We are to go to a football match. A friend is bringing me by car.'

Well, it was now Friday and I didn't give a damn if I was going to be late for work. I went straight down to see our friends Jo and Mary who lived in Carrington Street. They had indeed heard from Werner too and

65

confirmed that he was coming the following day.

I was so excited. After all this time we were to be together again. At last!

When I got to Jo and Mary's the next day Werner was already there. Mary showed me into the front room where he was waiting and left us alone together. His hair had grown a little bit but it was still very short. It was such a crime to shave off that lovely hair. The look on his face, that lovely smile which had always been so special to me, told me now that inside he was feeling exactly the same as me. And then we were in each other's arms. I wanted him to hold me for ever.

'Oh Muriel, it was been so long. Do you know how much I love you?'

'I know how much I've missed you, Wern. It's been awful.'

'Muriel, I don't know how to say this. But I think you feel the same way I do. Not being able to see you for so long has just made me realise that I don't want to ... that I can't live without you. When I'm free, *mein liebling*, will you marry me?'

I didn't even have to think. All I knew was that I wanted to be with him always.

'Yes.'

And then, out of his pocket, he took a little ring he had made out of a nail. I held up my hand and he slipped it on my finger.

'Later, when I have money, I will buy you a proper engagement ring.'

'But this one is lovely. It means as much to me as any diamond would.'

He smiled down at me and kissed me.

'Oh, and I have flowers for you too.'

Again, out of his pocket, he took three tiny flowers, also made out of nails and exquisitely painted.

'Oh Wern, they're so beautiful. Did you make these too?'

'Uh-huh.'

He was still kissing me when Jo and Mary came in.

'Everything's all right then?' Mary asked.

'Everything is wonderful, isn't it, Muriel?'

'Yes. But, Wern, you haven't told me how you managed to get over

66

here from Ollerton.'

'Well, funnily enough, I have found myself in a similar situation there to the one I was in here with Doug. One of the guards has a German girlfriend and I write his letters to her for him. Actually, I don't really like doing it this time because the man is already married to an English woman. But it was the only opportunity I could find. This man lives in Derby and it was he who drove me over here for the day. I have to meet him at seven tonight to go back again.'

'Oh, Wern. I knew you'd find a way sooner or later.'

'Yes and hopefully we can arrange more meetings. It is not difficult for me to get out of camp for a few hours. Do you think you might be able to come over to Ollerton sometimes?'

'Ooh yes. On Monday I'll look into how the buses run.'

'Come on then, you two. Let's go to that match if we're going,' Jo said. He and Mary were beaming all over their faces. I couldn't quite work out why they looked so pleased.

The match was good fun. Werner got quite carried away with his cheering for the Derby team, so much so that the mac he was wearing over his P.O.W. uniform rode up to reveal the yellow patches on his trousers.

'Hey, that bloke's a P.O.W.!' one of the crowd shouted.

'Well, as long as he's cheering for Derby let him alone. He's on the right side,' someone next to him replied.

What could have been a fatal moment passed off in really good spirits. I was so surprised. Maybe our luck had turned at last.

Back at Jo and Mary's I was expecting tea. They had left Werner and me alone in the front room again and we could hear preparations going on in the kitchen.

Then I got a second surprise. They came bursting into the front room not with tea, but with Jo carrying a bottle of wine and Mary with four glasses.

'Now let's drink a toast to the time, not too far away, when Werner will be free and you two can make a proper life together.'

'Oh thanks, Jo ... so you know ... you know Werner's asked me to marry him?'

'We knew he was going to, 'cos before you arrived this afternoon he was priming us to see if we thought you'd agree to it.'

'Then, when we saw the looks on your faces after we'd left you alone together before the match, we weren't left in any doubt,' said Mary. 'We are right, I hope, Muriel?'

'Yes, of course you are.'

'Here's to the two of you then.' Jo handed round the glasses of wine. 'And all the luck in the world to you both.'

Too soon it was time for Werner to leave again. But I was determined that I would get over to Ollerton, by hook or by crook, the following Saturday. He described a place, near the bus stop before the bus station, where he would wait for me until I arrived.

'My God, it's good to see some colour in your cheeks,' Joan said to me on the Monday morning. 'So he's managed to bring you back into the land of the living then?'

'More than that, Joan. I've got something wonderful to live for now. He's asked me to marry him.'

'Oh my God! And I suppose you said yes?'

'What do you think?'

'Well I wish you all the best, Muriel. You know I do. God knows you'll need it.'

'Don't tell me. Do you know he nearly got caught again? We went to the football match and someone saw his P.O.W. uniform under his mac.'

'Hasn't he got any civvies then?'

'No. He hasn't managed to get any over at Ollerton.'

'Tell you what. Let's go down to the three brass balls shop at lunchtime and see if we can't find him a suit.'

'The three brass balls shop?'

'Yes. You know. The pawn brokers.'

'Maybe next week. Today I want to find out about buses to Ollerton.

I'm going over there on Saturday to meet him. I thought I'd tell Mum I'm spending the day with you, if you don't mind.'

"Course I don't mind.'

'Thanks, Joan. You're a little clinker.'

I discovered I'd have to leave Derby really early on the Saturday and that I'd have to change buses once on the way. But I was so relieved that it was, after all, possible and I could be there by half past ten.

I left the house before seven that Saturday morning, telling Mum I was going to spend the day with Joan. I was so looking forward to seeing Werner again that the long bus ride seemed to take no time at all. And then I was there. The spot was exactly as Werner had described it. It was half past ten. I got off the bus and went to sit on the bench where Werner had asked me to wait for him. He'd said he'd be there between a quarter past and half past ten.

I waited for what seemed like hours.

CHAPTER 6

I was about to give up all hope of seeing Werner and began questioning whether I had the right bus stop. It must be right. It was exactly as he had described it. I looked at my watch. It was twenty to eleven. It seemed like ten hours I had waited, not ten minutes. And then I saw him. My heart began pounding. He came rushing up, took me in his arms and kissed me.

'I'm so sorry to be late. I've just seen my friend Max, another P.O.W., with his girlfriend. And she said the next time you come you can stay overnight with her if you like.'

'Oh! Well maybe ... or maybe I could stay in a bed and breakfast.'

'But I don't want you spending out your money because of me.'

'Well, we'll see. What shall we do now then?'

'Let's just walk for now.'

We walked along holding hands and after what must have been a long time, though it seemed like no time at all because we were together, we went into a café.

We chose a quiet table in the corner. When the waitress came over I was surprised to hear Werner ordering a pot of tea for two and asking me if I'd like a toasted tea cake.

'Yes, please.'

'Two toasted tea cakes as well.'

When the waitress had gone Werner explained.

'I have been writing poems for some of the guards to give to their girlfriends and they pay me for them. So now I have money and I can start paying you back for everything you have done for me.'

'Oh, Wern, you don't have to spend your money on me.'

'You know it is what I want to do, *mein liebling*.'

He took my hands across the table and held them. We were still gazing into each other's eyes when the waitress returned with our order. The tea cakes were delicious.

'Aach! What is wrong with this tea?' Werner grimaced when he tasted it.

I took a sip. 'Oh dear! It's Shamrock tea isn't it?'

'Shamrock tea? What is that?'

'Oh, haven't you hear of Shamrock tea? It's three leaves to the pot, or three leaves to the gallon!'

His face broke into that lovely smile and we laughed.

As we left the café I noticed the juke box was playing 'Saturday night is the loneliest night of the week'. Werner squeezed my hand and looked down at me knowingly. Without having to use words we both knew that we felt the same things. All we ever wanted was to be together for as much time as possible. As things were, we had precious little time together. That made it all the more important to make the most of every moment.

We went walking again and finally came to a park where we found a bench to sit down. It was then that we started talking about what we were really feeling inside.

'Werner, I know we both want to be together as much as we can, but please, will you promise me you won't take any unnecessary risks? I couldn't bear it if you were ever caught again.'

'All I want in the world is to be with you, *mein liebling*. And to do that I take a risk every time I step outside the camp. But I do promise to be very, very careful.' He looked down at my worried face. 'Always.'

'But you won't try taking guns off guards or anything like that again?'

'No. Now we are engaged I promise to be 150 per cent careful.'

'I'll try and get over here, every weekend, or every other weekend. Frank says he can come and pick you up for Christmas day if you can manage to get out of the camp.'

'Ah yes. Christmas is only a few weeks away, isn't it? Let's arrange it then. What time will he come?'

71

'He says he'll stop the car about a mile down the road from the camp about half past eleven on Christmas Eve. By then all the guards'll be so merry they won't notice you slip out.'

'That's true. It will be easy.'

'When he sees you approaching he'll flash his lights three times and then lift up the bonnet and pretend to be tinkering with the engine. Then you'll know it's him.'

'Very good. Ah, it will be our first Christmas together, Muriel. The first of many, eh?'

It was a lovely thought. After all, that was what Christmas was all about, surely - being with the people you love, sharing love. But why did the person I loved have to be a prisoner? Now the war was over the situation seemed so ridiculous. So unfair. Werner suddenly started waving.

'Look, over there. That's my P.O.W. friend Max with his girlfriend Ann.'

I looked over to see a short, fat man with a slight, willowy girl. They seemed an unlikely couple.

'Come and meet Muriel,' Werner said as they came up to us.

Max was all smiles and seemed to have enough to say for both himself and his girlfriend. She was very shy and just smiled faintly.

'Pleased to meet you, Muriel. Werner has told us all about you. Ann says you can stay at her place for the night if you ever want to come and stay over.'

I smiled at Ann. 'That's very kind of you.'

'I know what it's like trying to court a P.O.W.! Would you like to come home to tea with us now?'

All I wanted was to be alone with Werner. I didn't want to have to talk to strangers. Time was so precious.

'No, thanks. It's not very long 'til I have to catch my bus.'

'But Muriel is coming again next week. Perhaps we could take you up on your offer then?' Werner said.

At that moment I was thinking next week was a long time away, maybe I would stay with the girl if it meant I could spend more time with Werner. She seemed all right. Maybe it would be all right. But I was nervous about it. I didn't really fancy the idea of staying overnight with a stranger.

'That's arranged then,' said Max. 'You come next Saturday, Muriel, and stay the night at Ann's.'

There it was. All arranged. What could I say?

'All right then. Thanks, Ann.'

With that they went on their way. I became aware that I was feeling terribly insecure. I had Werner, that was true. But for how long? What if he were caught again? And, if he was, what was there left for me? Without him nothing was important to me. Suddenly I felt like going to the church I had seen just up the road. I don't really know why. Although I'd had the convent education, I wasn't exactly a religious person. It was a pure impulse.

'I feel like going into that church, Wern. I'm so nervous and mixed up.'

'We are both Catholics. Come on, I will come with you.'

I didn't have to say anything else. Werner always seemed to understand what I was feeling, without me having to say very much about it.

We went into the church and sat in a pew. As I sat down a prayer book fell down beside me and I picked it up to read it quietly. Werner was praying beside me.

For some unaccountable reason the number thirteen came into my mind. For a second I was filled with panic. Thirteen. Unlucky thirteen. Then I reasoned with myself. My relationship with Werner might be difficult and illegal and fraught with danger, but surely it wasn't unlucky. We were in love. Besides, thirteen had always been a lucky number for me in the past. I was half praying and talking to God about my insecurities. And, anyway, thirteen ought to be lucky; after all, there were twelve apostles and with Jesus that made thirteen. I didn't know what the future held for us but I prayed that God would bless us with luck.

It was so calm and peaceful in that church. We seemed in a different world there, safe and protected, whereas outside I was always so aware that walking with Werner was like walking on ice. It could crack beneath my feet at any moment and he could be taken away from me, perhaps for ever.

When we left the church Werner took me to a little restaurant and bought sausage, chips and peas for us both.

'The guards tell me they do a very good steamed bread and butter pudding here, with custard,' he told me. 'Would you like some?'

We had a portion each and it was rather good. The custard was weak and watery but quite a bit better than what we had been used to during the war. Things were improving, slowly.

We didn't talk very much. Since leaving the church that terrible feeling of insecurity had swept over me again.

And then I felt Werner watching me. I looked up and saw the gentle concern on his face.

'You know what your friend Joan says, don't you?'

'What?'

'You die if you worry and you die if you don't, so just stop worrying, *mein liebling*.'

He held my hands across the table and that transmitted a little of his strength to me. Oh, I was all right, just as long as I was with Werner. It was when I wasn't with him that I was worrying about.

Later, he took me to the bus station. My bus was already in but I didn't want to get on until the very last minute. We stood there, with his arm around my shoulders and me feeling really embarrassed because a lot of the people on the bus were watching us.

'I still feel ever so nervous, Wern.'

'If you are worrying about staying with Ann next week, we can always book you into a bed and breakfast.'

'No, it's not really that. I suppose it's just everything.'

'Would you like me to come on the bus with you a little way and then I could walk back after a couple of stops?'

'Oh no, Wern. Remember you promised. No risks!'

'All right then, *mein liebling*. There, you must go now. The driver has started the engine. I will see you next week.'

He kissed me goodbye and I got on the bus, hating to leave him.

That Tuesday lunchtime Joan and I did go down to the pawn brokers.

I looked up and down the street to make sure no-one saw us taking the side entrance into the shop.

'God. It'd be awful if anyone saw us going in here,' Joan said. 'Whatever would your Mum say?'

'I dread to think.'

'Listen, love, remember to haggle. You can always beat 'em down in price.'

'Yes, all right.'

There was an elderly man in charge of the shop. I could see rows and rows of suits behind the counter and began to feel hopeful that I'd be able to find Werner something suitable.

'Do you have any nice grey suits?'

'One or two, my ducks. One or two.'

The man showed us several but none seemed the right size for Werner and I was just about to give up when the man suddenly remembered something.

'Ah, now. I had a gentleman who was supposed to pick up a suit two weeks ago. It's upstairs. I bet that'll be the right size.'

He disappeared out the back. I felt awful. I didn't want to deprive some poor bloke of his suit because he couldn't afford to pick it up. But then Werner needed a suit too. My qualms disappeared.

The man returned with a really nice grey pinstripe.

'That's lovely. How much is it?'

'Twelve and six, my ducks.'

'Oh ... well I'll have to think about that.'

'Look, you can have it for ten bob. Can't say fairer than that now, can I?'

'Oh. All right. I'll take it then, thanks.'

When I got home I hung the suit in the downstairs cloakroom, hoping Mum wouldn't notice it amongst all the coats before Saturday. Of course she did!

'Muriel, what's that suit doing hanging in the hall cupboard? Does it have anything to do with you?'

'Oh, yes, Mum. It's Werner's. He wants me to keep it here in case he ever arrives from work and we want to go on to a dance. Then he can have a wash and change here.'

'You're still seeing him then?'

'Only very occasionally. He can't get over here very often.'

'Mmmm.'

I packed an overnight bag and parcelled up the suit on the Friday night, ready for the early Saturday morning start. I'd told Mum Joan had invited me for the whole weekend and she'd been quite happy about it. I waited until I heard her go out of the back door to peg out the washing and then I came downstairs with my overnight bag and the parcel. I just poked my head out of the back door.

'I'm off now, Mum. See you tomorrow.'

'Have a nice time. Remember, don't do anything to make me ashamed of you. Don't ...'

'Yes. 'Bye, Mother.'

On the bus I put the parcel and my bag on the seat beside me. I was still a bit nervous about staying away for the night at Ann's but I was so looking forward to seeing Werner that that kind of compensated in a way.

And then I was on the second bus and heading fast towards Ollerton. As the conductor came along to sell me a ticket, I put my hand down beside me and to my horror discovered I had left the parcel behind on the other bus. I felt literally sick.

'Oh, Mister, I've left a parcel on the Nottingham bus. What can I do about it?'

'Well, don't worry, love. People are always handing things in. When you get to the bus station at Ollerton if you report it missing, they'll make sure it gets back to you.'

I felt such an idiot. I'd really wanted to see the look on Werner's face when I gave him the suit. At Ollerton it meant I couldn't get off the bus at my usual stop as I had to go to the bus station to make my report. That meant Werner would be left waiting for me. All my insecurities came flooding over me again, and I must have been wearing them all over my face when I confronted the most unsympathetic brute I had ever met in my life at the bus station. I was such a little innocent abroad in the big bad world.

'Um, excuse me please ... but I left a parcel on the Nottingham bus.'

'Well, what did you bloody do that for? Bit stupid, wasn't it?'

'I didn't mean to.'

'Oh, didn't you? Well, what do you expect me to do about it?'

'I hoped you might be able to make enquiries and get it back for me.'

'And who the hell do you think I am? A bloody magician? Someone will have walked off with it by now. You might as well forget about it.'

'Oh. Thank you.'

I turned tail and ran. Why I said thank you I'll never know. What was I thanking him for? An unfair dose of rudeness? I suppose that's what comes of being a well brought up young lady. I ran and ran so that I would catch Werner before he gave up on me. And all the time I felt so disappointed about the suit. I decided that I wouldn't even tell Werner about it. It was bad enough just me being so disappointed.

It was a great relief to see him sitting there on the bench.

'Oh, Wern. I forgot to get off here and went all the way to the bus station.'

'I thought you must have missed the bus. I'm so glad you didn't, *mein liebling*. Here, I have something for you.' He pressed a little box into my hand. 'And don't ask where I got them. They are for you for your bus journey home.'

I looked in the little box to see some fruit sweets. I had never seen anything like them before. I felt so touched. If only I hadn't lost that suit.

In the late afternoon we met Max and Ann at the park. Werner carried my overnight bag and we set off for Ann's home. After about half an hour's walking we found ourselves in some allotments on the outskirts of the town. There didn't seem to be any houses around at all and I began wondering where on earth this couple were leading us. Ann must have spotted the puzzled looks Werner and I were exchanging.

'It's not far now. Look, there's my home over there.'

I looked but couldn't believe my eyes. Ann's home was an antiquated-looking railway carriage. Was that where I was to spend the night? Whatever would Mum say if she knew? The girl was obviously some kind of gypsy!

We were shown into quite a large living room-cum-kitchen, where a stove was the centrepiece. On top of the stove a kettle was steaming away. At least it appeared clean in there, I thought. Presumably this was a converted guard's van.

We were introduced to Ann's Mum and Dad. My first impression was that they seemed more like her grandparents, they were so old – in their seventies, I'd guess. But they seemed pleasant enough. Max started talking to the old man and the old lady made a cup of tea for us all.

Then Werner and I decided to go for a walk. By now it was dark but we just wanted to be alone together.

'I'm not sure about this you know, Wern. Mother would die if she knew where I was staying.'

'I think you'll be all right, Muriel. They seem nice enough people.'

'Oh yes. They seem all right.'

Werner started talking about some friends he'd made with other P.O.W.s in the new camp, I think he wanted to take my mind off things. It was certainly good to hear how he had managed to carve another nice little niche for himself in this camp too. But then Werner was like that. People always liked him. He seemed to make friends so easily with everyone. Not like me. I was quite reserved. It took me a long time to get to know people and to feel safe with them so that I could be myself. I certainly didn't feel myself with these new people and I dreaded having to spend the night in that railway carriage. Still, it meant I would be able to see Werner again tomorrow.

By the time we got back to the carriage it was time for Werner and

Max to leave, if they were going to get back to camp in good time.

Werner kissed me goodbye in front of everyone which made me rather embarrassed, but they didn't seem to notice. And then he and Max were gone.

'What time do we go to bed, Ann? I'm quite tired.'

I just wanted to get to sleep as soon as possible and shut out all my fears about my surroundings.

'Oh, when you like.'

Then there was a bang on the door and a young bloke in army uniform came in. For a second I imagined Werner and Max had been caught, but then I was introduced to Frank, Ann's brother.

I think he must have mistaken my look of relief for some real pleasure at meeting him, because we all sat and talked for at least another hour and Frank seemed to be trying really hard to make in impression on me. He seemed a nice enough bloke, but not my type. Anyway, there could never be anyone else, not now I had Werner.

The rest of the carriage consisted of a corridor with three compartments leading off it - the three bedrooms. I was to share with Ann. I took a little while getting to sleep. I heard the old couple go into the next compartment and then the brother go down to the end one. And then I slept.

Some time later I felt someone shaking my shoulder and woke with a start. When I saw who it was I was just about to scream.

'Shh. You'll wake everyone. Go back to sleep.'

To my horror it was Max. He had thought I was Ann. She was now getting out of bed. I heard them go off into the living room together.

The next thing I knew it was seven o'clock in the morning and Ann was waking me up with a cup of tea.

'Sorry about last night, Muriel. Max usually comes back to stay on a Saturday night. Come and have some breakfast when you're dressed.'

I got dressed quickly and went into the living room. As I went in Max came out and went down to Ann's bedroom.

'Now you're up Max can go and have a sleep in the bed,' Ann told me.

I shuddered, I hoped not visibly. The thought of that little fat man

79

sleeping in the bed I had just got out of horrified me. Did he always do that I wondered. Suddenly I just wanted to get home and have a bath. What happened next reinforced that urge ten thousandfold.

Ann opened the carriage door and went out to empty the teapot down the earth closet outside. I could see her doing it from where I sat. Then she came in and, without even rinsing out the pot, she put more tea in and filled it with boiling water from the stove.

'Would you like another cup, Muriel?'

'Uh ... no thanks ... uh ... I don't drink much tea as a rule.'

Actually I was parched. I could have drunk gallons as I usually did but the last thing I wanted was a dose of the turkey trots. Fancy emptying the teapot in the earth closet, where all that foulness splashed up, and then not even rinsing it after. God, what would Mum have had to say about that? Then Frank came in.

'Would you like a cooked breakfast, Muriel?' he asked.

'Oh no, thanks.'

'Go on. I'm having one. I'm starving. I'll cook you some as well.'

'No, really. Thanks all the same.'

I went outside to the earth closet, leaving the brother and sister alone inside for a few minutes. I hoped Werner would arrive early. All I wanted was to leave that place and never return. Then the rain started pelting down.

Back inside Frank had almost finished his breakfast.

'I'm going down to buy some Sunday papers, Muriel. Would you like to come with me?' he asked.

'Oh no, thanks. I'll wait for Werner. He should be here soon.'

'Doubt if he'll come in this rain. Just look at it!'

Well, clearly Frank didn't know Werner. Werner would come hail, rain or shine. Of that I was certain. Frank was beginning to annoy me. Soon he left to get the papers.

'Muriel?' Ann started tentatively, 'I'm three months pregnant you know.'

I think my mouth must have hung open. I didn't know what to say. I was just flabbergasted. Stupidly I said: 'Who's the father?'

'Max. We're going to be married when he's free.'

Well, you dirty little slut, I thought. And you seemed so sweet and innocent.

'Oh,' I said.

'By the way, Muriel, Frank asked me to suggest to you that you stay on here another night. You could pretend to Werner that you are going home on the bus as planned and then come back here for another night.'

'Frank suggested this?'

'Yes. He's really smitten with you, you know!'

This girl took my breath away, really she did. What did she think I was? A slut like her? I looked at her unbelievingly. And then I felt sorry for her. She didn't know any better. She really was innocent. Either that or six sheets to the wind. Well, there was no crime in Frank trying it on. I wasn't about to make a scene.

'No, Ann. I have to get home today. My mother's expecting me.'

'Oh, that's a shame.'

When Frank got back with the papers he was drenched. Werner arrived soon after him, also soaked to the skin. The old lady insisted he hang his coat by the stove to dry.

With the rain teeming down there was nothing we could do but wait for it to stop. We passed the time playing a few card games. I was so relieved when the rain finally stopped and we could leave. As far as I was concerned I would never be back.

'Do come and stay again any time,' the old lady said to me.

'Yes, come next weekend,' Frank said as he shook my hand and let his linger in mine just too long.

As Werner and I walked back to town I told him about Frank's suggestion. I told him because I didn't want him suggesting that I stay in that carriage ever again. But when I saw his reaction I began to wish I hadn't said anything at all. I had never seen him so upset and angry.

'The swine. I'll kill him. The nerve. *Mein Gott*, that man had better not come near me.'

'Oh, Werner, he was only trying it on. No harm's done.'

I held onto his arm, hoping he would calm down. He looked at me

81

then and his expression softened.

'I am sorry, Muriel. I am so sorry to put you through that. You must never stay there again.'

Then, to lighten the atmosphere, I told him about the teapot and the earth closet incident. He laughed.

'Poor Muriel. What people. What a way to live.'

Werner's reaction to Frank's suggestion had frightened me a little. There had been real anger and hatred there. I had never seen Werner like that before. I realised how possessive he had become of me then. But that didn't bother me. It made me realise just how much I meant to him.

'Come on, *mein liebling*. Let's go and have a nice lunch. And I don't want you passing me any money. I have money.'

We found a café that was open. Few were on a Sunday.

'Well, what would you like?'

As we had come in I had seen a waitress pass with a plate of mixed grill that looked very good, so I suggested that. Werner ordered two mixed grills and coffees.

Then he took a matchbox out of his pocket. I was puzzled. Werner didn't smoke. From underneath the matchbox he detached a ten shilling note that had been stuck on with Sellotape and he carefully unfolded it.

'See, *mein liebling*. We are well off!'

We laughed, we talked and we thoroughly enjoyed the meal. The horrors of the railway carriage seemed a long way away to me now.

When we left the café the pavements were still wet and it was drizzling a bit. But I felt so fresh, so free. The railway carriage had seemed clean when I first went in but I had soon discovered it was a stifling, steaming, sordid place. It was a den full of everything my mother had always done her best to steer me away from. Now I understood why. How wonderful it was to be out in that fresh air with Werner, even if the sky was full of heavy clouds, threatening to release a downpour at any moment. It was the story of my whole life. I had to learn to make the most of every fresh moment that was offered to me ... as long as Werner and I could be together we'd be all right. I just prayed any pending storm would hold off.

When I got inside our front door that night I couldn't help but appreciate my home and my Mum. She was strict all right, but now I understood why. My God, if I'd been pregnant like that Ann, what would I have done? I'd have had to emigrate to Australia. The shame of it. Even Australia wouldn't be far enough away for Mum. And our home, it was a lovely, clean, comfortable home. Mum had standards all right. Now I'd seen, first hand, where having no standards could get you.

CHAPTER 7

On the weekends I didn't go to see Werner I tried to keep myself busy in order to make the time pass more quickly. Peggy and I always did our fair share of housework to help Mum out.

Saturday was usually my cleaning the silver and ironing day. There was always masses of ironing and I hated it, Mum was very particular about us always wearing well aired, clean clothes. She was a very good mum in that way, trying to make sure we were always healthy and well looked after.

It seemed to take for ever doing that ironing. The neatly pressed clothes always had to be slung over the clothes pulley in our big kitchen and hoisted up towards the ceiling to air properly. It was a routine, a part of life.

Saturday was the one day Mum didn't cook. It was a free for all. She was often out for the day at my aunt's. Invariably Peggy would be out with her boyfriend, or at a friend's.

One Saturday I was due to go to the twenty-first birthday party of two of my mates who were twins, Jill and Jane. Mum and Peggy were away for the whole weekend. It took me all morning to do the ironing and silver cleaning and then I made beans on toast for my lunch. My tongue was hanging out for a cup of tea but blow me if Mum hadn't hidden the tea caddy. She always did that when the tea was getting a bit low and, because of rationing, we couldn't get any more for a while.

I had to content myself with drinking a couple of pints of water, I had that much of a thirst on me after all that ironing.

Before meeting my friends in town that afternoon, I changed into my nice skirt with matching jacket and snood. Joan, Jill, Jane and I were going to go clothes shopping for something nice to wear to the party that evening.

We all met promptly at two o'clock outside Marks and Spencers. We were in really good spirits, looking forward to the shopping spree and the party that evening. Afterwards Joan was to come and spend the night at my house and the next day the twins and some other mates from work were coming over for a knees-up. I was pleased that I had this weekend planned and filled. It helped to take my mind off how much I missed Werner.

The girls and I headed for a dress shop where I had previously seen a dress I had liked the look of. I tried it on. It was a beautiful, long-waisted linen dress with box pleats. It fitted like a glove.

'That's really lovely, Mu,' Joan said.

Jill and Jane were in agreement too, so I bought it for £2 10s. 0d. I decided as Mum was away I'd borrow her opossum fur coat to wear to the tea party and pub afterwards in the evening.

'You'll look really great,' Jill said to me. 'I don't know why you haven't got a boyfriend, Mu, you're very attractive.'

I caught Joan winking at me. The fewer people who knew about Werner and me, the better, I thought. It was a shame it had to be that way, though.

We set off to find Joan a dress. She finally settled on one she tried on in Newmans. I wasn't all that struck with it, neither were Jill and Jane, and we all said so, but Joan was adamant. That was the one she wanted, so she bought it.

Having traipsed round the shops for at least a couple of hours, we had quite a hunger on us and decided to go for a bite to eat.

'God, I'm starving,' Jill said as we went up the Gaumont steps to the restaurant.

I remembered one of Mum's favourite expressions and repeated it now.

'An empty sack won't stand. Hey, girls, let's have a proper meal instead of cakes and tea.'

We saw that cod, mashed potatoes and peas was on the menu and we all decided that would be just about right for us.

Trust Joan to find something wrong with the meal. The twins and I had almost finished ours when Joan poked under her batter with her knife, like a child trying to entice a crab out from under a rock.

'Bloody hell. Oh my God, look at that!'

We looked. To our horror there were two revolting white worms under the batter. Well, that turned my stomach. I hadn't thought the fish had tasted all that good, but then we were used to food not being up to par during the war. But actually seeing those worms! Well, it put me off fish for several months, I can tell you.

Joan called the waitress over. She was very apologetic when she saw the worms and said she'd bring Joan another meal. Actually the manageress, herself, brought it and said that it was on the house. How Joan managed to eat another fish after seeing those worms I'll never know. But she said it tasted all right this time.

As we left the restaurant the twins and I went over to the till to pay for our meals.

'Oh no, lovies. You can all have your meals on the house. We're so sorry about your friend's fish.'

Well, that was a nice surprise, but it did leave me wondering if all the fish had been off and I had a few worms wriggling about in my stomach at that moment.

Walking up the street we bumped into some of the Sisters of Mercy. Suddenly I felt guilty.

'I hope they don't know I'm going to the pub tonight,' I whispered to Joan.

She and the twins laughed. None of them were Catholics.

'Better behave yourself, Mu. Pub tonight and confession tomorrow, eh?' Joan teased.

After a bit more wandering round town, we finally made our way home to change. Then we set off to the twins' house for their birthday tea. Joan and I had bought them a lovely identity bracelet each. They were really thrilled with them.

Tex arrived a little later and a few other friends from work and then the twins' Dad brought out his home-made beer and poured us each a glass. I made sure I was sitting next to a convenient plant so that I could pour mine in there. I couldn't stand beer but I didn't want to appear rude by not accepting it. Tex had brought along a food parcel and we ate some lovely tinned pork sausages, much better than any sausages you could get in England at that time.

Later, we all set off for an evening in the Bateman's Arms. I couldn't help noticing the street lamp outside as we walked up to the pub. That was the lamp under which Werner and I had always stood to say our goodbyes before he had been caught. I wished Wern could be with me now. My mates were good fun, we had a really good laugh together, but if only Wern could have been there too.

Tex ordered the first round of drinks. I had a grapefruit juice. I never drank much alcohol, but everyone else was drinking a lot and getting very merry. Even the pub pianist had had a few too many and was playing all the wrong notes. Nevertheless we sang loads of songs, like 'Underneath the Spreading Chestnut Tree' and we did all the appropriate actions. Everyone was having a really wild time.

Quite a few of the blokes were complaining that they were tripping over in the gents' lavs because there was no light in there. At this Tex roared with laughter. Well, I thought it was funny too, but not quite as funny as he seemed to find it. He was practically rolling about with laughter.

And then it was time to leave. Tex came back to my house with Joan and I where he was going to be picked up by some of his mates. We had real difficulty trying to get him to be quiet on the way home, he'd had that much to drink. As soon as he flopped on our settee he fell asleep and started snoring. As his hand went limp we noticed an electric light bulb he had been carrying slip out of it. Then Joan and I laughed our heads off.

The jeep arrived a few minutes later and Tex's mates piled him in and drove off. Joan and I went straight to bed.

Poor Joan. The next morning she had a terrible hangover.

'Come on. The best thing for you is a walk in the arboretum. We'll take Judy,' I told her.

'Bloody hell, I feel awful.'

I gave her a cup of coffee and went to put Judy's lead on. Judy was my aunt's Pekinese dog that I was supposed to be looking after for the weekend.

We had quite a good walk until we came to the monkey cages. And then Judy just went wild, barking and carrying on. She didn't like those monkeys at all and they didn't like her. They were jumping about, squealing and screeching. We beat a hasty retreat home before we could be had up for causing an animal riot.

Then we set about preparing buffet sandwiches and bits and pieces for our afternoon knees-up. The twins and several other girls from work arrived about three o'clock. I brought my wind-up gramophone down from my bedroom and we had a great time dancing and jitterbugging ... until disaster struck.

Jane got so carried away with her jitterbugging that she bumped into Mum's beautiful porcelain aspidistra pot and knocked it flying. The pot broke into thousands of pieces and there were dirt and pieces of plant all over the room.

'Oh, my God, that's done it!' Joan voiced the horror everyone felt and the rest of us just stood there gaping.

'What am I going to tell Mum?'

'Let's get it cleaned up quickly,' Joan said.

She rushed into the kitchen and came back with the washing-up bowl and started scooping up all the dirt into it. I got the hoover. In no time at all, with us all working frantically, the place was spotless – but minus Mum's prize aspidistra and the beautiful pot.

'I just don't know what I can tell Mum.'

'Umm, she's bound to notice it's missing,' Joan said.

Terry, one of my mates, suddenly turned round and looked at Judy.

'Why did you knock that pot over, naughty doggie?'

The dog cocked its head on one side and looked so pathetic. We all began laughing with relief.

But I did feel guilty about blaming that poor, innocent-looking dog.

Then I remembered what the nuns used to say about white lies sometimes being necessary. In this instance, the white lie certainly would be necessary. Mum would never have forgiven me for holding a party at home without her knowledge. I could imagine the barrage I would have got.

As it happened, Mum didn't notice the missing aspidistra until the following evening. I had spent a tormented day at work wondering what she would say. It had only been a slight relief that morning to realise she hadn't noticed it yet.

Apart from the worry of the pending revelation of the missing aspidistra which hung over me all day, the general atmosphere at work was really unpleasant.

It started at lunchtime. On our way to the canteen Sid, the ex-merchant seaman, told us not to be too long.

'Bloody cheek,' Joan said. 'Who the hell does he think he is? The little runt. We'll make a point of taking our time, Mu.'

So we did. We overstayed our lunch hour by about ten minutes just to spite Sid. When we got back to work he was livid.

'You bloody bitches, if you shut your big gobs, you might get some work done round here.'

Joan couldn't stand for that. She always gave back as good as she got.

'You know your white beard's filthy from nicotine and coffee. Don't breathe on me,' and then she shouted for all to hear: 'He speaks to us as if we're P.O.W.s.'

'You bitches are worse than that - I wouldn't piss on you if you were on fire.'

'Shut your ears, Mu.' Joan was getting really worked up by now. 'My God, that little runt is so uncouth.'

Sid came over to me and started pushing one of my boxes around, looking to see if he could criticise my work in any way. He must have been really niggled because he couldn't find anything wrong with it and then he shuffled off down to the other end of the shed.

Meanwhile, the P.O.W.s up above were rolling around laughing. They had really enjoyed the spectacle.

There was nothing nice about that depot any more, not since Werner had left. In my eyes he had raised the tone of the place, created a special atmosphere all his own, right in the middle of all that nastiness. But then, as I say, Werner could fit in anywhere and people always looked up to him and liked him.

Back at home that evening I was expecting the worst as I went in the door. But to my surprise Mum was smiling.

'I've got a lovely surprise for you, Muriel. Cod and parsley sauce. Your favourite. And as Peggy's out to tea you've got an extra big bit of fish because she won't want any.'

Normally I'd have been delighted, but so soon after my Saturday experience of cod, if I never saw fish again it would be too soon for me.

'Oh, lovely, Mum,' I said weakly.

The place was laid for me in the dining room. I sat down and Mum brought the plate of fish in.

'I had mine at lunchtime. You don't mind if you eat alone, do you? I've got some sewing I want to finish.'

I not only didn't mind eating alone, I was ecstatic about it. As soon as Mum had gone out of the room I opened the drawer in the table and extracted a paper bag. The sight of that fish just made me want to be sick. Carefully I slipped the contents of the plate into the bag. I took the plate into the kitchen and slipped out to the dustbin with the paper bag. Carefully I placed it right at the bottom, underneath all the other rubbish. It was a wicked crime. I felt so guilty, but I'd rather have died than eat cod ever again.

When I'd washed up I went to join Mum in the lounge.

'How was your fish then?'

'Lovely, Mum.'

'By the way, what's happened to the aspidistra?'

'Oh yes, I meant to tell you, Mum. Judy came rushing in while you were away and knocked it over. It made such a mess and it took ages to clear up.'

'I thought that's what must have happened. We'd better make sure Judy stays in the kitchen next time she comes.'

I felt awful. What a little liar I was becoming. Somehow I could never present Mum with the blatant truth. And then I wondered what she would think if she knew how Sid swore up at the depot. She'd always made sure I'd led a sheltered life. She'd be horrified if she knew how I was having to face the world these days. That was what made things so difficult for me to face and to bear. Having led such a sheltered life, at anything unpleasant that confronted me I really felt ... as if a knife was sticking in me. It was always a shock. It always hurt.

And then it was Christmas. I had to get Mum's permission to stay at Alice's. I knew she'd think it odd, me spending Christmas away from home ... there would have to be more lies, more fabrications anyway.

'Why on earth do you want to stay at Alice's? She's a married woman. She's got a husband. It's families that should be together at Christmas.'

'That's just it, Mum. Frank will be working all over Christmas, taxiing people around, so Alice'll be on her own most of the time. I said I'd keep her company.'

'Oh well, if you've promised her I suppose you must go.'

I arrived at Alice and Frank's at teatime on Christmas Eve. Alice was just finishing off the icing on her Christmas cake.

'Don't say anything, Mu, but I ran out of fat, so I've had to use some liquid parafin in this cake!'

'I won't say anything but if we all get the trots after eating it I'll know why!'

We laughed. We spent a few hours making preparations for the next day and then we sat down to have a drink. By then it was almost midnight and I imagined Frank would be on his way back with Werner from Ollerton. One o'clock came and went, then two o'clock. By this time I was getting concerned. Where on earth could they be?

'Don't worry, love. They'll have been delayed. Have another sherry. They'll be here soon.'

We had another sherry and must have dozed off where we sat at the kitchen table because the next thing we knew there was a lot of commotion and the kitchen was suddenly full of three men.

Werner pulled me up out of the chair and held me tightly in his arms,

91

kissing me. At last he had arrived.

As he let me go I caught sight of the clock on the kitchen mantle. It was ten past four.

'Where on earth have you been all this time?'

'Hah. The guards were not as merry as we thought they would be, Muriel. We had to wait much longer than we had expected before we could slip out. By the way, Muriel, Alice ... this is my friend, Jo.'

We shook hands with Jo, Werner's P.O.W. friend. Clearly he and Frank were already firm friends as they had been joking and laughing together since they had burst into the kitchen.

'I told Werner you wouldn't mind if he brought Jo along, Alice. We always have room for one extra. And he's going to entertain us. He's brought his guitar. He's a professional, aren't you, Jo?'

'Well, I am, when I'm not a P.O.W.'

'You're very welcome, Jo,' Alice told him. 'Come on, all of you, sit down and let's have an early breakfast.'

It was wonderful to be sitting there with Werner, with his arm round me. During all the chatter that was going on around us he seemed to have eyes only for me. He was watching my reaction to everything that was said. And I was watching his. You could say we had eyes only for each other, and yet we were in such lovely company. Our friends just made us feel all the more together.

That Christmas day was quite magical. Alice had prepared all the usual Christmas food and trimmings. It was a real feast. We found a couple of packets of cigarettes to give to Jo as a present. He was delighted with them. For Werner I had bought a gold ring which I had taken to the engravers to put on his initials and the Christmas date. Alice had gone with me to buy the ring but, when she looked at it when Werner passed it round, a puzzled expression came over her face.

'Muriel, could you just come and help me in the kitchen for a moment?'

'Yes, of course.'

We slipped out to the kitchen, leaving the men in the lounge.

'Muriel, love, that ring you've had engraved isn't the same ring you bought when I was with you. They've fobbed you off with a cheaper version.'

'I thought it looked different, but I thought that was because it's been engraved ... oh no ... now I understand ... that Mr. Plunkett asked me at the time if it was for my German boyfriend. He didn't seem very pleased about having to do it.'

'Never mind, love. It's best forgotten. Werner's ever so pleased with it and that's all that matters.'

We went back to join the others. Jo and Werner were having a wonderful time. They hadn't had a Christmas like it for years. We played cards and Monopoly and Jo played the guitar. He really was very good.

But too soon it was all over and it was time for Frank to drive them back to Ollerton.

'I'd like to come with you, Frank. Do you think I could?' I couldn't bear to let Werner go after such a wonderful day.

'It's best if you don't, love. If I get caught driving P.O.W.s I can always say they were just a fare I picked up and how should I know they were P.O.W.s. But if you were there too it might be a bit tricky explaining you away.'

I saw his point but nevertheless I felt I would have risked anything just to be with Werner for a little longer.

Discreetly the others left us alone together in the front room to say our goodbyes.

'Soon *mein liebling*, the time will come when we won't have to say any goodbyes and we can be together always.'

As he held me close to him I longed for that time and wondered just how far away it was.

'I will try and get over again very soon, Muriel. You will always wait for me, won't you? You won't go out with anyone else, *mein liebling*?'

'Of course I won't, Wern. We're engaged. You know you're the only one I could love.'

'Then we feel exactly the same for each other still, eh?'

'Always.'

And then he was gone. Alice and I went off to bed, me with a very heavy heart.

The next morning I woke up wondering where I was and who was calling my name. Having had no sleep the night before and waking up in a strange bed had a very disorientating effect on me. And then I realised it was Alice speaking to me.

'Come on, Muriel. Wake up, it's half past nine. I've brought you a cup of tea and, look, there's a pressie for you - a letter from Werner.'

I sat bolt upright. Suddenly I had come to life. Alice left me on my own to read the letter Werner had sent back with Frank. More than anything I felt so touched that Werner had written to me when I most wanted to be with him. Clearly our parting had hurt him as much as it had me.

With trembling hands I tried to open the envelope carefully. But it was no good. I had to rip it open, I was shaking so much. And then I read the most beautiful letter.

'*Mein liebling*. How I miss you. No-one could possibly know how much. As these lonely days pass I love you more and more - deep, everlasting love. You belong to my heart now and forever. Keep smiling, *mein liebling*.'

The last two lines he had printed in block capitals.

I felt our love was so strong. When would we be together again?

Down at breakfast Alice and I sat talking for ages. Frank had already gone off to work.

'Frank said Werner told him to look after you for him.'

'Ah, he really wants me to be protected, doesn't he?'

'Yes. He's a really nice bloke, Muriel. You know Frank and I think the world of him.'

'Umm.'

'But, Mu?'

'Yes?'

'Don't get me wrong. We're only thinking of you. As I say, Wern is a lovely bloke. But we wonder if he's right for you.'

'There could never be anyone else, Alice.'

94

'I know that's how you feel now. Everyone always does when they're in love. It's not that there's anything wrong with Werner. But being engaged to him ... marrying him ... well it might make a very difficult life for you, love.'

'As long as I'm with Werner everything will be all right. It's when I'm not with him that my world falls apart.'

'I know how you feel, lovie. I know what it's like being in love. But you know there are a lot of fish in the sea. Why don't you go out with one or two other boys? Play the field a bit?'

'Oh, I couldn't do that, Alice. I've promised Wern. I just love him. I don't want anyone else.'

'It's a real shame. I mean it's a shame that there has to be all this anti-German feeling that you'll have to contend with. I don't think it's going to be plain sailing for you, Muriel, much as I wish you all the luck in the world.'

'Well, as I say, Alice, so long as I can be with Wern I just know everything'll be all right.'

'Umm.'

CHAPTER 8

'You look tired,' Mum said when I got home. 'Did you have a nice Christmas then?'

'Oh yes. I think Alice appreciated me being with her. Did you?'

Mum gave me the whole run down of the day's events with Peggy and all my aunts who had come over.

Later I phoned Joan to tell her about Christmas. Mum had gone up the road to visit a friend.

'Look, Mu, I've got tickets for a dance at the Plaza on New Year's Eve. Can you come over to stay with me and we can make a really good night of it?'

'Well, I'll ask Mum. I don't think she'll be very happy about me spending New Year as well as Christmas away.'

'Oh, you can butter her up. You must, Mu. It'll be a great evening.'

'I'll try, I'll certainly try.'

'I'll phone you later to see if you've wangled it then.'

When Mum came home I didn't think I'd better put it to her so soon after Christmas. I thought I'd soften her up first by being as helpful as I could.

'I think I'll polish all the hall furniture and the banisters, Mum. It looks as if it needs doing.'

'Oh, thank you, that'll be a help.'

I spent a long time making a really good job of it and then I told Mum I would clean the windows.

'Goodness, that two days away gave you some energy, didn't it? They don't really need doing, you know.'

'Oh well, I'll do them anyway.'

After a few more chores I felt it was safe to broach the subject.

'By the way, Mum. Joan wonders if I can spend New Years's Eve at hers. She's got some tickets to a dance.'

'I don't know about that. I'll have to think about it. You know I've heard Joan's mother lets her stay out until after eleven o'clock sometimes. I don't want you staying out that late.'

'Oh no, Mum. When I'm with her we're always in early.'

'Well, as I say, I'll see. Leave it with me for a while.'

That night I read all Werner's letters again. It was about ten o'clock when I heard Mum calling up to me.

'Muriel, are you asleep?'

'No.'

'Telephone. It's Joan.'

Quickly I slipped the letters under my pillow and ran downstairs.

'It's disgusting, phoning at this time of night,' I heard Mum muttering as she went into the kitchen. I picked up the phone.

'Well? Can you come then, Muriel?'

'I don't know yet. I'm working on it.'

We talked for only a short while and when I put the phone down again Mum came out of the kitchen.

'Joan ought to know better than phoning at this time of night, when decent folk are in bed. You'd better tell her not to phone so late again, Muriel.'

'Yes, I will,' I said, all meek and mild. I wanted to keep on the right side of Mum.

Finally, the day before New Year's Eve, Mum agreed that I could go and stay with Joan. She had a nice evening fixed up for herself with my aunts and I think she must have thought it would be mean to spoil my fun.

A group of us girls met at Joan's and dolled ourselves up to the nines for the dance.

'Let's go to the pub first,' Joan suggested.

'Which one?'

'Well, the Green Man's convenient for the Plaza.'

We set off for the Green Man, walking as briskly as we could in our high heels as it was a bitterly cold evening.

The Green Man was packed out. Everyone was getting into the New Year spirit in more ways than one. I had made up my mind to make the most of the evening and to try not to think about Werner at all, or to mention him. I didn't want my loss to put a dampener on the evening for the others.

'Ooh, look. There's Jim over there from the depot,' Joan said.

Jim was already heading towards our group with two other squaddies. Theoretically that made one each for us.

'Like a drink, girls?'

'Yes, please,' Joan was the first to say. Gwen, the other girl from work who was with us, smiled broadly. It was only me who was apprehensive about the whole thing. The last thing I wanted was a date for the evening ... after all I had promised Werner. And there he was, stuck in a dingy P.O.W. camp while I was out enjoying myself.

'What would you like, Muriel?' I heard Jim asking.

Oh well, one drink wouldn't do any harm.

'Grapefruit juice, please.'

We all shifted into a side room where there was enough space for some of us to sit down. One of the squaddies sat next to me and put his arm round me. I felt awful.

'You've had it, mate,' I thought. But it was difficult in all that squash for me to get away from him. He started chatting me up.

'Are you going on anywhere else after this?'

'No, we just came out for a quick drink, then we're going home.'

'That'd be a shame. I think you should stay here and see the New Year in with me.'

'Can't do that. We have to be home early, Mum's rule.'

'Never mind about Mum's rule. We could have a really good time together.'

I didn't know the bloke from Adam and I didn't want to. I didn't even look at his face. I was sort of talking straight ahead of me and all the time I was frantically wondering how I could get out of this situation.

'If Werner could see me now, he'd be so upset,' was all I could think.

Then Gwen said she was going to the lav. I caught Joan's eye and winked.

'Yes, let's all go and powder our noses,' she said.

We picked up our handbags and made for the lavs.

'Hurry back, girls, I'll get some more drinks in,' the squaddie who had put his arm round me called after us.

'Let's leave now,' Joan said in the lavs. 'We don't want them coming on to the dance with us. Tex is going to meet me there later.'

As we were about to leave we could just see the squaddies ordering us all a new round of drinks.

'God, I hope they don't follow us. We mustn't let them see us leaving,' I said under my breath.

We crept out of the back entrance of the pub and scuttled as quickly as we could all the way to the Plaza.

Tex and his mates arrived soon after us and we had a lot of fun, jitterbugging away the evening. I won a bottle of wine as a spot prize and Joan won a box of chocolates.

At midnight I offered to open the wine so that we could celebrate the New Year. But Tex produced a bottle of champagne and he insisted that we drink that. He poured it out and we all kissed each other and wished each other well for the new year.

I had managed to have a very pleasant evening without a date and with my mates. But if Werner had been there it would have turned into an evening nothing short of perfect.

Not long after that Joan came bounding into work one morning.

'Mu, there's a dance on tonight. You know that mate of Tex's you jitterbugged with a few times on New Year's Eve?'

'Yes.'

'He wonders if you'd like to go with him to this dance.'

'Oh no, Joan. I couldn't do that. I promised Wern. I'm just a one-man woman.'

'Oh, go on. It won't do any harm and it'll do you good to go out.'

'Well, maybe ...'

I half promised to go but by the evening I got cold feet. It just wasn't fair to Werner.

However, the next week I did go to a dance with Joan. I had discovered it was worse to stay in with nothing to do than to go out and have my mind taken off how much I was missing Werner.

We went to a really expensive do at the Friary hotel.

As soon as we sat down at our table a waiter pounced on us. It was expected that you buy a bottle of wine for drinking between dances. And the wine was incredibly expensive.

'Give us a chance,' Joan said. 'We've only just arrived, we want to study the wine list.'

The waiter walked away a little distance, then hovered, watching us.

'Look, we'll order the first bottle of wine and then we'll go on to the one I brought with me,' Joan said.

'What one you brought with you?' It was the first I had heard about it. But Jill and Jane were laughing and Tex and his mates laughed loudest of all.

'This, in my bag. I've got a huge medicine bottle full of home-made wine.'

'Oh Joan! You are a one. Talk about being prepared!'

We only drank half the first bottle of wine which we bought from the waiter and then, when the lights dimmed for the dancing, we surreptitiously filled our glasses from the medicine bottle under the table.

The evening was a real laugh. I had a few dances with Tex's mates. But I didn't notice what they were like as people. Werner, truly was the only one for me.

The following Saturday morning I was busy polishing the hall when I heard the front door bell ring. Looking up I saw a very familiar shape through the vestibule glass.

'My God, it's Wern,' I realised. I flung the door open and he stepped inside.

'Hello, Muriel. I can stay until tomorrow.'

'But how ... what ... what ...?'

'Look, do you want me to stay or not?' he laughed.

'Of course I do. But how have you managed it?'

'It's O.K. Everything is arranged. Where is your Mum?'

'Oh she's just gone to the butcher's.'

Werner closed the front door behind him and then he took me in his arms. I hadn't seen him since Christmas, not for two whole weeks. We held each other for ages and he kissed me passionately.

'I'll ask Mum if you can stay here tonight then.'

'Will she mind?'

'No. Peggy's boyfriend often stays over. And you know she likes you very much.'

Mum was delighted to see Werner again and said he could sleep downstairs in the front room. Two of my aunts were also staying for the night so all the bedrooms would be occupied.

At teatime Peggy arrived with her Army bloke, Jim. We introduced him to Werner.

'So you're Dutch, mate?'

'Yes.'

'Where are you working?'

'Over at Nottingham.'

'Oh, yes. What do you do exactly?'

'To do with engineering. Where are you based?'

Werner cleverly turned the tables on Jim who, thankfully, liked talking about himself and proceeded to do so for the next ten minutes.

'Mum,' Peggy said, 'can Jim stay tonight?'

'I'm sorry, Jim, Werner's having the front room tonight. I'm afraid I've got a houseful.'

I caught the look on Jim's face. He was looking at Werner with real malice. It made me very uneasy.

'Let's go for a walk, Wern,' I suggested.

We walked through the arboretum and eventually ended up in the

Bateman's Arms. We stayed out until ten o'clock. I didn't want Werner to have to face any more of Jim.

When we got home Jim had left and everyone else was getting ready to go to bed. I said goodnight to Werner in the hallway.

During the night I woke up and saw some kind of light flash across my window. I wasn't awake enough to think anything of it but the next morning I remembered it only too well and it was then that I realised what it was.

I saw the look on Mum's face as soon as I stepped into the kitchen. Whatever had happened?

'That so-called Dutch boyfriend of yours isn't Dutch at all. He's German. A German prisoner of war! You knew didn't you, Muriel?'

'No, Mum.'

What had happened? My heart was pounding as I waited for Mum to go on.

'Yes, you did. You knew all right. He was a German P.O.W. up at the depot. And you know what you are, don't you? A collaborator. That's what you'll be branded as. You wicked girl!'

How did she know? What had happened?

'Well, the police have been and they took him away. And they'll put you in prison too, Muriel. How dare you bring such shame on this house. You wicked, wicked girl. You'll burn in hell for this, you know. And deceiving me all that time ... telling me he was Dutch, indeed!'

I just dissolved into floods of tears.

'I tell you, you'll burn in hell, my girl. You'll go to prison for at least five years.'

'Oh, please be quiet, Mum. I can't take any more.'

I ran up to my room and buried my face in my pillow, sobbing uncontrollably. What I had always dreaded had finally happened.

And then I heard a knock at the front door. I heard hushed tones down in the front hall and recognised the voice of our local policeman.

'Oh, my God, he's come to get me,' I thought.

But then I heard the front door close again and Mum's footsteps on the stairs. She came into my room.

'That was P.C. Briggs. He seems to think you were innocent and they won't be charging you. You are a silly little fool, Muriel. Just think of the shame of it all.'

'But he's such a lovely person, Mum. You know he is. You liked him.'

'I didn't know he was a German, did I?'

'Well, what difference does that make?'

'What difference does that make? For heaven's sake, Muriel, we've had two wars against the Germans. Your own father had his right arm shot off by the Germans. Oh Muriel, how could you? How could you bring a German into this house?'

'All I know is that I love him, Mum, and when he's free ...'

Something made me hold back. Mum had had enough of a shock for one day. Now would not be a good time to tell her we were engaged to be married ... But it was too late. Mum had caught my drift.

'You surely don't think you can marry him! Over my dead body! You really are an innocent young fool. Well, for your information P.C. Briggs has just told me Werner's escaped again. He got out of the police station toilet window and disappeared. He's in very deep water now, Muriel. He'll never dare show his face round here again. And if he thinks anything of you at all he'll stay well away from you. He's already got you into enough trouble!'

With that Mum left my room and I had a chance to think. So Werner had escaped. Well, I knew where he would have gone. But I also knew the police would be keeping an eye on me and would follow me if I left the house to see if I would lead them to him.

I was certain he would have gone to Jo and Mary's in Carrington Street. Well, I had to see him. If we were going to have any future together at all I knew his best bet was to try and stay on the right side of the law. I also knew how hot-headed Werner was when he got into a tight corner. I remembered how he had panicked the first time he had been caught and had taken the gun off the guard. I just had to get to him before he did anything stupid. I had to tell him to give himself up. He would listen to me.

103

I got dressed quickly and left the house quietly. I didn't want any questions or warnings from Mum.

I walked into town and spent at least an hour window-shopping. Everything was closed because it was Sunday. Then I went and had a cup of coffee in a café – about the only place I could find open. After my coffee I went out the back to the lav and afterwards slipped out of the back door. I was very careful to make sure no-one could be following me and took a very long route through the side-streets until finally I arrived at Jo and Mary's. Sure enough Werner was there waiting for me.

'I knew you would come, *mein liebling*. I'm so sorry to cause all this trouble. Are you all right? You look so pale.'

'I'm all right, Wern. But what about you?'

He held me and kissed me and I started crying.

'What will happen to you now, Wern?'

'I don't know why I escaped from that police station. It was a stupid thing to do. But I had to see you, Muriel. I couldn't just be dragged away from you again to who knows where, like the last time.'

'You must give yourself up to the police, Wern. It's the only thing to do. You know that, don't you?'

'Yes, I know, *mein liebling*. But no matter what, you will wait for me, won't you?'

He looked down at me and I saw the tears in his eyes.

'You don't have to ask, Werner. You know I would wait forever for you. I love you.'

He kissed me passionately, then turned and rushed out of the house.

Jo and Mary came into the room. I was in floods of tears. Mary sat with me while Jo went to make a cup of tea.

'I know it seems like the end of the world to you right now, Muriel. But you wait. One day you'll be able to talk about this time to your grandchildren. In no time at all you and Wern'll be married and all this anguish will be forgotten. You'll see.'

'But when, Mary, when?'

'I'm sure it won't be long before the P.O.W.s are released. It doesn't make any sense to keep them very much longer. Everyone's beginning to realise that.'

'I hope you're right. Poor Werner. You should have seen his face when he left me. No human being should be made to suffer like that.'

'I know, love, I know.'

Jo brought in the tea and after about a quarter of an hour I had calmed down enough to face going home.

'Just where do you think you've been?' were Mum's first words as I stepped inside.

'Walking, just walking.'

'For three hours?'

'Yes.'

'P.C. Briggs has been round again. Apparently Werner has given himself up.'

'Has he? Thank goodness for that.'

The words came out of me without any expression. I suddenly felt very, very tired.

'I'm going to bed, Mum.'

I felt Mum watching me as I walked up the stairs. She was still seething with anger but strangely I felt no guilt about how she was feeling. All my caring was for Werner and what he must be going through at that moment.

In the middle of the night I awoke with a jolt as if something had suddenly struck me. Something had. In my subconscious state I had suddenly become aware of why Werner had been caught.

It must have been Jim. I remembered the look on his face when he heard that, because Werner was staying the night, he couldn't.

The rat. The rotten, lousy rat. There were two breeds on this earth. And everything about Werner, the way he behaved, the way he treated me and everyone else he came into contact with, told me that my particular German was definitely of the superior breed. So far above those rats of the sewers.

CHAPTER 9

Again the days and weeks passed so slowly. It was awful, not only because I couldn't see Werner but also because I didn't know where he was or what had happened to him. I knew he would have had his head shaved. They always did that to P.O.W.s who tried to escape, as a matter of course. But where was he? Would I ever hear from him again?

Often I would find myself twisting the little nail ring he had given me, twisting it round and round my finger in sheer anxiety. I'd catch myself doing it and remember how strong our love was, that Werner would do anything to be with me again. And then I'd start worrying about him doing something dangerous and stupid, like trying to escape again so that he could see me.

Those weeks were agony. My whole world seemed to have collapsed around me. Mum often looked reproachfully at me and I knew she felt hurt at me deceiving her about Werner. Joan was the only one who really gave me any support.

'You'll hear from him soon, love ... remember the last time. It's just a time you've got to get through,' she'd say to me time and time again.

I was leaving the house for work one day when I noticed a letter addressed to me lying on the doormat. I picked it up. The address was typewritten and the postmark was Wisbech. I was puzzled. I didn't know anyone in Wisbech.

As usual, these days, I was running a little late so I slipped the letter in my pocket, thinking I'd read it on the bus. As I walked briskly down Rosehill Street I suddenly thought the letter might be to do with Werner. I tore it open and I walked, praying that it was.

Sure enough, the letter was from an infant teacher called Audrey who lived in the village of Upwell near Wisbech. She told me she had a P.O.W. boyfriend billeted near her, called Herman, and Werner was a friend of theirs. Would I like to go and stay at her house the following week so that I could see Werner? Could I let her know by return of post?

My heart was pounding as I jumped on the back of the trolley bus. I looked around for Joan's face. I wanted to tell someone how happy I was. It was as if a ton weight had been lifted from me.

But Joan wasn't there. I thought about how I could get time off work to go to Wisbech. What would I tell Mum?

As soon as I got to the depot I went straight to the office and asked for a week's leave to go and stay with an aunt ... There was no problem about that. I was practically dancing as I went into J shed and over to Joan to tell her my news.

'Could I tell Mum I'll be staying with you for the week, do you think, Joan?'

''Course you can.'

'It might be best if you come to tea with me one day this week and I'll ask her then.'

'All right, if you like.'

That evening I wrote back to Audrey, accepting her invitation. Joan came to tea the next day. I was dreading asking Mum. She wasn't all that happy about me staying with Joan these days, not since she'd heard her Mum let her stay out late. Very tentatively I broached the subject.

'Mum, I've got a week's leave next week.'

'Oh?'

'Yes, I thought I'd spent it at Joan's, if that's all right with you?'

Mum looked straight through Joan with a really disdainful air.

'Yes, that'll be all right, Muriel. I can get your room decorated while you're away. But mind you behave yourself.' She looked at Joan then. 'I hope your mother is strict, Joan. I don't like Muriel staying out late at night.'

'Well, we haven't got any late evenings planned, Mrs. Webster.'

'Good, mind you keep it that way.'

The next day I bought my train ticket. I felt ten feet tall as I walked

107

home. Soon I would be with Wern again.

When I got home there was another typewritten letter waiting for me on the hall table.

'Who's that from?' Mum asked as I picked it up.

'Oh, it's one of my pen pals.'

I went straight upstairs to the bathroom and locked myself in so that I could read it in peace.

Audrey said she was very pleased that I could come. If I let her know my time of arrival she would meet me in Wisbech. She told me the P.O.W.s were allowed out at weekends until 8.30 p.m. and we would have a grand time.

Well, this was much better for Werner. To be legally free at weekends would make all the difference. I felt so happy.

I began packing my case straight away. One of my dresses that I wanted to take was missing. I knew it must be in Peggy's room so I went to get it. Peggy was reading a book on her bed.

'Have you got my blue dress?'

'Yes.'

'I want to pack it for my week away.'

'But I want it for next Thursday night.'

'It is my dress, Peggy, and I need it.'

'You're not going to stay with Joan. You're off to some hotel somewhere to see that Werner, aren't you?'

'Mind your own business.'

'You are. I know you are. You know Mum'll kill you if she finds out.'

'Keep your voice down, Peggy. She'll hear you.'

'Well, are you going to see him or aren't you?'

'Yes. He's in Wisbech now. I'm going to stay with a woman called Audrey, she's an infant teacher.'

'I think you should pack him up, Muriel. He isn't doing you any good.'

'He's asked me to marry him.'

'Marry! Marry you? Don't be so stupid, Muriel. Mum would never allow it ...'

108

'Oh, don't go on, Peggy. Can't you let me be happy? Please don't say anything to Mum.'

Peggy looked at me, shaking her head in disbelief. I took my dress out of her wardrobe and went back to my room. I knew she wouldn't say anything to Mum but I wished she wasn't so negative about Werner.

Why was it that everyone liked him as Werner Palmer but as soon as they heard he was German they couldn't see further than their noses? Suddenly that turned him into a ogre to be shunned. What was wrong with everyone?

The night before I left I had a bath and washed my hair and put my dinky curlers in. I laid out my clothes for the next day; my pin-striped, navy-blue suit and white blouse, my camel coat and my fur hat. I chose a pair of nice square-toed shoes with five-inch heels. I was so excited. Soon I would be with Wern again.

I left the house early the next morning and felt a million dollars, all dressed up and with somewhere to go. On the platform I counted every second until my train arrived.

Unfortunately, on the train, an old gentleman sat next to me and wanted to talk. All I wanted to do was think about my holiday with Wern. I didn't want to appear rude so I took a book out of my case and pretended to read. Fortunately the gentleman got off after a couple of stops. I put my book away and listened to the rhythm of the rattling train. It seemed to be saying, 'You're going to see Werner, you're going to see Werner.' I could hardly contain my excitement. In my mind I was already with Werner. I knew he would be thinking about me too as I sped towards him.

I got off the train at Cambridge and ran outside the station to catch the bus that was already waiting, the bus that would take me to Wisbech.

In no time at all we were on our way and I felt myself drawing closer to Werner. The conductor came up to me.

'Single to Wisbech, please.

'Not on this bus, dearie.'

'Oh no, have I got on the wrong bus?'

'Afraid so. But you're all right. If you get off at the next stop and cross the road to the other bus stop, your bus should be along in ten minutes.'

'Oh, thank you. How much is it to the next stop then?'

'That's all right, dearie. You needn't pay anything.'

The conductor was really charming. He actually got off the bus with me at the next stop to show me where to catch the right one. I felt a bit of an idiot. In my excitement to see Werner I hadn't even looked at the destination sign on the front of the bus.

When I finally alighted in Wisbech I recognised Audrey straight away, as she had described what she would be wearing. I liked her immediately. She had a broad, welcoming smile on her face.

'It has to be Muriel, yes?'

'Hello, Audrey!'

'Come on, that's my car over there.' She pointed to a little Austin seven.

'Thank you ever so much for inviting me.'

'Delighted to have you. Werner's a lovely chap. I can see you're made for each other.'

'I wish other people could.'

'Oh, I know. I get it all the time because I'm going to marry Herman. But don't let all this anti-German feeling get you down. The war's over. One day people will realise they have to forget their prejudices.'

'I just can't get over how narrow-minded people are. Everyone really likes Werner ... until they find out he's German. Then it's as if he's no better than a piece of dirt ... and me too for associating with him.'

'I can see we've got a lot in common, Muriel. We're going to get on well. We'll show 'em, eh?'

We laughed. Audrey seemed a very happy, strong person. She made me feel strong too. As we drove along she told me she was divorced and had a ten-year-old daughter called Jill. Her husband had left her to go off with another woman when Jill was only a baby.

Soon we were pulling into the drive of a lovely manor house.

'This is home. Werner and Herman are inside waiting.'

Even before the car stopped Werner came bounding out of the front door and in a couple of leaps he had my door open, pulled me out of the car and was holding me tight and kissing me.

'Oh, Muriel, my love, my sweet.'

We smiled at each other in utter joy.

'I'll carry your case in, my darling.'

I was in a whirl. I couldn't speak, but I didn't need to. Werner knew what I was feeling and I him. It was written on our faces, in our eyes.

Audrey took me upstairs to show me my room and Werner put my case in for me. Then we went on a quick tour of her lovely home. It was a fine, rambling, stone manor, filled with a happy atmosphere – or was that just inspired by the way I was feeling in those first moments?

Finally we went into the lounge and I was introduced to Herman. He had been reading a newspaper but he stood up as soon as we came in. He smiled warmly at me and shook my hand. He was not at all like Werner, being short and fair.

'You are right, Werner. She is pretty,' Herman said.

I felt myself blushing.

'You have made her blush now,' Werner said, putting his arm round me.

'Let's have drinks. Would you like a sherry or a gin and tonic, Muriel?' Audrey asked.

'A sherry would be very nice, thank you.'

Herman poured the drinks. Audrey had a gin and tonic and the two men had beers.

We sat and chatted for a while and I took in my surroundings. The lounge was beautifully furnished and the most prominent feature was an exquisite, very large chandelier.

'Jill is at her friend's house for the day but you'll meet her later,' Herman told me. 'She is a little darling.'

After a while Audrey and Herman discreetly left Werner and me alone together, saying they were going to see to the lunch.

Werner drew me close to him. For a long time we just sat there, holding each other. It was so good to feel his arms around me again.

'I'm sorry about my shaved head again, *mein liebling*, but this is the last time. I will never escape again. I want you to come and live here so that we can be together.'

That thought immediately struck me as thrilling. Of course. It was the obvious thing to do.

'Audrey says you can stay here with her.'

'That'd be great. She's ever such a nice person, isn't she, Wern?'

'Yes, and Herman too. They are a good couple together.'

'I'll have to find a job in Wisbech. On Monday morning, first thing, I'll go to the employment office.'

'Soon, soon, my love, we can be married. I don't want you having to work. We will go to Germany where I can teach and you won't have to work. It won't be long, I promise. Here I live in a billet, not a P.O.W. camp. It is a Nissen hut in an orchard and really we are more or less free to come and go as we like. I'm sure it won't be long until we are completely free, *mein liebling.*'

'I'm so glad. Things are a 100 per cent better here, aren't they, Wern?'

'Yes, we can start to breathe, I think.'

With that he covered my mouth with a kiss that actually took my breath right away.

When we had finished helping Audrey to wash up after lunch we all sat and chatted again and later played Monopoly and Ludo.

It was in the evening, when we were all dancing to a few records, that Jill arrived home and I was introduced. She was a very pretty little girl, full of smiles and with lovely manners, obviously beautifully brought up by her mother.

The next day Werner and I went for a cycle ride. We were going to meet his uncle, who was a P.O.W. camp cook over at Fridaybridge. It rained a little on the way but we didn't mind a bit. It just added to the thrill of being together. We had suffered worse adversities. The beauty was that we were free. Out together legally!

It was springtime and the hedges and trees along the narrow country lanes were sparkling with that lovely fresh green. The sight just filled me with hope of our future. I felt we had passed through the terrible winter and come out safely on the other side.

Werner's Uncle George was cycling from Fridaybridge to meet us. So, about half way, we stopped and sat on a stile to wait for him. The rain stopped and the sun came out.

I knew it was Werner's uncle as soon as I saw him approaching. He looked a jolly man and was quite fat, as I imagined a cook would be.

He greeted me warmly and shook my hand as soon as he got off his bike. He didn't speak much English but he seemed full of good will for Werner and me.

Then the three of us cycled back to Werner's billet. As we wheeled our bikes through the orchard Werner pointed out the different apple trees, telling me their names and whether they were cookers or eaters. He knew much more about apples than I did, or his uncle. But then I had always found Werner to be knowledgeable on any subject he was presented with. His boss, he told me, was a fruit farmer, a very nice man called Mr. Hunter-Rowe. He was very kind to all the P.O.W.s.

Werner led us towards the Nissen hut, outside which stood a very pretty Jersey cow. It had such lovely big brown eyes and a really soft expression. I stood for ages making a fuss of it.

'Mr. Hunter-Rowe has given us this cow to milk and to make cheese. That is the sort of man he is, very thoughtful.'

'My goodness, Wern. This is a step up on Alvaston and Ollerton, isn't it?'

'It certainly is. Like heaven by comparison.'

Inside the hut I was introduced to four other P.O.W.s. All but one spoke quite good English. One of them made coffee while we sat round a table and chatted. Werner interpreted for Hans when necessary.

One of the men told me he had a girlfriend in Nottingham. I told him that was quite near my home and he was really interested. He obviously liked to have another woman to talk to about her and I was a good listener.

As we drank coffee there was a knock on the door and a tubby, grey-haired man came in. Werner stood up to greet him.

'Ah, Mr. Hunter-Row, may I introduce you to my fiancée, Muriel.'

I stood up and shook hands, quaking in my shoes for fear that they would get into trouble for having me in the hut with them. But I needn't have worried. Mr. Hunter-Rowe was perfectly charming.

'Very pleased to meet you, my dear. Your Werner is a damned good worker and a very good fellow. Would you both like to come up to the house for dinner tomorrow?'

I looked at Werner.

'Thank you very much, Mr. Hunter-Rowe. We'd be delighted,' he said.

We cycled back as far as the stile with Uncle George, where he gave me an affectionate kiss as he said goodbye and then he said something to Werner in German which I didn't understand.

After he had gone Werner turned to me.

'He really likes you, Muriel. We have his blessing for our marriage.'

Back at Audrey's we played some games with Jill and then had a very tasty rabbit stew and Yorkshire pudding which Audrey had prepared.

Herman had spent the afternoon repairing a shed in the garden. We all ate the meal with great relish, having worked up good appetites. It was a long time since I had been cycling and I was ravenous.

That night I went to bed very happy. Things were so much better for Wern and me.

The next morning Audrey went off to school and I caught the bus into Wisbech to look for a job. I went to the employment office where the clerk offered me the possibility of three jobs. I took the three cards and mulled over them. A waitress at the Welcome Café on the riverside in Wisbech could suit, I thought.

I went to the Public Conveniences and looked at myself in the mirror. I had on my smart pinstriped suit but my hair was down. Long and flowing. I delved into the handbag and found a few hairpins at the bottom. Carefully I put my hair up in a fashion that seemed appropriate for a prospective waitress. I was pleased with the result but a little worried that I might look too smart in my suit. I unbuttoned the jacket. That looked better.

My appointment for the job had been set for eleven o'clock. I went and sat on a riverside bench until it was time. I felt calm and confident.

Inside the café I was greeted by a young waitress, about my age, who showed me into the lounge. The lady who came in next told me she was the proprietress as she looked me up and down. I could tell she was thinking I was overdressed. But I told her my experience – actually the first concoction that came into my mind – that my parents had had a small hotel where I had helped as a waitress. She seemed well satisfied.

Then she took me upstairs and showed me the bedroom.

'You'd be sharing with Celia, the other waitress.'

The room was basic but clean. There were two iron-frame beds, two chests of drawers, a peg-rug and a washstand with bowl and jug.

'The hours are 7.00 a.m. to 5.00 p.m. and you're off after three on Saturday and all day Sunday. The salary is £2 10s. 0d. per week, plus your keep. Well, would you like the job?'

I suddenly realised she was actually offering it to me.

'Oh yes. Yes. Ta very much.'

She laughed.

'We'll have to get used to each other's accents. Where did you say you were from, dear?'

'Derby.'

In the kitchen she introduced me to her husband and told me a little more about the job and that she would like me to start in three weeks' time.

I hardly took in what she was saying. It had just dawned on me that I had accepted a job in Wisbech and I had yet to give in my notice at the depot. And worse ... explain to Mum!

As I left, I saw Celia cleaning a table and called out to her. 'Ta-rah, duck.'

'What does that mean?'

'It's a Derby expression. Means goodbye! I'll see you in three weeks.'

'Oh, right. Glad you got the job.'

'Thanks.'

I felt so pleased with myself. Everything seemed to be working like clockwork now. Everything was going to work out for Werner and me.

He was so thrilled when I told him I had landed the job and so was Audrey. She said I could stay with her at the weekends.

The rest of my holiday week just shot by. Werner and I had a lovely meal at Mr. Hunter-Rowe's. I enjoyed listening to the two of them talking over the dinner table. They talked like equals, not like boss and labourer or Englishman and German P.O.W.

Mr. and Mrs. Hunter-Rowe were in their sixties but didn't have any children. They did have a niece, they told me, who was training to be a doctor and who often came to stay with them.

Werner and I spent a lot of time going for cycle rides that week. A couple of times we took a picnic – when it looked as if the rain might hold off. So near to the Wash, it seemed to rain a lot in that area at that time of year, Audrey had said.

One evening we went to a dance. It was a formal do where long dresses were expected. I knew I'd perish if I wore mine as it had turned so cold.

'Don't worry,' Audrey told me. 'You can wear a pair of longjohns underneath. I've got a pair of Herman's I've just washed. If I slip some elastic round the top they should fit you a treat.'

No sooner said than done. We were in stitches as I tried them on under my dress. But they really were effective. I was as warm as toast and Audrey assured me they couldn't be seen under my dress.

We went as a foursome to the dance at the Village Institute, Herman and Audrey, Wern and I. It was so wonderful to be able to enjoy ourselves without worrying about whether Werner would be caught. A whole new world was beginning to open up for us. For a moment I really felt all our worries were over. But only for a moment ...

As we were leaving we passed two elderly women who were standing in the doorway.

'Filthy Jerry lovers,' one said.

'Scum. That's what they are,' the other one agreed, looking down her nose at us.

'Remember what I said, Mu,' Audrey took me by the arm, 'we'll show 'em. Sanctimonious old maids!'

We laughed. But for me a perfect evening had been marred.

'They're so ignorant, Audrey.'

We walked along the dark lane towards the manor, me on Werner's arm, Audrey on Herman's.'

'I'm going to have to go behind the hedge, Audrey, before we get home,' I said.

'Me too.'

'Won't be a minute, Wern.'

'All right, *mein liebling.*'

Audrey and I went behind the hedge. I had just pulled my longjohns down when a dog started barking its head off, very nearby!

I didn't have time to pull the longjohns up again. Audrey and I shot out from behind the hedge, like two bats out of hell. We were all killing ourselves laughing at me with the longjohns round my ankles. Life really could be a great laugh. Who cared about stupid old maids and their petty prejudices? True. I had at the time. But that was ten minutes ago.

Back at home in Derby I didn't have much time to get things organized before taking up my new job. I knew the first priority was to hand in my notice. I could drop the bombshell on poor Mum later.

As I walked in the front door after my holiday Mum greeted me with words that chilled me to the heart.

'I've done a lovely job on your room, Muriel. All newly decorated. And I had a fire in your grate to burn all the old wallpaper scraps. Go and have a look. I think you'll be really pleased.'

I darted up the stairs. I hardly noticed the new decorations in my room as I flung myself with one leap to the grate. With both hands I delved up the chimney breast in search of my letters from Werner. All I found were the charred remains. Papers burnt to cinders. Not a word to see. I cried and cried and wiped my eyes with my sooty arms. All my beautiful letters gone! I couldn't believe it.

In the bathroom I washed off the soot in the sink and then ran a bath. Those letters had given me such comfort in the months Werner and I had been separated. Well, we would soon be together forever. I tried to console myself with the thought. But all those beautiful letters burnt was still an unbearable loss for me. I couldn't stop crying for ages.

At the depot the next morning I went straight to the office to hand in my notice.

'That's not so easy,' the boss told me. 'You have to have a medical certificate to hand in your notice here. Don't forget you were conscripted to come here.'

My heart sank. I'd have to find a way round the problem. I thought about it for a long time back at my work bench. Then it suddenly came to me. Once a month I always went to the medical room for a lie down because of my heavy periods. I decided that I would go and see my doctor for a certificate that evening.

Dr. Penny lived only a few doors away from us. He had known me all my life and was quite a friend of the family.

I told him I wanted to leave the depot because I had found another job but that I needed a medical certificate.

'Say no more, my dear,' he put up his hand in restraint. 'It's as good as done.'

He drew a form out of his desk drawer and hastily scribbled on it. Then he passed it to me.

'There you are. I think you'll find that'll do the trick.'

I was amazed at how easy it had been. I handed the certificate in at the office the following morning and was told I could leave two weeks on Friday.

CHAPTER 10

I had told Werner and Audrey that I would try and get down to Wisbech the next weekend. During my holiday week I had discovered I could get there by bus. Werner knew the bus was due to arrive in Wisbech at 9.30 p.m. I had told him if I wasn't on it not to bother to wait. It would mean I wasn't able to come. We had left it like that.

So that weekend I was happily sailing on my way to Wisbech aboard the bus. I was in my usual dream world which I always adopted when travelling, thinking only of Wern, so it came as quite a jolt to me when the bus came to a stumbling halt near Huntingdon. My dream was shattered and I was faced with the prospect of a delayed journey.

After tinkering with the engine for half an hour the driver accepted defeat and gave up altogether. There was no way this bus was going anywhere, probably ever again, he told us.

There was nothing for it but to continue my journey by train. When the ticket man at Huntingdon station told me there was a half-hour wait for the next train to Cambridge I began to panic. Would I get there in time to catch the last bus to Wisbech?

After a seemingly interminable age the train drew in and I got on. All the way from Huntingdon to Cambridge I was willing the train to go faster. Instead of indulging in a relaxing daydream about being with Wern, I was anxious as hell about whether I would even be able to be with him that night.

By the time the train sloped into Cambridge station it was 10.30 p.m. All my daydreams were shattered. I knew the last bus to Wisbech was long gone and that Werner, not finding me there at 9.30, would have given up, thinking I wasn't coming, and gone home. What a mess! What could I do? There was nowhere to go!

I asked the porter if he could direct me to a bed and breakfast place.

'You won't find anything at this time of night, young lady.'

Well, I wasn't going to sit on the bench outside the railway station all night so I began walking. I would have to find somewhere. After about ten minutes I saw a house with a bed and breakfast sign so I rang the bell. There was no answer so I tried the knocker. Still no answer. In desperation I tried bell and knocker together. There was no light coming on anywhere in the house. I had to accept no-one would come to the door.

I walked back to the station, not knowing quite what to do with myself. When I got there the porter was just locking up.

'Couldn't you find anywhere then?'

'No.'

'Look, that bloke's just pulled up in his lorry. I'll ask if he knows of anywhere for you. These lorry drivers know all the bed and breakfasts around.'

I watched him go over and have a word with the lorry driver. Then he smiled and beckoned to me. I went over.

'He says he's managed to get a room for himself for the night so you can sleep in his cab, if you like. He's got a little dog here that'll keep you company.

I looked up at the lorry driver as he jumped out of the cab. He was a very ordinary-looking, middle-aged man.

'I must have got the last room in town,' he said, 'but you are welcome to sleep in my cab. It's quite comfortable, I've often slept in it.'

'Are you sure you don't mind?'

I was so relieved to have found a billet, I'd been beginning to think I'd have to walk the streets all night. The lorry cab seemed to be the best offer I would find.

'No, I don't mind. Go ahead and make yourself comfortable.'

As I climbed up I saw the porter disappearing home to his bed and the lorry driver put up a hand to wave goodbye to me. I slammed the cab door shut and watched him head off in the opposite direction to the porter. Then I snuggled down on the seat. The little mongrel had been sitting quietly on the floor all this time but after about five minutes it began wagging its tail. That's funny, I thought. This dog's reactions are a bit slow if he's only now decided to greet me. I patted it on the head. But it seemed to be looking beyond me. Then there was a muffled sound behind me and I realised, in utter horror, that someone had come in the back of the lorry.

My hand was on the door handle even before I heard the lorry driver's voice behind me.

'Thought you might like a bit of company, love.'

Grabbing my bag I jumped out of that cab and shot off down the road faster than I had ever moved in my life. As I ran I realised what a fool I'd been ... the man would have raped me ... murdered me ...

I didn't dare slow down to look behind to find out if he was following me. I just ran and ran until I shot round a corner and straight into the arms of a policeman. After spending the best part of two years deliberately avoiding policemen, I was never more pleased in my life to find myself actually in the arms of one now. I must have slumped with relief.

'Now then, love. Whatever's the matter with you?'

It all came out in a jumble and I realised I wasn't making any sense to him.

'Come on, let's get you into the police station.'

It was then that I noticed we were right outside the police station. He took me by the arm and marched me in.

The duty sergeant made me a cup of tea and after a few sips I was able to tell him and the constable exactly what had happened. The constable went off straight away to see if he could find the lorry driver. Meanwhile, the sergeant sat and talked to me.

'Always remember, if you ever get stuck like that again, go to the nearest police station. You don't want any more nasty shocks like that, do you? Look, so you're safe tonight you can sleep in the cell we have here.'

The constable came back and reported that both the lorry and driver had disappeared. I was just thankful that I had managed to escape.

I slept in the cell for the night and the next morning the sergeant brought me a cup of tea at quarter to six.

'I'm afraid I'll have to turn you out now, the other sergeant comes on duty at six.'

I thanked him for everything he had done for me and went for a little walk round Cambridge until I found a café open at seven o'clock. I went in and ordered a cooked breakfast. Thank God I was still alive!

With a good breakfast inside me I felt much better and by the time I was on the bus, bound for Wisbech, I had just about recovered from my fright. I decided I wouldn't tell Werner or Audrey about it. Werner worried enough about me as it was.

That weekend passed too quickly. I had less than a day with Werner and then it was time to return home again. We decided there was little point in me travelling all that way for the following weekend, especially as it would only be one week after that when I would be there for good.

On my way home I worried about how I would tell Mum I was leaving home for good in two weeks' time. The dreaded moment was drawing near. I couldn't delay it for much longer.

But I waited for another week before telling her. Every night I prayed desperately for help in doing so. And when I did her reaction was just as I had expected.

'If you leave here to go to that Werner, Muriel, you'll never come back here again.'

I tried to reason with her, to tell her how much we loved each other, but it was like talking to a brick wall. She wouldn't give at all.

Some time later, when I was in my room, Peggy came in to talk to me. I soon realised Mum had got her to try and change my mind.

'Can't you see it won't work, Mu? He's German. You won't be accepted as a couple anywhere. If you go Mum won't have anything more to do with you. She means it!'

I had heard Mum say it. I had heard Peggy say it. But I didn't really believe it. And anyway there was no turning back now. It was too late. Werner and I could not live apart.

The atmosphere in our house was very tense for two or three days after I had told Mum. I was quite glad to get to work each day, just to get away from it. Mum and Peggy kept on trying to talk me out of my decision. And then they just became silent, regarding me with hurt, disdainful airs, and that was even worse. I couldn't stand those silences.

But at work my mates couldn't have been nicer. By now most of them knew about Werner and me and they all wished us well.

One person who surprised me was Sid, when he heard that I was leaving. He came over to my work bench on my last day.

'In a way I'm glad you're leaving.'

'Oh, why?'

'So you don't get corrupted by them Nazi bastards.'

'Well, ta, Sid.'

He smiled and shuffled off. I think he actually meant well but I thought: that's rich ... coming from him ... what about all the foul language he uses?

In the canteen cook told me she was sorry I was leaving.

'We'll miss you, Mu. You've always been a friendly, smiling face about the place ... quiet and polite ... it shouldn't be you leaving. It should be that other one,' she said, nodding in Joan's direction. 'We'd be really pleased if that bloody-minded one left.'

The girls threw a bit of a party for me in the Main shed canteen at lunchtime on my last day. We had wine and cakes and someone played the piano for us to sing and have a knees-up. They gave me a really good send off. There was a lot about that depot in Derby that I'd miss after all, I realised. I'd made some good mates there, mates I'd remember all my life. They gave me a lovely leather handbag and a diary with all their names and addresses in. I would keep in touch with them all.

Next, Joan arranged another farewell party for me – dinner at the Friary hotel with two or three girls from work and then dancing at the Assembly Hall after, where Tex and his mates were to join us.

For the occasion I put my hair up in a French style. As I sat in front of the mirror, slipping the hair pins in and seeing the incredibly glamorous effect I was creating, I felt a sudden pang of regret. I had always wanted to be a professional hairdresser. I really did have a flair for styling hair and it was something I would very happily have done all day long, every day of my life. But Mum had put her foot down. No daughter of hers was going to be a hairdresser. She had always wanted me to be a nurse. Poor Mum. I really hadn't matched up to her expectations at all. How I wished she could have just let me be and do what I felt was best for me. How very different our relationship would have been then. I knew Mum meant well, that she only wanted the best for me. But her idea of what was best for me was so very different from my own.

I slipped the last pin in and went downstairs to find my handbag, which I had left in the lounge. Mum was sitting in there sewing.

'You know, I had a premonition you'd leave to go off with Werner.'

It was the first time she had actually spoken to me for days, and then she burst into tears. I felt so sorry for her. I knew I was letting her down again. I went over and put my arms round her.

'I do love you, Mum. You know that, don't you? But I love Wern too. Please forgive me for deceiving you when I told you he was Dutch, but I just knew you wouldn't look at him twice if I told you he was German.'

'Oh, I forgive you, love.' She patted me on the back. 'But listen, if you ever find yourself in trouble, give me a ring. I'm only a phone call away.'

'I know, Mum.'

'Sit down a minute, Mu. I've got something for you.'

I sat down and she went over to the table drawer. She took out a little box and came back to me with it.

'These are for you. I was going to save them for when you get married but you might as well have them now. Don't ever part with them, whatever you do.'

I opened the box to discover a beautiful string of pearls and earrings to match.

'Oh ta, Mum! Ta ever so much. They're really beautiful.'

'Wear them tonight if you like, love.'

'Yes, I will.'

Back in my room I put on my charcoal grey wool suit. The pearls complemented it perfectly. They made me feel really classy. Dear Mum. She had class. She always had had. She had always tried her best to pass it on to us girls.

I felt so much better now. I'd always known Mum would meet me half-way in the end. She might not be happy about what I was doing but at least now I knew for sure that she wished me well.

I felt a million dollars as I sat in the Friary Hotel with my mates, eating a turkey dinner with all the trimmings and drinking wine.

Later, at the Assembly Hall, Joan, typically, was still trying to pair me off with Tex's mate whom I liked jitterbugging with. I think she thought I might suddenly see the light at the eleventh hour, realise the error of my ways and settle for an ally rather than an enemy.

She might have known that, after all Wern and I had been through as enemies in love, we weren't about to throw it all up now.

'Oh, Mu, we'll miss you,' she said as she kissed me goodbye. 'We've had some great times together.'

'We have, haven't we!'

'I really hope it all works out well for you and Werner, Mu. But are you sure you won't change your mind? Just think, if you married Tex's mate and I married Tex we could all live in America. We could be neighbours, Mu, and raise our children together.'

'It's a lovely thought, Joan ... just one problem ... Tex's mate isn't tall and dark and called Werner Palmer!'

Neither wild horses nor all the words of persuasion in the world could possibly drag me away from the course in life I had now set myself. For me it was simple. Wherever Werner was, I wanted to be. He was still and, I was convinced, would always be, the only important thing in my life. I couldn't see anything beyond being with him, being married to him and him being a free man. That was my goal. Once that had been achieved I imagined life would be a bed of roses. Never again would I have to face the agonies of being separated from him, of living in fear of him being caught.

I finished packing my two suitcases that night. Peggy came into my room carrying a bag, just as I had shut the second case.

'A little going away pressie for you, Mu.'

'Oh, ta! What is it?'

'Open the bag and see.'

I did. It was a very pretty pair of soft blue slippers.

'They're lovely, Peggy. Ta ever so much. I'll save them for best.'

'The house won't be the same without you here. Mum and me'll be rattling around.'

'No more sharing stockings and clothes, eh! I wonder how we'll manage on half each of the wardrobe we're used to!'

'No more arguments about who's having the blue dress anyway!'

'No, that's true. Ta for everything, Peggy. All the sharing ... all the white lies!'

'You take care, love. I still don't approve of what you're doing but I hope it'll turn out all right for you. I hope Werner'll look after you properly.'

'I'm sure he'll do that.'

'Ummm.'

That night I didn't get to sleep for a long time. I knew I would miss Mum and Peggy and all my mates. I was leaving a way of life and people I had always known to go to a place I hardly knew, all because I had fallen in love with a German P.O.W. Was I being a fool to leave my security and start a new life far away which almost everyone was warning me against? Should I stay? Would that be safest? In the darkness of the night all sorts of doubts came flooding into my mind. How could I be so rash? How could I throw up everything for a German P.O.W.?

Then I remembered. That German P.O.W. was Werner Palmer, the man I loved above everyone and everything else in the world, the man who made me feel happy and safe, the man who made me know I was alive.

I had arranged for a taxi to pick me up and take me to the station the following morning. It arrived punctually.

Mum kissed me goodbye in the hall.

'God bless you, child. Remember to phone if you get into trouble.'

'Don't worry about me, Mum. You know I've got a good little job to go to. Perhaps you'll come and visit me soon?'

'We'll see.'

''Bye, then!'

Mum waved from the front door and I had tears in my eyes as the taxi started off down Rosehill Street. I glanced over at the arboretum. It looked really lovely with the dew on all the leaves, sparkling in the early morning sunshine. Would I ever see that sight again? I remembered how I hardly ever used to notice the arboretum. How it had just been there; something I had grown up with. Then I had met Werner and we'd had some lovely romantic walks in there in the sunshine. And now I thought it had never looked so beautiful ... now that I was leaving and might never see it again.

Soon we were passing along Regent Street. I hadn't been down here for ages. Now, as I looked at all the bombed-out houses, fingers of ice seemed to clutch tightly round my heart. I didn't want to look at houses which had been smashed to smithereens ... or any other reminders of the war ... it wasn't Werner's fault ... I shut my eyes for several minutes until I was certain Regent Street was far behind.

And then I was standing on the station platform with my two cases beside me. There I was in my camel coat, my brown leather shoes with the five-inch heels and my lovely new handbag, tucked under my arm.

That was me, Muriel Webster of Derby, about to set out on a whole new adventure in life.

CHAPTER 11

The sun was still shining in Wisbech when I stepped off the bus. Audrey and Werner were already there, waiting. Seeing Werner rush up to greet me swept away all the anxieties I had been suffering on the journey. When I saw his happy, smiling face I knew it was all worth while ... all my agony of leaving my Mum, my sister, my home, my friends, my Muriel Webster of Derby life. I loved Werner Palmer. I would do anything for him.

And then, with the strength of a lion, he had hoisted one of my cases under his arm, held the other in his hand and wrapped his spare arm around me.

'*Mein liebling*, thank you for coming to me. I'm so proud of you.'

'It's because I love you so much that I'm here, Wern.'

He bent down and kissed me lightly and then we walked over to Audrey's little Austin Seven where she was waiting at the wheel. She leant out of the window: 'Come on, pile in. Let's get home for some lunch. Isn't it a beautiful day? That's a good omen for you, Muriel ... having such a lovely day to start a new life!'

'Now we are together, all our days will be sunny, even when its raining,' Werner said as he loaded the cases into the car.

I had to agree with him. 'That's just how I feel, Wern.'

As we set off I looked about me. Everything was so perfect. I admired Audrey in her smart blue costume. I thought it must be new as I hadn't seen it before. And I admired the way she was, so self-sufficient, such a nippy little driver. One day, I dreamed, I would have a little Austin Seven like hers. Yes, the future was certainly beginning to look rosy.

At the manor Werner carried my cases up to my room and Audrey

128

and I went into the kitchen to make coffee. The sun hadn't yet penetrated round that side of the house and the kitchen was quite cool and dark after the brilliance outside. Suddenly I remembered Mum, would she be in our sunny kitchen now? My eyes filled up with tears and I began sobbing, just as Werner came in.

'Now, now, *mein liebling*, what's all this about?'

He came over to me and took me in his arms. I was aware of Audrey going quietly into the lounge with the coffee tray.

'I'm sorry to be so silly, Wern,' I sobbed into his chest.

'No, no. You tell me what is the matter.'

He put his finger under my chin and gently lifted up my face so that we were looking into each other's eyes. I saw his deep concern. I knew I could tell him anything and everything and he would understand.

'I ... I thought I had it under control. On the journey here and last night I felt awful about leaving Mum and Peggy and all my friends ... and my home ...'

'Oh, I understand, *mein liebling*. You are feeling homesick.'

'I suppose that's what it is.'

'Of course. It is only natural. You know, I too felt homesick when I was conscripted into the German army and had to leave my family and my home. But I got over it and you will too. Just remember your family, your home, they are still there. You haven't lost them.'

'I'm just being silly, I'm sorry.'

'No, you aren't. You cry, *mein liebling*, I'll hold you.'

He gave me a huge bear hug. I forced myself to stop sobbing and pulled myself together enough to smile up at him.

'Are you all right now?'

'Yes, I think so.'

'Good. Then I will leave you for two minutes to go and find Herman for coffee. He is down the bottom of the garden.'

'All right.'

As he went out of the back door Audrey came in from the hall.

'I'm sorry I broke down like that, Audrey. It was just so sad to leave my Mum this morning.'

129

'Don't you worry, Mu. I think you're a very brave person. I really admire you for the decision you made in coming here. It took a lot of guts. But it'll all be worthwhile. You'll see. You and Werner will be so happy together. Come on, let's go and have that coffee.'

The four of us sat and chatted and joked over coffee but I still felt the niggling pain of homesickness. I told the others I was just going to go upstairs to change out of my travelling clothes. First I went into the bathroom and had a really good cry. That must have done the trick and got it all out of my system because, when I went downstairs for lunch, I was able to join in the chatter and joking and discovered the niggling pain had completely gone.

After lunch Werner went outside to help Herman with the gardening while Audrey and I washed up.

'It's so good of you to have me here, Audrey. I'd never have managed all this if it hadn't been for you.'

'You know I'm only too pleased to help.'

'Well, I really appreciate it. I'd like to take you and Herman out for a really nice dinner with Wern and me. Do you know of a good place - somewhere you'd really like to go?'

'It's a lovely idea, Mu. But only if you let me pay for Herman and I.'

'Oh no. I want to treat you, for all you've done for me.'

'No. I insist we go halves. There's a very nice hotel just outside Cambridge that does very romantic candlelit dinners. Would that suit?'

'That sounds just the sort of place.'

'I'll go and phone and book a table for tomorrow night then. All right?'

'Yes. We'll have a candlelit dinner to celebrate our futures.'

Werner came in just then to get some string so I told him about the dinner.

'What a good idea. But you must let Herman and I help pay.'

'No. It's our treat.'

'But ...'

'No!'

'Oh, you are a tinker. All right then. But we'll make it up to you

130

somehow.'

He kissed me without holding me because his hands were all muddy from the garden. Then he went back to join Herman. Audrey came back in from the hall.

'That's all arranged. Eight o'clock tomorrow night.'

'Lovely.'

We watched Werner and Herman from the kitchen window.

'I think Werner's just telling Herman about the dinner. I told him when he came in just now ... look at them looking at us ... whatever are they up to?'

'They've certainly adopted a conspiratorial attitude ... they're plotting something!'

The following evening, before we set off for the dinner, Herman came into the house carrying a parcel and looking very pleased with himself.

'What's that?' Audrey asked.

I craned my neck round to get a better look but Herman headed off to the kitchen, saying, over his shoulder: 'Don't you and Muriel be so nosey.'

'They're up to something,' Audrey whispered to me.

But soon we were on our way to the hotel and thought no more about Herman's mysterious parcel.

Both men had spruced themselves up. Again Werner succeeded in taking my breath away. He looked so good in a suit. I felt really proud being with him. Audrey and I may have paid for the dinner but the two men entertained us beautifully. We drank champagne and talked and laughed. We got a few looks from the people sitting at the next table. They seemed to be showing a little too much interest in our conversation. Werner leant over to whisper to me, 'I think I had better start talking about my Dutch family!'

And that is exactly what he did, in a loud, clear voice.

'Of course, my grandfather ran the business in Utrecht before my father took it over. You girls must come and visit us in Holland sometime. We Dutch are very hospitable!'

It was amazing. The people at the next table seemed to take no further interest in our conversation after that. Werner was so clever. He always knew how to handle a situation.

Audrey had ordered a taxi to take us home. We were in high spirits and singing songs all the way home. We didn't stop when we went inside. There was no fear of waking Jill up because she was staying with a friend for the weekend.

'Go and sit in the lounge, girls,' Herman said and whispered something else in Audrey's ear.

'What?' she said, clearly not having heard him.

'Never mind.'

He and Werner disappeared into the kitchen and Audrey and I went into the lounge. She put a record on the gramophone. Just as it started up Werner and Herman came waltzing in with a bottle of champagne and a plate of cheese sandwiches.

'Our little treat for you,' Herman told us.

We didn't get to bed until about half past two that night. It had been a wonderful evening. Just as I was getting into bed I noticed an envelope on my pillow. Opening it I found a card inside which read: 'My darling, never more than a thought away. I'm longing for you by night and by day. The love in our hearts always keep burning bright. It won't be long because I'll be with you tonight ... Werner.'

Typical of Wern! I thought, he wants me to know he's always thinking of me. I hope he knows I'm always thinking of him too.

The next day I set off for Wisbech with one suitcase and arrived at the Welcome Café at 10.00 a.m., as arranged, to start work.

Celia greeted me with a smile and the proprietress, Mrs. Green, took me up to the bedroom.

'Is that all you've got?' she asked, looking at my one suitcase.

'Yes.'

She left me to change into a black skirt and white blouse and then I went downstairs to join her in the café.

'Right, I'll just show you the ropes, Muriel. Then I'll leave you and

Celia to get on with it.'

'Ta, very much.'

'Pardon?' she said, laughing.

'Ta ... thanks!'

'Of course, that's another of your Derby expressions, isn't it?'

Mrs. Green showed me what I had to do and told me to just ask Celia if I wasn't sure about anything.

'When things get slack you can stop for a cup of tea or a meal. Do you think you'll be all right?'

'Oh yes, ta ... uh ... thanks!'

That day passed very quickly. The café was busy and I worked very hard. But I enjoyed the work and I enjoyed Celia's company. She took it upon herself to put me wise about practically every customer who came in and made me laugh at all the nicknames she had cooked up for them: like Octopus for the fat man with the wandering hands and Mrs. Teacake for the old lady who came in every afternoon for a pot of tea and a toasted teacake.

At the end of the day Mrs. Green told me she was very pleased with me.

'You're good at nipping about, Muriel. I can see you'll be an asset to the place,' she told me as she and her husband carried in an extra table.

'Looks like we'll be nipping about even more tomorrow!' Celia said, winking at me.

I quickly got into the routine of working in the café. Some evenings I would cycle to meet Werner, but two or three evenings a week I'd just sit in the café lounge and read a book or talk to Celia. Occasionally I would pop along to the church. It was beautifully cool in there on those summer evenings. I liked listening to my footsteps as I walked down the aisle. That was me, Muriel Webster, no longer of Derby, now an independent working woman, in love with Werner Palmer. I would pray for my family and for Werner to be freed so that we could marry.

Before long I got to know all the café customers as well as Celia did – especially I got to know the ones to avoid. Several young men tried chatting me up. Some had seen me out cycling with Werner. Some began to be a real pain. They'd ask me where my boyfriend was from. I'd say he was Dutch. They'd say, no, he wasn't, he was a Jerry. Then they'd ask why I preferred a Jerry to an Englishman. I tried to ignore them. Sometimes Mrs. Green would ask me if the customers were insulting me. I always said no. I wasn't sure if she knew my boyfriend was a P.O.W. If she didn't, I didn't want her to find out in case she decided to give me the sack. So I just got used to the insults and tried not to let them bother me.

But one day I got a letter. It was addressed to 'Muriel, the waitress'. It came in a filthy envelope. I read it in my tea-break and then I tore it up and flushed it down the lavatory. It said: 'You bleeding old cow, going with a Jerry. You need shooting. I hope someone will rape you to death. Watch out. We may be waiting for you.'

Of course it wasn't signed. I was shocked and frightened to start with. Should I go to the police? Should I tell Werner? I just didn't know what to do. When I went back into the café I found myself wondering about every man that came in. Was it him? Did that one send the letter?

By the end of the day I had convinced myself that the best thing to do about the letter was ignore it. I wouldn't even tell Werner about it. I had seen how angry he could get when I had told him about Frank at Ollerton. I didn't want to see him setting himself up as a one-man vigilante force.

The letter was just one of a score of episodes I found myself having to cope with. I soon realised that everyone around must know Werner was a German P.O.W. Who was I trying to fool by saying he was Dutch? Just myself. The number of times I was spat at in the street told me I wasn't fooling anyone else.

One afternoon I was just cycling along the street when someone opened an upstairs window and threw the contents of a chamber pot at me. Fortunately it missed but that person had sent her message loud and clear.

I found myself seeking out the cool peace of the lovely old church more and more often. Why, I asked in my prayers, did I have to suffer all this abuse? No direct answer came but somehow I found the strength to let it all slide over me, and I found I could cope.

The only person I did talk to about it was Audrey, at weekends. She suffered the same kind of abuse. She understood. But we both agreed our men were worth it. The world could sling all the insults it liked at us ... we'd show 'em it didn't matter.

And then the day came when Werner told me he had asked for permission to marry me.

'There is a procedure to go through, *mein liebling*,' he said as we pushed our bikes into a field and sat down to chat. 'An officer will have to come and see you and question you. He will talk to me too, separately, and then it will be decided if we may marry.'

'Do you think it'll be all right then? Do you think they'll give permission?'

'I don't really see why not. I have heard of other cases where permission has been given. But I'll tell them we'll get married anyway, with or without their permission.'

'Oh, don't do that, Wern. It's not right. Don't get all hot-headed on them.'

'It will show them how much I love you.'

'But, Wern ...'

'It's all right, *liebling* ... I'm only teasing!'

At last our marriage looked as if it might become a reality. I didn't fancy being questioned by an officer but, if it meant getting one step closer to being Mrs. Werner Palmer, then I would face it.

We set off on our bikes again. Werner always cycled back to the café with me before returning alone to his billet.

We started down quite a steep incline. Werner was way ahead of me because I was using my back brake to slow me down and his brakes didn't work very well. At the bottom of the hill I saw his bike skid on an oil patch. He went head over heels over the handlebars and straight into the deep ditch at the side of the road.

It all happened so quickly I could hardly believe my eyes.

'Good God! What are you doing there, Wern?'

I pulled up sharply beside the ditch, relieved to see the grin on his face as he clambered out. He was covered from head to foot in muddy slime.

'I was practising a commando jump.'

'Don't be daft!'

I couldn't help laughing at the sight of him now that I knew he was unhurt. He looked himself up and down.

'No. Really and truly I think I was fixing drains!'

Good old Wern. He always made a joke out of any mishap. That was one of the things I loved so much about him.

The next couple of weeks I spent on tenterhooks, waiting for the officer to come and question me. One minute I'd be dreading it, the next I'd be wondering why he hadn't come yet. Then one day Mrs. Green came over to me in the café and said she had an Army C.O. in the lounge to see me. She patted me on the arm.

'It'll be all right, dear.'

Those words told me a lot. They told me the C.O. had already spoken to Mrs. Green, that she knew Werner was a P.O.W., that she knew why the C.O. wanted to question me. And the way she had patted my arm and given me that kind reassurance told me she wished me well.

I was quite surprised when I saw the C.O. standing in the lounge. He was a very short man, not much taller than me and he had a tiny moustache and wore glasses.

'Good afternoon, Miss Webster.'

'Good afternoon.'

'Shall we sit down?'

'Yes.'

We sat facing each other in two armchairs.

'I've come to see why you want to get married.'

'Yes, Werner said you'd be coming.'

He looked me up and down in a way I didn't quite like.

'Why is a girl like you doing a waitressing job?'

'To be near Wern.'

'Umm. He's had his head shaved twice, hasn't he? Did you have anything to do with that?'

136

'Not actually. I didn't actually shave it.'

He laughed.

'No, I wasn't exactly suggesting that.'

'No. I know you weren't.'

I didn't like this questioning and was quite relieved to hear a knock on the door. Mrs. Green came in with a teapot and cups on a tray.

'I thought perhaps you and your friend would like a cup of tea, Muriel.'

'Oh ta ... thank you very much, Mrs. Green.'

She left the tray and went out of the room again. I poured tea for us both. The C.O. didn't question me at all while I poured. In a way that silence was worse than the questions, or so I thought until he asked me the next one.

'I have to ask if you are pregnant, Miss Webster?'

I felt utterly shocked. I slammed my cup and saucer down on the tray.

'No, I'm not. If you like I'll go and be examined by a doctor to prove I'm a virgin. I wouldn't go into a church to be married if I wasn't a virgin. I'm a Catholic and I've been brought up strictly.'

'I'm sorry, Miss Webster, but I'm afraid I had to ask. Let me go on ... You do know if you get married to Mr. Palmer you won't get any allowances ... how will you live? You know you can't live together even after you are married.'

'I work. I earn my living. And when Wern's free we will go to Germany together where he will teach.'

'Please believe me. It will be very hard in Germany. You won't survive. There are terrible food shortages there. People are begging for food on the streets. I've seen it. I've been there. Many a young girl turns into a prostitute to get money for food.'

I must have been looking at him blankly. Was he trying to frighten me off? Obviously he didn't understand how much Wern and I loved each other. I said nothing.

'I don't tell you all this to frighten you, Miss Webster, just to make sure you are aware of the reality ... and then there is all the anti-English feeling there ...'

I found my voice.

'I've managed to cope with all the anti-German feeling here and I'm still determined to marry Wern. We love each other. Don't you understand?'

'I'm sorry if I have upset you, Miss Webster. I'll go now.'

He went. I was all in a fluster and quite upset. In all honesty I didn't know how the interview had gone. Would Wern and I get our permission or not? Mrs. Green came in.

'Are you all right, Muriel?'

'I think so.'

'Let's have another cup of tea together before you go back to work.'

Mrs. Green was very kind. She sat and talked to me for half an hour, about everyday things. I needed that. When I went back to work I felt calm again.

That evening I cycled to meet Wern and told him the C.O. had been.

'How did it go then?' he asked me.

'I don't know.'

'I do. It went very well!'

'How do you know?'

'He came to see me this afternoon too. He told me I was a lucky man, as if I didn't know! That you were a nice, decent girl.'

'Huh, he treated me as if I was a common tart to start with. He asked me if I was pregnant, Wern!'

'Oh, *mein liebling*, he shouldn't have asked you that. He probably thinks all girls are the same. He told me not to take you to Germany. He said we wouldn't survive there. But I told him that was where I trained, the only place I could get a good job and provide well for you. Anyway, I think it looks good for us.'

'Oh, I hope so, Wern. I do hope so.'

CHAPTER 12

Werner was right. It was not long after our interviews with the C.O. that we got our permission to marry. We went to see Father Paul of St. Mary's Church. Like the C.O., he spent a lot of time pointing out the pitfalls we would have to face as a married couple, especially the anti-German feeling that was so rife, not least in Wisbech. But, as we had done with the C.O., we managed to convince him too that we were deeply in love and could not live apart.

'Well, we'd better set a date then. You two have a talk about it for a moment,' he told us as he went out of the room.

Werner took hold of my hand and looked excitedly into my eyes.

'Muriel, I wonder if we could be married on my Mother's birthday, the 23rd of September? It would please her very much and it is a date we would always remember. Would you mind? It's only a few weeks away.'

'That's a lovely idea, Wern. All right, let's ask him for the 23rd of September.'

And so it was settled. We were to be married on the 23rd of September 1947.

How it happened I don't know, but, somehow, the news spread like wildfire that an English girl was going to marry a German P.O.W. Our names began appearing not only in the local rags but also in the national press. I had never thought our very personal and deep love would become so public. It was the last thing we wanted, and me working in a public place like the café made it even worse. People flocked from all over. They came in and bought cups of tea as an excuse to ogle me. I knew that was what they were doing. They were not our normal customers and some of them dropped the usual abusive comments which I had become accustomed to.

Nevertheless, I was so excited about my forthcoming marriage that I managed to rise above the ogling and the abuse. There were a lot of preparations to be made.

Celia asked me if I would like to borrow her sister's wedding dress as she was about my size. It would have been impossible for me to have bought a new one on my wages so I jumped at the offer.

'Ooh yes, Celia. You bring it for me to try on and if it fits I'll hire it off her.'

Not only did it fit. It was as if it had been made for me. It was a very good quality, gorgeous satin dress.

'And don't think of paying her anything for it,' Celia told me. 'She's only too happy to lend it to you.'

I was so thrilled. All my friends were so good to me. I went and bought a lovely white, feathered headdress, like a tiara, to wear with it.

My next thought was the bridesmaids' dresses. I was going to have four bridesmaids. Audrey and her daughter, Jill, and the little daughters of two old friends from Derby.

I soon realised this wedding was going to incur several expenses so I withdrew all £28 from my Victory savings account. I stashed the money under my mattress and took from it whenever I needed to and added to it from my wages whenever I could. That way I managed to buy the bridesmaids' dresses and all the food for the reception.

As August turned into September it was still light when Celia and I went to bed. She liked to sleep with the curtains open but I couldn't sleep when it was light. I would lie in bed for hours, mulling over the road my life was taking ... Mum had said she didn't want to come to my wedding for, even though she wished me well, she just couldn't approve of what I was doing. I thought over all my growing-up years. Now that I was away from home, I realised just how much Mum had done for us kids. Now I missed her terribly. Often, on those light evenings, I would cry myself to sleep with these thoughts.

Then it was time for me to go back to Derby, just for the day. I was going to Joan and Tex's wedding. I left Wisbech very early in the morning, dressed in my smart navy-blue suit with white piping and a little navy pillbox hat. When I got to Derby, around ten, I just had time to go home and have a coffee with Mum before going on to Joan's.

It was the first time I had seen Mum since leaving to take up the job in Wisbech. We hugged each other and we both cried. I knew she was as pleased to see me as I was her. We sat and talked for an hour, catching up on all the news. Then it was time for me to leave in a taxi for Joan's.

'I'm sorry, Muriel, but I can't come to your wedding. You know I don't agree with it.'

I had tears in my eyes.

'I know, Mum. But I do wish you would. It might be the last time I'll see you because we'll be going to Germany soon after we're married.'

She kissed me goodbye, saying, 'You've made your bed, you must lie on it.'

Her saying that really hurt me deeply. But there was no time for me to mope about the way she had virtually rejected me with those last words: soon I was at Joan's and being greeted excitedly and warmly by all my old mates from the depot. It was great to see them all again and not least Joan. She hugged me.

'Come and have a drink, Mu. You look as if you could do with one!'

'It's lovely to see you, Joan. You look radiant!'

'Well, it's not because I'm pregnant, at least I don't think I am. But I have to tell you, Mu, tonight won't be the first night for me!'

'Oh, Joan! You are a one!'

We laughed. Even though we were so different, like chalk and cheese really, we were the best mates ever.

It was a lovely day. Joan and Tex were so obviously happy together. We all trooped off to the registry office and then back again to Joan's for the reception. Tex had had food parcels sent over from the States and there really was a good spread. The two of them were setting off for the States the very next day, after staying at Joan's for their wedding night, so they and all my other mates came down to the station to see me off back to Wisbech that night. I hated leaving them all. They were such a cheerful, carefree lot. I felt as if I had the weight of the world on my shoulders as the train pulled out of the station with all the "Bye, Mu's ringing in my ears.

I burst into tears. Would I ever see Joan again? She was off to the States and soon I would be in Germany ... worlds apart! And all my other mates ... yes, we could write ... but that wasn't the same as being with them. We had had such great times together. And Mum ... would I ever see Mum again?

I went along to the toilet where I dried my eyes and powdered my nose. I looked at myself in the mirror, saying: 'Come on, Muriel Webster. You'll be Muriel Palmer soon. Your life is with Werner now. Pull yourself together.'

Mr. and Mrs. Green met me at Wisbech station to drive me back to the café. It was very kind of them but they asked me questions about my day and all I wanted to do now was forget my past and look forward to the future. I was so glad to get into my bed that night where I could be alone with my thoughts. I had a really good cry and got some of my sorrow out of my system.

The next day Werner and I went for a cycle ride. We were going to meet his Uncle George, who was to be his Best Man. I was still very subdued after my visit to Derby and, of course, Werner noticed.

'What's the matter, *liebling*? You aren't changing your mind about us getting married, are you?'

'No, course not. I'm just so sad that my Mum won't be coming to the wedding. And none of my Derby friends will be there, except the bridesmaids and their mums.'

I felt absolutely desolate and even Werner wasn't able to find the words to console me. Dear Uncle George gave me a great big hug when we met. He sensed my unhappiness but thought I was suffering the effects of all the abuse I had been getting.

'You not worry, Muriel,' he told me, 'you be fine in Germany, they not call you names there.'

He was so kind and I began to feel that I really belonged to Werner and his family. That helped me a lot. I knew I had to face up to letting go of the past and just head for the future. I just wished it wasn't so hard.

Mr. Hunter-Rowe was to give me away and Mrs. Hunter-Rowe had very kindly arranged the cake for me. I bought several bottles of wine and prepared ham, tongue, salads and trifles for the reception.

On the morning of my wedding day I took all the food down to the house where the reception was to be. Audrey had wanted me to have the reception at her house but Upwell was a bit too far for people who had come all the way from Derby by train to trek. A very kind lady, Minnie, who did the church flowers, had told me I could have the use of her front room in a terraced house in Wisbech for the reception, so I had gratefully settled for that.

As I was styling my own hair, I had it in curlers and it took me several trips to transfer the food from the café to the house. Each time people seemed to be waiting on the street for me so that they could spit at me or call out, 'You Jerry-loving bitch.' I just ignored them. At least, outwardly I ignored them. Inwardly I felt so hurt, so insulted. It was purgatory.

Finally I was ready to change into my dress in the reception room. Then I remembered I had left all our letters, cards and telegrams at the café. I would have to make one more trip. We had had some lovely messages ... 'Roses are red, violets are blue, don't get yourself tight and land in a stew', from Jill and Jane, the twins; 'Today's the day, tonight's the night, we've shot the stork, so you'll be all right', from Joan and Tex; and many, many more.

I shot up the street again, collected the pile of messages and headed back.

I should have avoided that window. I knew about that window from previous experience but I was in such a hurry that I forgot all about it, until it was too late ...

The old witch flung the window open and threw the contents of her chamber pot at me again. It caught me this time, on the side of the face.

'Wait till you get in church,' she shouted at me. 'We've got a booby trap for you there!'

I was in tears as I rushed into the house. Audrey was standing in the doorway, already in her bridesmaid's dress.

'You stupid old maid! You ought to be ashamed of yourself,' she shouted at the woman.

There was just time for me to have a good wash and put on my wedding dress before the cars started arriving. The bridesmaids went off to the church first and then Mr. Hunter-Rowe helped me into his car. I was so nervous. I know all brides are supposed to be nervous on their big day, but for me it was torture. Now I was frightened to death about what booby trap might be waiting for me in the church.

The car pulled off down the street, which was now crowded with hundreds of people. They were all ogling me, not to see what I was wearing with normal human interest, but just to see what this 'Jerry loving trollop', as they called me, looked like. And still they spat and hurled verbal abuse at me.

Outside the church the crowds were the thickest. There must have been over 200 people there, more people than I had ever seen gathered in Wisbech. The vibes were awful. I felt them hating me. I longed to get inside that church ... to be standing beside Werner.

To my amazement the church was also packed out. I knew they had come to see Werner's 'horns' and me, 'the trollop'.

As 'Here comes the bride' started every face in that church turned to stare at me. I focused on Werner who I could see standing, waiting for me up at the front. It seemed a mile down that aisle until, about half-way down, I caught sight of one face in the crowd I recognised – the last face I had expected to see. My heart leapt. It was Mum! She had come! Suddenly all the hatred and the negative vibes melted into nothing. My Mum was there to see me married! That meant everything in the world to me.

Father Paul conducted the service beautifully. It was well over an hour long and he smiled at me reassuringly throughout. Werner too, kept gripping my hand to give me reassurance. He had no nerves at all, standing there to attention throughout, looking so smart in his brown suit.

Amongst that overwhelming crowd were just a few invited souls. It was their love and kindness that came shining through to me during the

144

service, effectively blocking out everything else.

At last 'Ave Maria' was played for us to leave the church. Outside our photographer had to compete with many others from the newspapers. Ours was about the first case of an English girl marrying a German P.O.W. They wanted to make the most of it.

Mum came over to give me a kiss.

'You look lovely, Mu. I want you to be happy, love.'

'I'm so glad you came, Mum. Are you coming to the reception?'

'No, love. I couldn't face it,' she said, looking round at the crowds.

I understood. I was just so happy that she had come.

'I can't tell you how much it meant to me, Mum, having you here.'

'You write to me, love. Remember.'

'Of course I will.'

'Take good care of her, Werner.'

'You can be sure I'll always do that, Mrs. Webster.'

And then she was gone, disappearing through the crowd. The P.O.W.s from the orchard billet rushed up to us and filled my arms with three lovely bouquets of flowers. I was so touched.

At the reception Mr. Hunter-Rowe read the messages because Uncle George's English wasn't really good enough.

Everything seemed to be going all right, with a lot of laughter and chatter, when the living-room door suddenly burst open and a young man swung in.

'What the hell are all you people doing in here with a filthy Jerry?'

A deathly hush came over the room. Before anyone could say anything Minnie stepped forward, took the man by the arm and led him out into the hall. I followed.

'What's the matter?' I asked.

'Wait there a minute,' Minnie said.

She took the man into the kitchen and closed the door behind the two of them. Within a minute she was back in the hall again.

'I'm ever so sorry, dear. That's my son. He's just arrived home. He didn't know I'd invited you to have your reception here. Please don't take any notice, go back in and enjoy yourselves.'

145

I went back into the living room but I couldn't enjoy myself. My wedding day had been spoilt. It seemed forever until the end of the reception.

Mr. Hunter-Rowe ferried the Derby guests up to the station and then he drove Wern and I back to the billet where the P.O.W.s had another reception for us. Audrey, Jill and Uncle George also made their way there. For me that was the best part of the wedding day. I felt at home in the orchard. Safe.

The P.O.W.s had organised a real feast with cheeses, cakes and custards and a wonderful buttercream tart, as they called it, which was a kind of gateaux, over a foot high. It was delicious.

Towards the end Mr. and Mrs. Hunter-Rowe came down from their farmhouse to join us and I thanked them for everything they had done for Werner and I.

'It's been a memorable day, Muriel,' Mr. Hunter-Rowe said.

'Yes. I'm just sorry it's over.'

'Over?' Mrs. Hunter-Rowe said. 'It's not over, dear. You're coming up to our house now and you and Werner are staying there together for three days.'

'What?'

I was so surprised. I was supposed to be going back to the café ...?

'It's all arranged. The Greens are quite happy for you to be off work to have a bit of a honeymoon. We've squared it with them!'

I couldn't believe it. The Hunter-Rowes were so very good to us.

'I don't know what to say ... ta ever so much!'

I looked at Werner, who had been keeping very quiet throughout all this.

'You knew, didn't you, Wern?'

'Yes. But Mr. and Mrs. Hunter-Rowe wanted it to be a surprise for you.'

'Oh, it's so kind. It's such a lovely surprise.'

The four of us set off through the orchard towards the farmhouse. On the way I noticed a large wooden shed. I'd seen it a hundred times before but it suddenly struck me as having potential as somewhere for Wern and me to live together. I piped up: 'You know, that old place could be made quite habitable.'

'Yes, it could, couldn't it?' Mr. Hunter-Rowe said, winking at me.

I knew he knew what I was thinking. Werner smiled at me. Without saying anything else we all knew the kind of potential that shed obviously had.

Up at the house we listened to records until about half past ten and then Werner and I went up to bed.

The Hunter-Rowes had given us the big front bedroom. Laying on the bed, waiting for me, was a really beautiful negligée made out of parachute silk and trimmed with lace. I picked it up and held it to me.

'Mrs. Hunter-Rowe made it for you, *mein liebling*.'

'Oh, Wern! Everyone has been so kind. We've got some marvellous friends, haven't we?'

'We certainly have. And I have a marvellous wife.'

He came to me and held me tightly, covering my face and neck with kisses.

I was frightened of making love. I didn't have to tell him. He knew, and he accepted it. He didn't force me. We loved each other as much as two human beings possibly could but we didn't make love properly that night ...

The next day we went to church with the Hunter-Rowes and for the next two days we spent most of the time going for walks with their dear little wire-haired terrier, Rags. The weather was good, perfect for walking. All we wanted was to be together and that, thanks to the Hunter-Rowes, had been fixed for us.

But, back at the café, after our honeymoon, I felt so lonely. My room, the café, seemed so empty without Werner beside me. It was awful being parted so soon after our wedding. I prayed that it wouldn't be long before we were allowed to be together.

About two weeks after the wedding an Army truck pulled up outside the café and a colonel jumped out. As I watched through the window, I noticed it was the same man who had interviewed me before. A few minutes later Mrs. Green came in and asked me to go through to the

147

lounge. I went in with her.

'The colonel has come about Werner, Muriel. He says he's very poorly. The paraffin fumes in his billet have made him ill and he's been taken to the military hospital.'

My heart missed a beat. Wern! Poor Wern! Was he very ill?

'Is he all right?' I asked the colonel.

'He's very poorly, but they say he'll pull through. Come on, I'll take you to see him.'

I was taken in the Army truck to the military hospital, near Fridaybridge. All the way I was imagining Werner lying in bed, at death's door. Why was life so cruel? We had had so little time together. Surely he wouldn't be taken away from me now! Not after all we had been through!

In the hospital I was marched down a long corridor with a guard on either side of me. At Werner's room one guard stayed outside the door and the other one came inside with me. He sat on a chair by the door. I went over to the bed, took Wern's hand in mine and sat beside him.

'Oh, Wern, Wern. What have you been up to?'

When I saw that lovely smile of his I knew he was far from being at death's door.

'I'm all right, *liebling*. All the better for seeing you!'

I bent down and he kissed me.

'Guess what, Muriel? After this nasty little episode, Mr. Hunter-Rowe is now lining the inside of that shed. He has managed to get permission for us to live together there!'

'Really?'

'Yes, *mein liebling*. You can give up your job at the café and come and live with me!'

'Oh, that's the best news I've heard for ages.'

'Isn't it good?'

I went back to the café so much happier than when I had left it. Then I had thought I was in danger of becoming a widow. Now I knew I was shortly to become a fully fledged live-in wife.

Mrs. Green accepted my two week's notice very graciously. She said she would be sorry to see me go but she understood my position.

That same evening I saw an advertisement for a job at an hotel in Upwell, only a fifteen-minute walk from the orchard. I knew we would be very badly off without my wages so I made up my mind that the next day I would go and apply for that job.

CHAPTER 13

I got the job as general assistant at the little hotel. The hours were 9.00 a.m. until 12.30 p.m. daily and for that I would be paid £1.10s. 0d a week. That, plus Werner's rations which Mrs. Hunter-Rowe doled out, always generously adding a little extra, would be all we had to live on. It wasn't much at all but we were so in love that being together was the only thing in the world that mattered to us.

As Werner recovered in hospital and Mr. Hunter-Rowe finished lining the shed and getting the old stove into good working order, I hunted around for all the bits and pieces we would need for setting up our first home.

The first thing I bought with some of my savings was a very good double bed. A local family who were emigrating had a sale and I got it there for 7s. 6d. From them I also bought a couple of kitchen chairs, a peg rug, two blankets and some pots and pans. I bought new sheets and made pillowcases out of washed and bleached sugar bags.

The shed was about 22 feet by 18 feet, with a large window. It had a very large barn door. In the winter months we were to discover the full implications of that barn door, when gales blew so fiercely through it that the peg rug lifted a good four inches with every gusting blast.

The floor was brick tiled. Just before we moved in Werner painted it up with red tile paint. I painted the window ledge white and out of pinafores made pretty check curtains with frills on the bottom. I bought an old card table for five shillings and covered it with a table-cloth. Always I had a vase of flowers or greenery on it.

Werner found some orange boxes which he cleverly made into storage cupboards and I bought some little hooks from Woolworths to hang cups and pots and pans inside these cupboards. We also had apple boxes for storing our clothes and linen and to make two bedside tables, one on either side of our bed. We ran a big curtain across the width of the shed to divide the bedroom from the living area. On my bedside table I had a candlestick with a box of matches and in the living area we had a paraffin lamp.

We did all the cooking on the stove, which also heated our water. There was no supply of water to the shed so Werner always had a couple of buckets in his hands, to fetch water from the tap near his old billet. He kept our big tank topped up so that we always had a constant supply.

The only real luxury we had was our radio, which we ran off an accumulator. Actually we had two accumulators, as there was nothing worse than if one went before the end of a story, but usually one was in the shop being recharged so we would miss it anyway. The recharging sometimes cost me 3d., sometimes 6d., depending on which shop assistant served me. One of them hated Jerrys so he always charged me double.

A friend of Audrey's said she had an old tin bath and mangle we could have. Werner and I carried it, with the mangle inside, over two miles to get it to our little home. Fortunately there were not many people about that day. Those who were, watched with amused interest as we passed. Only one old witch spat at us, but then she always did, whenever she saw us, apart or together.

That tin bath served us really well. Not only for doing the weekly washing, which always had to be done when the weather looked good, but also for our Friday night baths. Werner would put the bath beside the stove and fill it with hot water. I would get in first and then he would have to use the same bath water after me.

I used to buy blue bags, which I used not only for whitening the washing but very often for wasp and bee stings. Living in an orchard we got a lot of those.

At the back of our shed was a lean-to where we kept our bikes and at the side we had an earth closet, which Werner had the pleasant task of emptying every so often.

151

The day before we moved in I felt on top of the world. I was going to our very own home. It might not be a mansion but it was clean and pretty and ours. All ours! I decided I would buy a few little luxuries so I invested 6d. on some Pond's Snowfire face powder, 9d. on some lipstick and 6d. on a tin of Kiwi shoe polish. For the enormous sum of 2s. 6d. I sent a telegram to Mum to tell her my change of address. I really hoped she might come and visit us now we had a place of our own. I was still missing her terribly.

It was about the middle of October when we moved in. All the apples in the orchard had just been harvested and the falling leaves were beginning to turn colour, both on the trees and the grass. Our shed was overhung by a lovely walnut tree. The whole place looked so mellow and warmly welcoming. Our little home in the orchard, our little bit of paradise, well away from all the parochial snoops.

I was so happy unpacking all our things with Werner. He was as thrilled as me.

'Where would you like me to put these bowls, *liebling*?'

'In that middle part of the cupboard, I think.'

'Don't you lift that! It's too heavy for you.'

'It's all right.'

He came over and took the box from me.

'Now, where do you want it?'

'Just on the bed, so that I can unpack it there.'

There was a knock at the door just then. We had left it wide open and looked round to see a young lad about ten standing there. He was carrying a sack.

'Hello, young man,' Werner said.

'Hello, Mister. Would you like a rabbit? You can buy it alive or I'll deaded it if you want.'

Werner and I couldn't help laughing.

'Is that what you've got in your sack?'

'Yes, Mister. Caught it this morning.'

'Did you now? Well, how much do you want for it ... deaded?'

'Sixpence.'

'That sounds a good price to me. What do you say, Mrs. Palmer?'

'Yes, that sounds a very good price.'

'All right, young lad. You deaded it and hang it on the side of the shed there.'

The boy's face lit up. I gave him sixpence out of my bag and Werner took him round the side of the shed, out of my view!

Later I wanted to go up to the village shop to buy some margarine.

'I'll walk up with you,' Werner said.

It was a pleasant walk along the lane but always better when we walked together. We never wanted to be apart, not even for a few minutes if we could help it.

'I'll wait outside,' Werner said when we got to the little wooden shop.

I went in. There was just one woman being served. As soon as she saw me she spat at me, picked up her bag and strode out of the shop. I felt awful. I wished, at that moment, I was in the safety of our little home in the orchard.

'I'm sorry about that, Mrs. Palmer. There's so much bad feeling about you two round here. Look, do you think in future you could make sure you come in when no-one else is about?'

She made me feel like a criminal, but I could see the sense in what she had said, both from her point of view and mine. She obviously didn't want to lose any customers - neither me nor those that might be put off at the thought of going to the same shop as me. From my point of view ... well, I was always looking to avoid tactfully unpleasant situations, rather than confront them. That had always been in my nature.

In future weeks and months I often had to wait, sometimes as long as half an hour, before it was safe for me to go into that shop.

Not long after we had got into bed on that first night in our orchard home I heard a scratching noise.

'Wern, listen. What's that?' I whispered.

He didn't reply and I realised he was fast asleep. But then again, out of the still silence of the shed, came the noise.

'Wern, wake up!'

I shook him.

'What, *liebling*?'

'Listen, what's that noise?'

We listened. There it was again, a scratching and scuttling noise.

'Oh, it's just a mouse.'

He got up and went to light the paraffin lamp. I peered over the blanket and in the flickering light saw two mice scurry along the ledge behind our bed. I screamed.

'They're just little field mice. They won't hurt you.'

'Oh Wern! I hate the thought of mice in our home.'

'Look, tomorrow you go up and ask Mrs. Hunter-Rowe for some traps and poison. They keep them up at the house.'

He got back into bed and held me tightly, but I didn't sleep all night. I didn't hear the mice again but I kept listening for them, straining to hear that scratching which I dreaded and yet was certain would start up again.

The next morning I went straight up to see Mrs. Hunter-Rowe.

'Oh heavens, we should have thought about field mice. Look, dear, why don't you take Rags down to live with you? I know you're very fond of him and he's an excellent ratter and mouser. You wouldn't have any problems with him around.'

And so we adopted Rags, the wire-haired terrier, and we never again saw a mouse in that shed. We did see something worse though, just once ...

The Hunter-Rowes had invited us up to lunch one day. Before going, Rags and I went round the back of the shed to see if Werner had managed to fix the puncture on my bike. I left the shed door open for about twenty minutes, a fatal mistake, while we chatted as I watched him finish off the job. Then I went to get my bag and, together with Rags, we strolled up to the Hunter-Rowes' house.

When we came home in the evening, Mrs. Hunter-Rowe presented me with a chicken to cook. We went into the shed and I put the chicken down on the table. Werner hung up his coat in the bedroom and I turned to do the same. Suddenly there was a heavy thud and scuffling noise and I saw a huge rat jump onto the table from the top of an orange

154

box cupboard. Before I could even scream Rags growled and pounced. He had that rat by the scruff of its neck and was shaking it to death. Werner flung open the door, chased the dog out and found a piece of wood to finish off the rat. Thank goodness it hadn't had time to touch the chicken. That was going to feed us for the next four days! I made Werner pull out our bed to make sure there wasn't another rat hiding there. I never left that shed door open again without Werner, Rags or me being in there.

When I got paid my wages on a Saturday morning I would feel rich. But that £1. 10s. 0d. had to stretch the whole week and, come Thursday, I usually had only a shilling left and often no food in the house.

We didn't have electricity bills or water rates, but we did need paraffin for the lamp, coal for the stove, our accumulators and our food. And, at the same time, I was trying to get enough things together to take to Germany when we went, because I knew money would be even scarcer there.

One thing I desperately needed was a new pair of shoes.

'Make sure you get a good pair,' Werner said. 'It is always important to get good shoes and look after your feet.'

Well, one good pair wouldn't have been an insurmountable problem but the three pairs I wanted to acquire for Germany almost was. It took a lot of scrimping and saving.

My Mum had a motto I was always recalling in those months in the orchard. 'Never throw anything out' ... We never had anything to throw out!

But we really learnt about thrift, about making do, making the most of everything and having an eye for a bargain.

A little bit of breast of lamb could be stretched for three or four days. I would roast it, then stew it with vegetables and then make soup with the bones. The fat would be used for frying chips.

To supplement our coal fuel supply we would never go for a walk without collecting wood on our way. We were lucky with milk because of the Jersey cow and with our supply I would make butter and cheese. There were always plenty of cooking apples, of course, but you can only

155

eat so many apples a week! By the time we left the orchard I wouldn't have been sorry if I never saw an apple again!

One real boon was discovered on the morning after the night of the plonk-plonking on our roof. It had been a windy night and the walnut tree had shed almost all its nuts. We gathered them in baskets and sold them to a shop in Wisbech.

Saturday was my baking day. Mostly I would make a week's supply of lemon curd or jam tarts which I would store in two tins, so that even if there was nothing else there would always be a tart to eat. We would pass the tin round if ever anyone came for a cup of tea, like Audrey and Jill, the P.O.W.s or the Hunter-Rowes. But always, by Thursday, they would all be gone. Yes, by Thursday we definitely felt very poor.

Many a time Audrey, Herman and Jill would come and play cards in the early winter evenings. Then Werner would stoke up the stove with a good lot of coal and we would toast crumpets or have baked potatoes.

One day I decided I would go and visit Mum. I hadn't seen her since the wedding and, despite all my letters asking her to come and visit, she didn't show any keenness to do so.

For two or three weeks I saved hard to buy my ticket for a day trip to Derby. I wondered what we could do without so that I could save enough. As I wondered I looked out of my window and saw a pheasant strutting in the orchard. It seemed to me that God had answered a prayer! I sidled over to the orange box cupboard and picked up Werner's dobber (catapult) and a stone from the supply next to it, all the time never taking my eyes off the bird. Quietly I opened the door, took aim and fired. The pheasant fell sideways and I ran over to it. But I was horrified to find it wasn't dead, only stunned. Its little heart was fluttering away with fright under its warm breast feathers. I felt awful and rushed back to the shed to find some bread for the poor thing ... bread we badly needed!

I crumbled it up and put it down in front of the bird, but it wouldn't touch it. I was almost frantic. I didn't know what to do. I went back to the shed to fetch some water and, as I came back with it, I saw the bird hobble a little and shakily fly up. I noticed its poor wing was obviously

156

hurt, as it flew off very uncertainly. Well, that was it as far as I was concerned. I vowed I would never try to kill an animal again, even if we were starving to death.

Two weeks later I had saved enough money and went to Derby to visit Mum. I told her how happy Wern and I were in our little home and how I wished she would come and see us.

'I'm sorry, Muriel, I just can't do that. You can come here whenever you like, but please don't expect me to go down there.'

I was really hurt. Why wouldn't she come? Then I felt her looking me over. I had always been slim but I was aware that I was probably on the skinny side then, after cutting down on things so that I could make this visit.

'Have you got enough money, Muriel?'

'Oh yes. I've told you, I've got that good little job at the hotel.'

I didn't want Mum to worry, even though I only had two shillings in my purse to last me until my next wages.

When I got home I decided to look for a job that would pay more. I liked the little job at the hotel and I liked the people there, but we desperately needed more money if I was going to get things together to go to Germany. I saw an advert for a similar job at another hotel near Upwell. It paid more because the hours were longer.

I felt quite confident as I walked along on my way to the interview. So far I had managed to land every job I had ever applied for and I couldn't see any reason why I shouldn't be offered this one, especially as I had had experience as a general assistant.

The receptionist showed me into an ante-room and asked me to wait there for the proprietress. I waited about twenty minutes and began to wonder if she was ever coming.

At last a tall, elegant woman came in. She looked at me as if she had a bad smell under her nose.

'Good afternoon ... uh ... Mrs. Palmer, isn't it?'

'Yes, that's right. Good afternoon.'

'Aren't you the young girl that married that Jerry?'

'Yes.'

'Well, you ought to be ashamed of yourself. Have you no shame, marrying a Jerry?'

I was so surprised. The woman was well spoken – educated, as they say. I had always believed 'educated' people were above such prejudices. I was lost for words but it really didn't matter. She wasn't about to give me a chance to say anything.

'I couldn't possibly consider YOU for this job. Please get out now before anyone around realises who you are.'

She swept out of the room and I followed her. I couldn't wait to get back to my poorly paid job where the people were so nice and friendly.

Not that that little job was without its problem or two. I was once going to put some rubbish in the dustbin out the back when I was confronted with a swastika daubed on the dustbin and a dead rat lying beside it. The message was plain to me. Obviously one of the customers had sent it. As usual, it hurt me deeply. When would these terrible things ever stop?

At home I told Werner about it.

'Ignore them, *liebling*, soon we will be in Germany, well away from all this bad feeling.'

The happy times we had living in the orchard more than made up for the nasty incidents. The Christmas season was particularly happy.

I made all my own Christmas decorations because we couldn't afford any, and Werner and I collected masses of holly and red berries. Our little home looked magical after we finished putting up the trimmings. Werner even made a wreath for the door.

One night carol singers came round. Those children were too young to know about prejudice. We stood at the door, enchanted by their well-scrubbed, earnest faces as they sang their little repertoire. We found them a sixpence which we couldn't really afford but it was well worth it. They were really delighted, thanked us and skipped off through the orchard.

On Christmas Eve Audrey, Jill and Herman came round and we played cards and sang carols. I had begun to learn German so Werner and I sang 'Silent Night' in German.

158

Werner was very insistent that I should learn the language well before going to Germany and he gave me lessons every evening. At first I had found it very difficult but then Werner, knowing how much I loved singing, had the brilliant idea of teaching me German songs and their meaning; I loved that and began to find the language much easier after starting that way.

When our guests had gone that night, Werner opened one of the bottles of beer I had bought him for Christmas. I only had a sip as I didn't like beer and we exchanged our presents. He had bought me a lovely scarf from Marks and Spencer's and I had bought him a nice white shirt. Mum had sent three pairs of silk stockings for me and three pairs of Wolsey socks for Werner. Peggy sent me a jumper and Joan and Tex had sent us a food parcel, all the way from the States.

We hadn't been so spoilt for a long time and were like two little kids, we were so excited. We listened to the radio until 2.00 a.m. before finally turning off the lamp.

On Christmas Day we went for a walk in the orchard. One of the P.O.W.s was milking the Jersey cow. We stood and watched him and then he handed us a big jug of lovely thick, creamy milk. As we walked back to the shed with it, I felt Werner turning my wedding ring round my finger as he held my left hand.

'You know, in Germany, *liebling*, you will have to wear your wedding ring on your right hand or they will think you aren't married.'

My heart almost missed a beat. I never wanted to have to take my wedding ring off. To me that meant bad luck. Oh well, I would cross that bridge when I actually came to it.

'Umm,' I said.

I cooked chicken for our Christmas lunch and in the afternoon we went over to Audrey's for tea. From there I phoned Mum, wished her a happy Christmas and asked her again if she would like to come and visit us. But again she said I was welcome to go and see her but not to expect her to come to me. Again I was upset about it. But not for long. I was with the lovely company of Werner and my friends - all fully into the joy of the Christmas spirit.

The fun, games and food were repeated again on Boxing Day at the Hunter-Rowe's. It began to feel as if this wonderful season of feasting and merriment would go on forever, but of course it didn't. We were soon back to our usual thrift-conscious style of life and really enjoying every minute of it because we were together. Even the mishaps and hardships were not really bad because we shared them and laughed over them together.

Perhaps the most frightening incident was the night the tin chimney in our shed caught fire. I suppose it wasn't really surprising, with all the wood and coal we had been burning and never thinking to clean it out. Werner managed to put out the fire but we didn't sleep a wink that night for fear of the odd spark still lurking in the roof and causing another fire.

The next day Werner dismantled the chimney and cleaned it thoroughly. We didn't want a scare like that again.

Of all the things that happened I think the one that worried me most was the day one of Mr. Hunter-Rowe's workmen came by on his bike. Rags rushed out of the shed and pulled him off the bike by grabbing his leg in his teeth. The man wasn't hurt but there was a terrible hole in his lovely grey flannel trousers.

'You'll have to pay for these, Missus,' he told me.

It was the end of the week and as usual I only had two shillings to my name. To pay for a new pair of trousers would take several weeks' wages. I was frantic. I didn't know what to do. In the end I went up to talk to Mrs. Hunter-Rowe about it.

'Don't worry, dear. We'll see about it,' she told me.

It was the greatest relief. What we would have done without the Hunter-Rowes I shall never know.

And so winter turned into spring and we watched, first snowdrops, then crocuses appear in the orchard grass, where the autumn leaves had lain on the day we had moved into our little nest.

But there was no offspring on the way – not only because we couldn't afford a baby but also because we still hadn't made love properly yet ...

But we were busy and happy and so very much in love. We did

everything together and not least my German lessons. By now I was learning it night and day, during every spare minute we had.

Mr. Hunter-Rowe had helped us greatly by arranging my pass to Germany with the Home and Foreign Offices. However, it soon became clear that I would have to travel ahead of Werner.

Because of this, Werner wanted to make sure I knew enough of the German language to get by on my own on the journey. He also taught me Dutch and French for my passage through these countries. However, I found Dutch quite impossible and ended up filling a notebook with phrases I might need when travelling through Holland, so that I could point to the appropriate one.

We had a letter from Werner's Mum, saying how much she was looking forward to meeting me, but I wondered how on earth I would manage on that journey without Werner beside me. Me, who had never been further than to Wisbech from Derby on my own before ...

CHAPTER 14

The P.O.W.s had made me a large trunk with a handle on either end. While Mr. Hunter-Rowe dealt with all the paperwork for my pass to Germany, I began packing. We didn't know exactly when I would be going but I wanted to be ready. Clothes, tinned food – as much as I could muster – my three pairs of shoes and a hundred other things we had scrimped and saved for went into that trunk.

It was fairly brimming, difficult to shut and weighed a ton. Wondering how on earth I was going to manage it, I did consider dispersing the contents into several smaller cases.

'No, *liebling*, it will be much easier for you to keep your eye on one big trunk than several smaller cases,' Werner advised me.

I was sure he was right about that but just how I was going to manhandle it, all on my own, was a problem I couldn't solve myself and so I placed it in the laps of the gods.

Several times I was called up to Mr. Hunter-Rowe's office to sign papers. The process to get my travel pass seemed to take forever. I began to think it would never actually happen. In a way I suppose I hoped it wouldn't. I was very happy in my life with Werner, living in the orchard. And now that it was springtime everything was so fresh and green, so beautiful. Daffodils had replaced the snowdrops and crocuses I had picked for the vase on our table. The days were warmer and our home looked so pretty, bathed in the sunshine. I would be leaving this little paradise for a country I knew little about, a place so many people had warned me against going to. But I had always known Germany was where my destiny lay. Right from the very beginning Werner had spoken of the time when we would be living in Germany. That was where our future lay. I had never really seriously considered that it could possibly be otherwise.

One evening Werner came bounding into the shed and flung his arms round me.

'Now, Mrs. Palmer!'

'What? Whatever is it, Wern?'

'Tomorrow, *mein liebling*, you will be going on that long journey to your mother and father-in-law's!'

'Tomorrow? No!'

'Yes the date has been fixed. Mr. Hunter-Rowe has just received the confirmation. It's tomorrow!'

'But I can't go tomorrow, I haven't said goodbye to Mum and all my friends ... I ... I haven't given notice at the job!'

I began to panic as I thought of everything I wanted to do before I left England ... before I left? Was I really leaving Wern? My home? England? Did I really want to go at all? Was all this real?

I burst into tears. Werner held me tightly.

'It's all right, *liebling*. I know it's a shock. It is very short notice. But your trunk is packed. Everything is ready. My parents will be at Frankfurt station to meet you.'

'But I haven't said goodbye to anyone.'

'You can go and telephone. We will go and see Audrey together and I will come up to the hotel with you to tell them. You know they said they wouldn't mind if you could only tell them the day before.'

I dried my eyes. Werner was telling me all the practical things I had to do. At least he was with me now. What would I do without him beside me to give me strength? At that thought I burst into tears again.

Werner made us a pot of tea and asked me to sit down with him for five minutes.

'It's not so bad, Muriel. In a way it's a good thing to be told one day and go the next, especially in your case. I know if you had been given a date for a week's time you wouldn't have slept all week, worrying about it.'

'That's true. This way I'll only have one sleepless night!'

163

We laughed at that and he held my hand reassuringly across the table.

'You'll be fine, *liebling*, I know you will. And Mr. Hunter-Rowe says it should be only a couple of weeks now and I will be able to join you in Germany.'

'Oh, Wern, how will I ever survive for two whole weeks without you?'

'Just think of it this way. It won't be as long as it was that first time I was caught and sent to Ollerton!'

'I'll miss you so much, Wern.'

'And me you. But at least we will be together most of tomorrow. Mr. Hunter-Rowe says I can come too when he drives you down to Harwich.'

As soon as we had finished our tea, I went to the public phone box. First I phoned the twins, Jill and Jane. They were very cheery, insisted we keep in touch and said they would say goodbye for me to all my old Derby friends.

Then I phoned Mum. We seemed to have too brief a conversation. Just 'goodbye' and 'take care'. Afterwards I was in floods of tears again. You can't say proper goodbyes on the telephone.

Werner came with me up to Audrey's and then to the hotel. Everyone was very kind. They all said they would miss me. I knew I would miss them terribly too.

As predicted, I didn't sleep a wink that night. I kept going on that journey to Germany, putting my mind through every possible eventuality of it, forming all the different phrases I might need to use ...

At eight o'clock the next morning I said goodbye to Mrs. Hunter-Rowe and her housekeeper. Then Wern and I got in the back seat of Mr. Hunter-Rowe's Rover. The P.O.W.s stowed my trunk carefully in the boot and we set off.

I had a large shoulder bag containing all my documents, a change of clothes, a couple of sandwiches and an apple. Werner told me to cling on to it at all times. No way must I lose that.

Throughout that drive to Harwich Werner held my hand. We spoke very little, both of us dreading our parting. As we travelled I watched the lush English countryside in its full springtime glory. This was the English countryside I now realised I had always been a part of. I had

164

never felt so strongly how much I belonged to it and it to me ... not until now ... now when I was about to leave it far behind me!

What would it be like in Germany? Would it be so very different? Would I feel I belonged there too? Well, I belonged to Wern. It was his country I was going to. I felt sure that when he arrived to be with me there I would feel that I belonged there too ...

We had lunch with some friends of Mr. Hunter-Rowe in Harwich. I took little part in the conversation. I don't even remember what we ate. All I could think of was that too soon Werner and I would be saying goodbye.

I had to board the ferry by 6.00 p.m. Werner and Mr. Hunter-Rowe came as far as the barrier with me.

'Good luck, Muriel,' Mr. Hunter-Rowe said and kissed me goodbye.

Then I was in Werner's arms.

'God bless you, *liebling*. I'll see you in two weeks time!'

He kissed me and before I could say anything he let me go and turned to join Mr. Hunter-Rowe. I boarded the ferry with the crowd of passengers, feeling utterly alone.

I suppose it was best that there was no time for a prolonged goodbye. I knew this was going to be the longest, hardest journey of my life. I reasoned that the sooner I got on with it the sooner it would be over. But I did wish it could have been arranged for Werner to travel with me ...

My trunk was installed in a two-berth cabin which I discovered I was to share with a Dutch girl of about my age.

She came in all bright and breezy, obviously excited about returning to her home country. Her emotions mirrored the exact opposite of my own.

In no time at all I felt the boat begin to move out of the port. We were on our way. I sat on my bunk with a book in my hands while my cabinmate changed her clothes. I wasn't really reading but I needed an excuse to be left alone with my thoughts.

'Would you like to come up on deck with me for some dancing?' she asked.

'Oh, no thanks, love. I've got a long journey tomorrow. I think I need

165

an early night.'

'See you later then.'

'All right.'

She skipped out of the cabin, leaving me alone with my thoughts. I was grateful for the peace of being on my own. I had a quick wash and hopped into bed. Then I remembered how insistent Werner had been that I keep my eye on my trunk at all times. It was as well that I hadn't gone up on deck, I thought. I knew there would be dire consequences if I didn't get all my valuable possessions and foodstuffs safely to Frankfurt.

I lay in bed for hours, unable to sleep for the second night running, trying to imagine the events I would encounter the following day. At about 1.00 a.m. the Dutch girl came back.

'Are you awake?' she whispered.

'Yes.'

'Do you mind if my friend comes in and shares our cabin?'

I looked over the blanket. Her friend was a burly male, looking as excited as she did at the prospect.

'Well, this is a two-berth cabin. I'm sorry but I do mind.'

'All right, just thought I'd ask.'

To my very great relief she and her friend departed. I was put in mind of my night in the railway carriage at Ollerton. Why did I keep attracting the company of girls with moral standards so very different to my own? Or was it me? Was I the odd one? Well, I was me and that was that. At that moment I had more important things to worry about ... would Wern's Mum and Dad be there to meet me? Would I like them? Would they like me?

About an hour later the Dutch girl came back, alone. She got into bed quietly and just five minutes later she was snoring loudly enough to wake the dead. I didn't sleep a wink for a second night.

In the morning I had a good wash down and changed into the clean clothes I had in my shoulder bag, putting the ones I had worn the previous day back into the shoulder bag. There was no way I was going to open my trunk. I might never get it shut again. Now I felt fit to face the long rail journey.

The Dutch girl and I left the cabin together to go up for breakfast in the restaurant. I locked our cabin door securely so that my trunk would be safe inside.

Not knowing when I might be able to have another meal, I indulged in a really good breakfast of bacon, eggs and tomatoes, followed by toast and coffee.

When it was time to disembark at the Hook of Holland, I made sure I had all my travel documents to hand. Feeling ever so nervous, I watched as the people in front of me handed their documents to the immigration officer. He checked them all very carefully before handing them back, as if looking for some little point he could dispute.

Then it was my turn. To my horror a more puzzled expression came over his face than any I had noticed when he had been dealing with the people in front of me. He shook his head and then looked at me frowning.

'This isn't right,' he told me.

'What isn't?'

He beckoned to an English Army officer who came over and they spoke together in Dutch.

'You don't have a visa to travel through Holland,' the Army officer said to me.

'But my husband's employer arranged it all for me with the Home Office and the Foreign Office.'

He smiled kindly at me. I was almost in tears. What was going to happen to me now?'

'Wait here a while. I'll just go and see about this,' he said.

I sat on my trunk, feeling utterly devastated. No sooner had I set foot on foreign soil than the trouble had started. I felt sure my worst fears and nightmares were about to become reality.

But the officer came back all smiles. To my great relief he said everything was all right.

'Off you go. You can get on the train now.'

I found an empty compartment and with enormous difficulty I lugged my trunk, by the handle, up the steps. There were many sturdy-looking men milling around on the platform but not one offered me any help. Everyone was too busy looking after himself and his own baggage. Of course I knew times were hard after the war; that there were thieves just waiting to pounce. But did it really have to mean the end of male chivalry? Evidently it did.

I plonked myself down on the seat, keeping the handle of my trunk firmly in one hand and my shoulder bag gripped tightly in the other. Then I allowed myself the luxury of catching my breath, sitting back and taking in my surroundings.

Thank goodness I had found a seat. I would stay in this compartment until I got to Germany, I thought: my trunk was just too heavy to lug anywhere else.

By now there was quite a crowd out on the platform but most of them must have been waiting for other trains as no-one else came into my compartment.

Then the train lurched forward. As it chugged out of the station I continued to grip my trunk and bag tightly. I was on my way to Germany with all my worldly possessions and only a few pounds to my name. Whatever would I do if I didn't like it there? There was no turning back now!

The train stopped at several stations in the first hour or two. After another hour or so we arrived at the Belgian border. A guard came into my compartment and told me everyone on the train had to get off here to have their documents checked.

Again there were crowds on the platform. I knew I couldn't leave my trunk unattended on the train so I had to drag it down the steps again and, with terrible difficulty, pull it through the massing people. They couldn't bother themselves to give me room to pass. They were all too busy pulling and shoving their own luggage about. I had never seen so many hard-faced people grouped together. It was a horrible atmosphere of 'look to yourself or watch out!'

An officer at the checkpoint, who was about six and a half feet tall and almost as broad, asked me what I had in my trunk.

'Not a lot.'

I prayed he wouldn't ask me to open it and take everything out. I'd never be able to get it shut again. Thankfully he said I could get back on the train.

By the time I got my trunk up the steps again I felt as if my back was broken and I was terribly hot and thirsty, but there was nothing to drink.

Now there were other people in the compartment with me, a middle-aged woman with a little girl of about ten and a courting couple, who sat directly opposite me. The train pulled off again and I continued to hang on tightly to my possessions. I noticed the man was a Yank and his girlfriend probably German. They were very wrapped up in each other, holding hands and kissing, looking lovingly into each other's eyes. Suddenly tears welled up in my eyes. If only that could have been Wern and me, if only he was here with me, how much more tolerable this journey would be. I lowered my head as the tears started rolling down my cheeks.

The middle-aged woman bent forward and patted my arm. She smiled at me and said something in a foreign language that I didn't understand. I felt sure she had known what I was feeling with her woman's intuition - words were not really necessary and I was slightly comforted by her gesture of reassurance. After seeing all the hard-faced people at the station, my faith in the better side of human nature was slightly restored.

The little girl looked at her mother and asked her something in their language. The mother spoke back to her and then the little girl smiled so sweetly at me. Yes, there were one or two good folk around after all. I dried my eyes.

As we passed through the countryside I thought it didn't look so very different to England. But it was when we stopped at stations that I realised there was a contrast and how very much harder life was here. I saw painfully thin children begging for food. They banged on the window of our compartment shouting: '*Bitte, bitte*, please give us food.'

By now we had crossed the German border and the people looked more desperate than any I had ever seen in my life. Everywhere there were hoards of refugees moving about with enormous quantities of luggage. Some seemed to have all their worldly possessions stacked high on barrows on the platforms, with one or two children perched right on top.

But it was their faces that really shocked me, all so hard, all so desperate. The poor things. I thought; God they must be hungry here. Surely it won't be the same for me ...

After a few stations the middle-aged woman couldn't stand the faces at the window any longer. She would yank down the blind just before we pulled into a station and not let it up again until we were steaming away on the other side.

At one point an American and a British officer came into the compartment to check documents. They discovered the German girl didn't have any papers.

'Right you ... out!' the American told her.

'Oh, please let her stay with me,' her boyfriend pleaded.

'Absolutely not. Now move along.'

I gathered from the next few exchanges that the girl was not travelling long distance and so she should be in one of the carriages that was fitted only with benches. The couple had moved along to our compartment because the bench carriage had been like an overcrowded cattle truck. Reluctantly they left to return to it.

During the next few hours I kept feeling I was about to drop off to sleep. I would start suddenly and will myself to stay awake. I knew I mustn't take my eyes off my trunk for an instant.

By five o'clock I was feeling very hungry, having eaten nothing since breakfast. I opened my shoulder bag and took out my sandwiches. The apple went only a little way to quenching my thirst. I looked at my watch. In about four hours I would be in Frankfurt and Werner's parents would be there to meet me.

Five minutes later the train halted in the middle of nowhere. I looked out of the window. We were right out in the open countryside. Just as I was wondering why we had stopped a German guard came into the compartment to check our papers. When he had gone I waited, estimating how long it would take the guards to check everyone's papers the length of the train. When that time was up we were still stationary. We waited and waited. I looked at my watch. We had been waiting nearly two hours. I would be late! Would Werner's parents wait for me? I began sobbing. I should have insisted Werner came before me. What would I do if there was no-one there to meet me? Why was I coming here anyway? Did I really love Werner? Of course I did but suddenly I realised I really didn't want to come to Germany.

Finally the train started moving again. It seemed to be travelling more slowly now. Or was that my imagination? Was I hoping it would never arrive? I was dreading finding myself alone in Frankfurt.

We arrived about midnight. I tugged my trunk off the train and along the platform to the barrier. Then I flopped myself down to sit on it and wait. Soon all the people who had got off the train had dispersed. Obviously there was no-one to meet me. I got up and dragged my trunk over to a guard. In my best German I asked him:

'Excuse me please, is there a train to Kriftel?'

'No, it went at 9.30.'

'How far is it?'

'About twelve miles.'

I pulled the trunk over to the side of the station, all the time pushing people away who were trying to get hold of it. I didn't know if they were trying to help me or to take it from me. I wasn't about to take any chances so I held onto it tightly and dragged it outside the station to an American taxi rank. By now it was 12.30 a.m. I called over to a taxi driver: 'Please, can you help me? I have to get to Kriftel.'

'Yes, I'll take you if you can pay me in American or English money. I just have to make one trip to the other side of Frankfurt first. I should be back about one, about half an hour.'

'All right I'll wait here for you.'

I sat on my trunk and waited. At 1.00 a.m. there was no sign of the taxi. By 1.15 a.m. I decided he wasn't coming back. But then, five minutes later a taxi pulled into the rank again and the driver got out.

I couldn't remember what the driver who had spoken to me looked like.

'Are you the one that's going to take me to Kriftel?' I asked.

'Yes, I'm the one.'

He opened a back door of the car for me to get in and then he opened the boot for my trunk.

'Oh no! I want the trunk in here with me please.'

One thing I had learned, since knowing Werner, was to be ultra cautious. I remembered my naivety with that lorry driver in Cambridge. I remembered Werner's words – never take your eyes off that trunk. I imagined the taxi driver speeding away with it in his boot as soon as he had dropped me at my destination. With quite a lot of difficulty he managed to stow it in the back seat with me.

'If you can get me there I'll give you five pounds and a tin of margarine.'

He beamed at this and then I realised I had probably offered him far too much.

It seemed to take forever to get to Kriftel. As we travelled through a quiet, forested area I realised there wasn't another car on the road and began to panic. Why on earth did I get into this car on my own with this man? He could murder me!

Even after two sleepless nights I didn't feel tired now. My wits were pitched more finely than they had ever been before. I was expecting danger to spring out at me from any direction.

But then we arrived. The taxi pulled up outside a house. It looked a nice quiet little place. There was no-one about. The driver got out to check it was the right address. Then he came back nodding and smiling.

'Oh, Wern, I'm here,' I thought. 'I wish you were here with me. How will I be greeted?'

CHAPTER 15

'Come out, come out,' the taxi driver shouted to me in his broken English.

My God, he'll wake the dead, I thought, as several lights came on in the house. Then I saw my father-in-law come hurrying down the path. I knew it must be him. He was exactly as Werner had described him. He had thick grey hair and was shorter than Werner, about five foot, eight inches. As he came up to me I saw Werner's smile on his face. Yes this was definitely Werner's Dad.

'Muri, Muri!' he said and gave me a welcoming hug.

Then he put his arm round my shoulder and spoke in rapid German; far too fast for me to understand. But I felt so relieved to have found Werner's family at last and I knew I was going to get on with this man. I liked him at once.

He and the taxi driver carried my trunk to the house and then I saw my mother-in-law hurrying down the stairs to greet me, accompanied by a little dachshund dog. She was the image of her most recent photograph, which Werner had shown me in England. She also hugged and kissed me and spoke in rapid German. I must have looked a little flummoxed so they spoke to the taxi driver. Again, in his broken English, he told me they were sorry they didn't speak English but I was very welcome.

'Dank,' I said, smiling.

I turned to the taxi driver and gave him five pounds from my shoulder bag.

'And I'll find you that tin of margarine.'

I fumbled for a couple of minutes, getting the trunk open but once it was I knew exactly where to find the prized tin.

The taxi driver was so thrilled he hugged and kissed me and then he left.

Mother started speaking to Father and I managed to understand what she was saying ...

'Go on your bike and fetch George from Hofime.'

I knew Hofime was the next village, about three miles away. Much as I looked forward to seeing Uncle George, who had returned to Germany a few months before, I didn't want poor Father to have to bike there at this time of night. It was about half past two!

'No, no ... wait until morning,' I said in German.

'Yes, yes, I am going now,' Father said and he was gone.

Then a lady came into the hall from a downstairs room. She was wrapping her dressing gown round her. I was so surprised. I hadn't expected to find anyone else in the house and wondered who she could be. Then I found she could speak English.

'I am Mrs. Hertz. I live in the front room with my husband who is a judge in Frankfurt.'

I shook hands with her but I didn't like her disdainful air. I sensed immediately she wasn't fond of the English. Werner hadn't said there were lodgers in the house. How would there be room for all of us, I wondered.

Mother took me upstairs to show me my room, accompanied by the dachshund I had heard her call Heidi. All the time she was speaking excitedly in rapid German. It was far too fast for me. I couldn't understand a word.

'Please speak slowly,' I asked her in German.

Well, at least my German was effective. She understood and from then on spoke nice and slowly for me. Now I understood the gist of what she was saying. She had been trying to tell me that Father had been to the station to meet me but when I hadn't arrived by 9.30 the station master had told him there would be no more trains that evening so he had come home. I told her it didn't matter.

We went into the bedroom. I could see it had obviously been Werner's and that they had gone to some trouble to prepare it for us. There were

174

twin beds, our wedding photo hung in a nice frame on the wall and several of Werner's knick-knacks were placed here and there.

'I'll leave you here. Come down when you are ready,' Mother said.

I smiled and thanked her. As soon as she had gone I sat on my bed and cried. I must pull myself together, I thought. I saw Mother had put a jug of water and a bowl on the side so I got up and washed my face. I felt better after that and went downstairs.

Soon Father arrived back with Uncle George. It was wonderful to see a face I knew. We hugged each other. He seemed as pleased to see me as I was him. He and Father carried my trunk up to my room and I went with them to unpack the foodstuffs.

When I took them down to Mother in the kitchen she was so pleased. In fact, she was almost ecstatic about it. It was then I realised how very short of food they must be here. Uncle George confirmed it.

'Food shortages are ten times worse than in England, Mu.'

'I thought it must be bad here when I saw all the starving children at the stations we passed through.'

'I know. Never have I seen anything like it.'

Looking at Uncle George now I realised he wasn't as fat as he had been in England when he had been a camp cook. That told me a lot too. While Mother and Father packed away the food Uncle George and I sat and talked.

'Who are the two people living in the front room?'

'Ah, everyone with house, have to take in refugees from Russian Zone. That couple, they lost everything. Don't worry, they not interfere with you.'

Suddenly I felt very tired. There was so much for me to take in all at once and I realised I hadn't had any sleep for over two days.

'Would it be all right if I go and lie down, Uncle George? I'm that tired but I don't want to look rude.'

'Of course. You go.'

I smiled at Mother and Father and tried my German again.

'I am very tired. I must go and lie down.'

'Yes, you go up,' Mother said.

175

I practically fell onto that bed, without even getting undressed. The next morning I awoke, after a very deep sleep, to see the sunlight streaming through the shutters. Downstairs I heard voices so I quickly got dressed and went down. There I met Uncle George's wife and daughter, who had just arrived. Everyone was sitting round the breakfast table but all I saw to eat was black bread. I was ravenous, having had nothing to eat since my sandwiches on the train.

'Is it all right if I have a piece of bread?' I asked Uncle George.

'Yes, go on.'

I helped myself and spread it with some of the margarine I had brought. Mother passed me a cup of black coffee. Then she spoke in her rapid German. I couldn't understand.

'What did she say, Uncle George?'

'She say they save rations for party when Werner returns.'

I ate the bread because I was so hungry. It tasted very strange to me but I guessed I could get used to it. Not so the coffee, though. It was even worse than the stuff they used to serve up in the canteen at the depot. It was certainly the most disgusting concoction I had ever tasted in my life. I would far rather have had water, but I drank it to be polite.

That first day shot by. Mother and Father showed me over the house and outside. They had a lovely garden, quite a large one where even the path had been taken up to make more room for growing vegetables. This was Father's domain. I knew I would enjoy helping him there as I too liked gardening. At the bottom of the garden they kept a few hens and rabbits. Some lovely pear, plum and apricot trees clung to the house. Father saw me looking at them with wonder.

'This year the crop will not be so good but last year it was excellent,' he told me.

Then he took me down to the cellar and showed me all the bottles of preserved pears they stored there. Also they had rabbits preserved in these same very large bottles and meat from their pig!

'We had a pig,' Father said. 'When it was slaughtered we had to give half the meat to the government and half we could keep ourselves. That pig would eat anything, but mostly grass and hay, like the chickens. Each

176

family is allocated a strip of verge along the lanes to grow grass and hay for the animals.'

'Doesn't anyone ever steal from another person's strip?'

'No, never, Murel. Everyone is very honest in that way! When I take the waggon to collect my hay, you can come too if you like.'

'Oh yes, I would like to.'

Father showed me the little outhouse where there was a copper.

'Here I dye army blankets, bright pretty colours for people. I used to work at a chemical plant, you know.'

'Yes, I know. Werner told me.'

'Well, now I do this chemical dyeing. The people don't pay me in money but they give me food or other useful things we need. It is how we live, Murel.'

Well, things were scarce but I could see Werner's parents tried to be as self-sufficient as they could. Obviously they had to be to survive.

At seven o'clock in the evening Mother served up our meal. It was potato soup and black bread. I couldn't face the potato soup. It looked like watery slush and turned my stomach.

'I'm not really hungry, you have mine,' I told Father. 'I'll just have a slice of bread.'

So I did. My hunger pangs got worse!

Every morning the judge and his wife left the house about eight o'clock to go to Frankfurt, not returning until about half past four in the afternoon. When they were in the house I could tell they didn't really like having me there. Oh, they smiled, but they were false smiles, for the benefit of my parents-in-law, no doubt. I wondered what it would be like if I ever had to be on my own with them. I didn't relish that thought. I tried to be nice to them, put a lot of effort into it. But you can't change people who are naturally prejudiced. I had learned that lesson in England.

For me the worst thing in those first few days, apart from the constant hunger pangs, was the lack of a decent beverage. There was absolutely no milk to be had and I had never been able to drink tea or coffee without milk in it. I told Mother and Father it was an English custom to drink tea with milk in it. I didn't want them to be offended because I didn't drink it. Then, after a few days, Mother arranged for a girl down the road to bring me some of her goat's milk every other day, so I had a very precious quarter of a pint of goat's milk to last two days for my tea. To start with, it tasted very odd to me, but I got used to it and found it infinitely better than black tea.

That first week we all went to a dance in Hofime. There was a huge crowd of elderly, middle-aged and young people there and, because this was the American Zone, many Yanks came.

Werner had taught me how to dance German style so I was not afraid to get up and dance with Father when he asked me, and then with Uncle George. I really enjoyed it. When we sat down a strapping young blonde German bloke came over and spoke to me in perfect English.

I was shocked. I was a married woman. I couldn't dance with a stranger. I looked at Mother and Father, hoping they would help me out and ask the bloke to go away.

'Go on, you dance,' Mother said.

Father nodded too.

So I did.

'When will Werner be home?' the man asked as we danced.

'A week or so, we hope.'

'Can I take you out in the meantime?'

'No!'

The dance finished and I was relieved to sit down again. How did the young devil have the bare-faced cheek to ask me out? I was a little confused. Was it that customs were different here? I just didn't know. But then he came over again and asked me to dance the next dance.

'Go on,' my parents-in-law said in unison.

So again I got up. Again the man tried to ask me out. By now I had had enough of this. I went and sat down before the dance ended.

When he came over for the third time to ask me to dance I refused.

'He's a cheeky one,' Mother said to Father.

By now my feet were aching that much. I kicked off my five-inch-heeled shoes. Mother noticed and laughed.

Werner had so many relatives I was introduced to in that first week. Uncle George's wife and daughter were lovely, but also living with them were a sister and brother-in-law. The brother-in-law had been a P.O.W. in Russia and I realised the first time I met him that he regarded the English with as much contempt as he did the Russians. He hardly ever deigned to look at me, let alone speak to me – that was if George and his wife were around. If I was left on my own with the man, then he would speak. He would insult me in the same kind of way I had been insulted in England. But I never said a word about it to anyone. I knew the only thing to do was ignore it. How many times had Werner told me to ignore abuse? He had always managed to himself. Somehow it didn't seem to effect him inwardly as it did me.

Werner had another aunt, Aunt Fena, and she was lovely. We took to each other right away when she came round to the house to meet me. She was middle-aged and had a ten-year-old son who could speak quite good English because he was learning it at school.

'Come and visit us tomorrow,' Aunt Fena said. 'You could walk Heidi the dog up to our house.'

The next day I was in high spirits as I set off with Heidi. Already I felt really close to Aunt Fena, something I didn't feel with Mother, somehow, though I wished I could.

Aunt Fena welcomed me warmly and introduced me to her son.

'I will show you my rabbits,' he told me straight away, in English, and proceeded to do so with great enthusiasm. Later Aunt Fena and I sat and drank coffee.

'How do you find Werner's mother?'

'Oh, I think we get on all right.'

'Good. But don't forget he's an only son. His mother would really have liked him to marry a German girl, here.'

She said no more on the subject but I suddenly felt I had better be a little wary of Mother.

I used to take Heidi for lots of walks or go cycling to visit Uncle George, but I soon learned not to pass a certain house if I could possibly avoid it. That was Herr Reinholdt's house. I knew that was his name

179

because Father had told me once when we had passed him at his gate as we pushed the little waggon to the verge to collect grass. The second time I passed Herr Reinholdt at his gate I was alone on my bike.

'You filthy bastard English,' he shouted at me. 'It's because of you I've only got one leg.'

I was so shocked I nearly fell off my bike. He hadn't said a word when I had been with Father.

After that I passed him again on a couple more occasions. Each time the abuse he hurled at me got worse, but if I ever passed with Father he never said a word.

For once I didn't keep the hurt to myself. I mentioned it to Mother.

'Ah, well, the poor man was shot in the leg in his own garden by an English plane. He had to have his leg off. I expect he is on morphine for the pain. You must make allowances for him,' she told me.

I didn't feel like making allowances for him. It wasn't my fault he had been shot in the leg, just as it wasn't Werner's fault my father had had his arm shot off. I knew the only thing to do with such unreasonable people, the Herr Reinholdts of this world, was avoid them, and that is what I tried to do whenever I could.

Far from finding life easier in Germany, as far as abuse went I was finding it just as bad as Uncle George had told me in England I would.

But my first two weeks in Germany passed very quickly. There was so much to learn, so many people to meet. I didn't find it as difficult as I had imagined to pick up the language. But the thing I couldn't get used to was the constant hunger pangs. Often I'd slip down to the cellar and eat one or two of the bottled pears. I could have eaten the lot in one go but I knew Mother was saving them for Werner's 'Welcome Home' party. Sometimes I found it so difficult not to eat more than two at one time. But after several days I noticed the bottle was emptying considerably. 'Oh my God,' I thought, 'they'll see how many I'm eating. I'd better stop.'

Three weeks passed, then four. I began to wonder if Werner was ever coming. Then one day his mother came rushing in.

'Werner is on his way. The woman down the road has her son back who travelled some of the way with Werner. He should be here tomorrow, or the next day!'

My heart leapt for joy. At last Wern was coming.

'Come on, Muriel. We had better get the fruit up and take it round to the baker,' Mother said.

We fetched the fruit from the cellar, together with all the other ingredients Mother had been saving, and took them round to the baker. This was a common custom, to take ingredients to the bakers, where they had the huge ovens and the huge baking trays for baking massive quantities.

At half past ten that night I heard a commotion outside. I flung on my dressing gown and rushed downstairs. Somehow I knew it was Werner. Sure enough there he was, being greeted in the street by a neighbour. When he saw me he didn't open the gate but jumped over it! How typical of Wern, I thought, as I ran into his waiting arms. We held each other in a tight embrace, and then he kissed me for longer than he had ever done before, or so it seemed. He took my breath away.

Then Mother and Father came out to greet him. Mother was crying as she hugged him.

'I'm all right. I'm here. Stop that now, Mother!'

In those first moments I realised how possessive Mother was of her only child. A sudden wave of apprehension came over me.

'Enough, enough, dear,' Father said. 'Leave the boy now. Remember he's got a wife!'

Mother reluctantly let Werner go and started to dry her eyes. Then her arm was round him again as she directed him into the house.

Everyone came in to see Werner, neighbours and relations. We sat up all night talking. I wasn't alone with him until we went to bed the following night.

'Everything will be all right for us now, *liebling*. Now we are here together in Germany everything will be fine,' he told me as he held me in his arms.

But I wondered if it would be. I didn't tell Werner but I was finding people were abusing me as much as they had done in England, and

181

living in this house with his parents and the judge and his wife was not an ideal situation for us. I desperately wanted to be alone with Werner. Even in our room we had to whisper as his parents were only next door. No, I wondered if things really would be all right.

The next morning I awoke to the sound of a lot of comings and goings downstairs and outside. I got out of bed and flung open the shutters to see what was going on. There was Mother carrying a huge baking tray covered with a slab of cake. Werner joined me at the window and put his arm round me.

'Come on, *liebling*. We'd better get dressed and go and help.'

We spent all day preparing for Werner's 'Welcome Home' party that evening. The men brought long trestle tables, which I covered with Mother's best cloths, and then I gathered flowers and greenery from the garden to make posies for the tables.

There was so much food! Enormous slabs of cake and pie to cut up. There was enough to feed a nation! When we were so short! Well, that was the way Mother wanted it. This was the return of her only child. She would have given him the world if she could.

Just before five I went upstairs to change. I had noticed many of the women wore black for evening wear here, so I put on my little black crepe dress, together with my pearl necklace and earrings. When I came downstairs Mother was in the hallway.

'Oh, you look lovely,' she told me.

Werner came over and put his arm round me.

'She always looks lovely, Mother.'

'Murel, you look beautiful,' Father said as he came out of the kitchen.

'Father, come here.' Werner put his other arm round his Father's shoulders. 'Her name is Muriel, M-U-R-I-E-L, not Murel!'

'Ah, let me say it ... MURIEL!'

'That's it.'

We all laughed. I had become used to Father calling me Murel. I had really quite liked it!

The guests began arriving and Father handed each a glass of apple juice or schnapps as they came in. All the relations were there: Uncle

George and his wife and daughter and Aunty Fena and her son and several others who I had met a few times before.

Then I was introduced to Aunty Marie for the first time. She was about forty-five, a very attractive looking woman, wearing a lovely black dress which suited her really well. I liked her right away and she came to sit with Wern and me later.

All evening I was sipping apple juice, because I thought it was innocuous. Actually I discovered later that its sweetness disguised its strength.

As the evening got underway we fell into a sing-song. I shall never forget us all singing, 'Hear my song, Violetta'. It was so very beautiful it brought tears to my eyes. Afterwards Aunty Marie put her arm round Werner and gave him an affectionate kiss. Jokingly I piped up: 'Now, now, he's my husband!'

Utter silence fell on the room. I realised I had said something terribly wrong, but I didn't understand why. Werner looked at me apologetically and whispered: '*Liebling*, I'm so sorry, I forgot to tell you.'

'What? Tell me what? What have I done?'

'It's all right, nothing. Nothing at all.'

But I felt very uneasy. I knew something was wrong and I wanted to know what it was.

Probably to clear the air, Mother and Father began clearing the tables to the side of the room so that we could all dance. But I didn't feel like dancing.

'Werner, I feel so uncomfortable. What have I done?' I asked him again.

'I can't tell you.'

'Well, I'm going upstairs then. I can't stand this.'

I slipped quietly out of the room. I didn't want to make a scene by making a dramatic exit. A few seconds after I arrived in our bedroom Werner came in.

'Muriel, I'm ashamed of you! Come down! You can't leave our guests like that.'

'I'm not coming down until you tell me what I have done.'

'All right. Aunt Marie's husband was a P.O.W. in Russia where he was almost starved. When he came home a few months ago the doctor said he must only eat a very few ounces of food at a time, as his stomach had shrunk so much. So Marie kept the food locked in the pantry. One night she woke up and found her husband wasn't lying beside her. She went downstairs and found him lying on the living-room floor, unconscious. He had broken the lock on the pantry door and eaten all the food in there. The doctor came immediately but there was nothing he could do. My uncle died.'

'Oh Wern, how awful! Why didn't anyone tell me? Poor Aunty Marie. Oh, I do feel terrible!'

'Will you come down now?'

'Yes, I will. I know what I'll do. I have an unopened bottle of 4711 Eau de Cologne I brought from England. I'll take it down and give it to Auntie Marie.'

'That's a nice idea.'

It took a few minutes for me to pluck up courage and go down again but I knew it had to be done and I really wanted to make amends.

As I went down the stairs Mother shot me a filthy look and I saw Father give her a sharp word. I went straight over to Auntie Marie.

'I'm so sorry. I didn't know, you see,' I said.

'Oh it's nothing, dear,' she smiled and hugged me.

'Here I want you to have this.'

I gave her the 4711. She was so pleased and hugged me again. From then on Aunty Marie and I were the firmest of friends.

Later in the evening I began to experience terrible stomach pains. Very soon I was doubled up in agony.

'*Liebling*, you had better lie down,' Werner said.

I went to lie on my bed for a while but after half an hour instead of feeling better I was much worse.

'Oh, Wern. I feel so ill. My stomach hurts so much!'

'It might be that apple juice, how much did you have?'

'Several glasses.'

'Oh darling, that's powerful stuff. I should have warned you.'

184

Mother came in to see me and said she would find me some medicine.

'Oh no, just some hot water, please. I have some peppermint drops I brought from England.'

Werner brought me the hot water and put the peppermint drops in. I sipped the concoction. Five minutes later I felt even worse. It was the most terrible pain I had ever experienced in my life. I literally felt I was about to die. All I could say was: 'Oh, Wern, Wern!'

'I'm going to fetch the doctor.'

'No, don't leave me.'

'Yes, I'm going right now.'

His mother sat and held my hand while he went for the doctor. It didn't seem very long before he was back again.

'The doctor is just coming.'

'Oh, Wern, Wern!'

And then the doctor came in. He asked Mother to go outside and came over to the bed to examine me. As soon as I set eyes on him I knew he was an English hater. He didn't smile. He had that awful look in his eyes that I knew so well. I had seen it a thousand times before in other people's eyes.

'Oh, Wern, Wern, don't leave me. Send him away, please!'

'Don't be silly, *liebling*. I'm here. The doctor will help you.'

'No, Wern. Send him away, please!'

But the doctor examined me, all the time with that same look of pure hatred in his eyes. Then I saw him take a syringe out of his bag and fill it with something.

'No, Wern!' I screamed. 'Please don't let him inject me!'

'Relax, *liebling*, everything will be all right.'

Before I could say another word the doctor stuck the needle in me and I lost consciousness.

185

CHAPTER 16

In the middle of the night I woke up feeling very groggy and shouted for Werner.

'It's all right. Everything's all right. Stop worrying,' he told me.

'God, I feel weak. Don't let that doctor come near me again.'

I slept after that and felt much better the next day. In the afternoon the doctor came to see me again. Still he had the hatred in his eyes. I was glad to see the back of him when he finally went.

After he had shown the doctor out Werner came and sat with me.

'Tomorrow I'm taking you into Frankfurt to see a lady doctor,' he said, putting an arm round me.

'No, not another doctor!'

'Yes, we're going and you know why.'

Yes, I knew why. It was the sex business. Werner and I still hadn't made love fully. I didn't exactly know why this was. All that I knew was that I was as nervous as hell about it. At that point I didn't want children, while things were so hard, with rationing and terrible food shortages. But I guess there was something more as well. As I say, I didn't know what it was.

'*Liebling*, I put up with it in England, but I'm not putting up with it anymore. I'm your husband.'

So the next day we caught the train into Frankfurt. I still felt very weak, not just from my problem with the apple juice, but also because I had had nothing at all to eat. The Frankfurt doctor had instructed Werner that I must not eat until after my examination.

We didn't speak much on the journey. I was so nervous, but I knew I had to get this over with. It was a bright sunny day and we walked from

186

the station. Normally I would have been really happy walking along on such a day with Werner beside me, but today I stumbled along in dread and so weak with hunger.

'I'm so hungry, Wern!'

'Well, when we've finished with the doctor we'll go and have something to eat.'

At that moment we were just walking past the zoo.

'And if you behave yourself I'll take you in there when we come back!'

I knew he was trying to cheer me up and give me strength but, as I say, I was stumbling along with sheer dread. Nothing he could have said or done would have made me feel any better unless it was: 'Let's turn round and go home.'

Finally we arrived and we waited in the reception area.

'Oh, Werner, I am frightened.'

'There's nothing to be frightened of. Nothing at all.'

Just then the lady doctor came in to greet us.

'Pleased to meet you, Mr. Palmer.'

Then she spoke in English as she shook hands with me. She seemed very pleasant.

'So this is Muriel?'

'Yes. How do you do.'

'Would you like to wait here, Mr. Palmer, while I examine your wife?'

She showed me into her examination room and closed the door behind us.

'Just pop behind the screen, dear. Take your clothes off and pop the robe on.'

Two minutes later I was lying on the hard examination couch, more frightened than I had ever been before. Consequently the doctor was totally unable to examine me.

'Just stay there a minute, dear,' she said and went out of the room.

I lay there for a good five minutes wondering what was going to happen next. Would she say there was nothing she could do and I would have to go home? I hoped so.

When she came in again Werner was with her.

187

'The doctor is going to have to spray you, *liebling*. It's like a scent spray, that's all. I will hold your hand.'

So, my ordeal wasn't over yet! Before I could even think about it my hand was in his firm grasp and the doctor had sprayed me. I did feel a sensation as she examined me and then I fell into a deep, short sleep. When I woke up I felt very dizzy and sickly. Both Werner and the doctor were smiling at me.

'All right, Muriel?' she asked me.

'I think so.'

'She'll be all right now but don't give her anything to eat or drink for three or four hours.'

Werner helped me off the examination couch and I got dressed.

'Can we go home now? I want to go home.'

I felt really ill as I tried to walk. I just wanted to get out of that place and into my own bed.

It was obvious I couldn't walk to the station so Werner called a taxi.

The doctor saw us to the door.

'Thank you, doctor,' Werner said.

They exchanged smiles and she patted him on the back. From that I gathered our problems were over but at that moment I felt so ill I couldn't share Werner's pleasure.

When we got out of the taxi at the station I saw a barrel of apples. My nausea had passed by now and I was just left with the weakness of hunger.

'Wern, please buy me an apple, I'm famished.'

'*Liebling*, you mustn't eat for a few hours, you heard the doctor.'

'Oh, Werner, you're horrible. You're so spiteful.'

Werner ignored this, put his arm round my shoulders and firmly directed me towards our platform.

Again we hardly spoke on the train journey home. When we got inside the house I flopped onto the living-room settee. Werner brought a small bowl of water and some cotton wool. He soaked the cotton wool and sponged my lips with it but he wouldn't let me drink. Then I drifted into an exhausted sleep.

When I awoke I felt much better. I could smell Mother's cooking and got up to eat the most longed-for meal of my life.

That evening Mother and Father went out to visit some friends. The judge and his wife were also out.

'Isn't it wonderful to be on our own?' Werner said as we sat together on the settee.

'But will we ever be really on our own, Wern? I don't think we will. And what about your mother ... she didn't want you to marry an English girl, did she?'

Both these points had been troubling me for ages and now, I felt, was the right time to voice them.

'Oh Muriel, don't be so silly. It's just your imagination. Of course Mother doesn't mind that I married an English girl!'

'O.K. We'll forget about it.'

I wished I hadn't mentioned it. I hated making Werner piggy in the middle between his mother and me. Obviously he didn't see the side of his mother that I did, the one I had been wary of ever since Aunty Fena had first mentioned it to me. Werner changed the subject immediately to talk about what he really wanted to talk about.

'*Liebling*, there is absolutely nothing wrong with you. The doctor says we can have children. From today we are man and wife.'

He went off to the cellar and came back with a bottle of champagne.

'This is to celebrate with when Mother and Father get home. We'll open it then.'

'Can't we have it now and celebrate on our own, Wern?'

'Well, I thought it would be nice to share our news with them.'

'What news?'

'That we can have children!'

'Oh, all right.'

I would have preferred to keep it private but Werner was so keen to share it and I didn't want to crush him at all.

When his parents returned he told them. They were delighted and fairly beamed at us as we drank the champagne.

'We hope you will have many, many children,' Father said.

Mother went upstairs and came back down with a large box.

'This is your wedding present from us,' she said.

Inside we found a whole collection of lovely things: tablecloths, porcelain and glassware.

I was delighted and gave them both a hug. It seemed our news had somehow softened Mother towards me, just a little - not that she hadn't always been kind to me, but there had always been something, something not only Aunty Fena's words had alerted me to. I couldn't put my finger on it but I did feel I couldn't really get close to Mother, not as I could with Aunt Fena and Aunty Marie. That saddened me.

That night Werner and I made love fully for the first time. He was so pleased and I was pleased because he was.

The next day Werner started work in Frankfurt. He had been given a job in telecommunications until a teaching post came through for him.

I found the days long and tedious without him. I still felt very much that I was in someone else's house. Mother did the cooking, the housekeeping, everything. I helped her but I was her assistant, I wasn't running my own home. I longed for the days Werner and I had shared in our shed in the orchard.

Mother told us she had been to see the mayor about getting the judge and his wife out, as we needed the room they occupied, but the law was the law. There was no way she could get rid of them.

One day I was peeling potatoes in the kitchen and Mother had her hands in flour when the insurance man came to the door.

Because Mother's hands were floury I answered the door and showed him into the kitchen.

'Oh, Muriel, would you mind going up to my chest of drawers and fetching my insurance book from the top left hand drawer, please?'

I ran upstairs and into her room. At the back of the drawer I found a long envelope which I pulled out. It was the only item in the drawer that wasn't clothing so I assumed it was the book. But to my astonishment there was a London postmark on the envelope. I realised immediately that it couldn't be the insurance book, it was a thin letter. My curiosity got the better of me and I opened it.

190

The crest and address on the letterhead bore into me ... it was from Buckingham Palace!

I scanned to the bottom of the page ... it was from Queen Elizabeth (The Queen Mother)!

Then I read it. The gist of it was that the Queen was sorry to inform my Mother-in-Law that she could not interfere in regard to her son marrying this English girl!

I was numb. In a flash everything made sense now. My intuition, Aunty Fena ... both had been right. Mother had hated the thought of Werner marrying an English girl so much that she had even written to the Queen, asking for help in stopping our marriage!

My God, I thought, how Mother must hate me deep down. I knew I could never, ever trust her now. Certainly I would never be able to get close to her, as I had hoped might happen eventually.

Quickly I replaced the envelope in the drawer. Realising I must have gone to the wrong chest of drawers, I went over to the other one, where I found the insurance book and took it downstairs. While Mother dealt with the insurance man I went to the shed to watch Father dyeing his blankets. He looked up, smiling warmly at me.

'Hello! Is Werner home yet?'

'No, not yet.'

'This is thirsty work!'

'Would you like a cup of tea then?'

'That would be lovely, Muri.'

I went into the kitchen and made a cup of tea for Father and myself. I didn't make one for Mother. I didn't feel I could ever do anything for her ever again.

When Werner came home I asked him to come up to our bedroom.

'What is it, *liebling*,' he asked as he sat beside me on the bed.

I had brought the letter from her drawer to show him.

'It's your mother.'

'Oh dear, what has she done now?'

'I was right, Wern, she does hate me for being English, she didn't want me to marry you.'

'I've told you before, that's nonsense.'

'Is it? Read this then!'

He read it. He was furious. I knew that look on his face. I hadn't seen it since I told him about Frank's advances at the railway carriage in Ollerton.

He stormed downstairs with the letter in his hand and me at his heels. I was petrified about what he would do.

'What the hell did you do this for?' he shouted at his mother, waving the letter at her.

She burst into tears.

'How dare you interfere in my life. How could you do this? How do you think my wife feels about it? It was a wicked thing to do!'

Father came running in, wondering what all the shouting was about. As soon as he saw the letter in Werner's hand a look of sudden understanding came over his face.

'I told her to burn that letter! I told you you would only cause trouble if you tried to interfere.'

Now, with both the men in her life shouting at her, Mother collapsed in a melodramatic heap. Father got her to her feet and helped her upstairs to her room. I couldn't feel sorry for her.

Five minutes later Father came down again, said Mother had had a turn and went to get the doctor.

It was the same horrible doctor who had attended me. I had hoped I would never have to lay my eyes on him again. When he came downstairs after examining Mother we were all in the kitchen: Father, Werner, I and the judge and his wife.

'It's that young madam's fault,' he said and turned to me. 'You have caused your mother-in-law's illness by mentioning some letter,' he turned to the others, 'but what can you expect of the English? They have absolutely no regard for the feelings of others.'

The judge and his wife nodded in agreement. I burst into tears and Father hugged me. Werner showed the doctor out.

After that episode I begged Werner to find us a room, somewhere else to live. I just couldn't stay in such an atmosphere. He understood my

192

feelings now and went so far as to check at the mayor's office.

I told Father we wanted to find a place of our own and that Werner had gone to enquire about it.

'It would be for the best,' he said. 'Mother is too possessive of Werner.'

But when Werner came home he was very downcast.

'I'm sorry, Muriel, but there is just no hope. There's no accommodation available anywhere. It isn't even available for some German couples, who are at the top of the list, let alone for us.'

It was then I realised my being English was a major factor preventing us finding a place of our own.

Mother was somewhat contrite when she finally felt well enough to get up. She suggested that we take over a little side room that had been used for storage and have it as our own private dining room. I could cook Werner's meals, instead of her cooking for us all, and we could eat separately in there.

I suppose it was a step in the right direction but, as it turned out, it didn't work at all. Yes, I would cook Werner's evening meal and we would sit eating it together in our room, but then Mother would come in with a pancake or some such treat, that she had cooked especially for her son.

Time and time again I heard Father tell her she shouldn't do this but she never took any notice.

Life became a terrible strain for me and it was obviously showing. Werner did his best to try and make me cheerful but he was struggling against the odds. Really he was powerless to change our situation. To me it began to look as if everything was against us. For the first time ever I began to have doubts about whether our marriage would work and that perhaps our relationship had been fated from the start.

'*Liebling*, I have a surprise for you,' Werner told me one day. 'Put your best clothes on, we are going out for the day to Wiesbaden where there are some lovely shops.'

Just the thought of getting out of the house and being alone for the day with Werner really gave me a lift. I put on my smart dog-tooth patterned jacket, styled my hair nicely and we set off on the train to Wiesbaden.

We spent some time looking in shop windows. There were some lovely things even though there were still shortages. Of course everything was very expensive and many items you could still only get with coupons.

I looked at the mouth-watering cakes in one window.

'Oh, I'd love one of those, Wern.'

'Yes, don't they look good, but we haven't got any coupons, *liebling*. Never mind, we'll go to a good place I know for coffee.'

I knew, as soon as we walked in, it was going to cost a bomb. It must have been the most exclusive place in Wiesbaden at that time to have coffee and gateaux. But coffee and gateaux were what we had and they were exquisite. It was the first good cup of coffee I had tasted in Germany and the gateaux was delicious, enough to fill me up for the next couple of days. I felt really pampered. And I really loved Werner for wanting only the best for me.

I could have walked on air for the rest of the month after that treat. Little did I know that Werner had an even bigger surprise in store for me.

'Come on, *liebling*, there's a special shop I want to take you to,' he told me after he paid our bill.

We walked briskly along the street; Werner knew exactly where we were going but I remained mystified.

'What kind of shop is it, Wern?'

'Wait and see, *mein liebling*.'

I couldn't imagine what it might be ... until we found ourselves standing outside a jeweller's.

'Now, *liebling*, you know I always meant to buy you a proper engagement ring, to replace that old nail one, when I had enough money. Well, today is the day. You can choose any ring in the shop.'

'Oh Wern! What a lovely surprise!'

'Come on, let's go in. Remember you can have whichever ring you like.'

I didn't have to look very far before my eyes alighted on a very pretty solitaire diamond ring. I knew that was the one I wanted but I guessed it would probably be too big for me.

'May I try that one?'

The assistant took it out of the case and I tried it on. I couldn't believe it, it fitted me perfectly.

'Oh, this is absolutely perfect, Wern. I would love this one.'

'Are you sure? Wouldn't you like to try any others?'

'No, this is the one for me.'

'All right, darling.'

I gave him a hug. Then he held my hand out and admired the ring on my finger.

'You are right. It really suits you. It's lovely.'

Werner paid for the ring and we set off up the street again. All the time I kept looking at the ring. I couldn't take my eyes off it. Having that on my finger made me feel a million dollars. Werner spoke then and reminded me of something I had put to the back of my mind, I had hoped forever.

'You know, if you think anything of me you'll put your wedding ring on your right hand.'

'I'd forgotten all about that, Wern.'

Inside I was suddenly in a turmoil. How could I refuse him when I knew how much it meant to him? I still felt superstitious about taking off my wedding ring to put on the other hand. But how could I refuse after he had bought me such a beautiful engagement ring?

'I'll think about it, love,' I told him sincerely.

'All right. I'm just popping in the Gents' over there before we catch the train home.'

'All right, I'll wait here.'

When he had gone I thought for all of two seconds. It was now or never. I would do it for Wern. It meant so much to him. I twisted my wedding ring round and round my finger until it came off and I replaced it on the other hand. There! The deed was done! Such a simple, quick operation which would mean the world to Wern. I prayed it wouldn't cast a cloud over mine ...

195

When he came back I didn't say a word about it. We walked to the station and sat on the platform to wait for our train. It wasn't until we were on the train and almost back to Kriftel that Werner looked at my hand.

'You've done it, *liebling.*'

He had that lovely smile of his and his eyes danced with joy.

'Yes, I did it while you were in the Gents'.'

Since being in Germany, and especially in the last few weeks, I hadn't seen that smile of Werner's half so often as I did when we were on our own together in England. At that moment I felt my simple gesture, which went so much against my better judgement, had been well worthwhile.

CHAPTER 17

For me the day in Wiesbaden had been like an oasis in a never-ending desert of hunger and tension. I knew Wern and I loved each other deeply, but would that be enough to see us through all the terrible difficulties facing us?

I began to hope we would have a baby. With Werner away working all day a baby would distract me from my loneliness. But who was I fooling? How could I think of becoming pregnant when there wasn't enough for me to eat? What sort of an undernourished child would I produce?

One day, when Werner had gone off to work, Mother told me she was going to the underground caves at Zielziem, where the Jews sold cheese and butter on the black market.

'I'll come too,' I said.

'No, you can't. Werner wouldn't like it. It's illegal, Muriel. Sometimes if the police come we have to run.'

'That's all right. I can run fast.'

'Well, if you really want to I suppose you can come, but don't tell Werner whatever you do.'

'No, Elise, don't take Muriel. Think about Werner,' Father said.

'I'll be careful,' I told him.

'Well, I tell you Werner won't like it if he finds out.'

Mother and I set off regardless, together with a friend of hers from up the road. We had to catch the train from Kriftel to one stop further on and then get out and backtrack over some fields until we came to the caves. There we managed to buy half a pound of cheese and a quarter pound of butter each. We were so pleased. Cheese and butter were like gold to us.

When we got home it was after five o'clock and we could hear the judge and his wife in their room. Father was out collecting hay with his waggon. On realising this, Mother rushed out to the bottom of the garden. I knew what she was doing. She was checking to see if the hens had laid. If ever Father, Mother and I happened to be out at the same time when a hen laid an egg, the judge or his wife would make sure they got it. Usually we arranged it so that there was always someone in. Sometimes if Mother felt a hen in the morning and found it was going to lay that day, she would wait in until that egg was laid for fear of the judge and his wife getting it. That is how desperate we were for food.

Often I'd be so hungry I'd go into the garden and pick some raw greens to eat, so the cheese and the butter really were a boon.

When, a few weeks later, Mother said she was going to the caves again I said I would go too. We went through the same conversation as the last time about Werner not being happy if he found out about it. But nevertheless I went.

We had just got to the caves when someone shouted that the police were coming. Without having bought anything at all, we took to our heels and ran.

'Come on, Mother. If we keep close to the hedge we won't be seen!'

Mother staggered behind me and finally we came out on a road. Once on the road we walked slowly, to look innocent. It was then that the police car passed us and fortunately they didn't look at us twice.

I never went with Mother to the caves again. Danger had come too close for comfort for me. I knew how ashamed of me Werner would have been if I had been caught. A little bit of extra food just wasn't worth the risk, I decided.

My days became endlessly tedious, waiting for Werner to come home in the evenings. Sometimes I would walk Heidi over to Aunty Fena's or cycle over to Uncle George's. One day when I arrived at Aunty Fena's she said: 'Today I'm going to show you how to make a pair of rabbit-skin slippers.'

'Oh, poor thing,' I thought as she placed the rabbit skin and a sharp knife in front of me on the table.

198

But I cut it as she directed me and then stitched it. By the time the slippers were finished they actually looked lovely but I knew I could never wear them. Only a few weeks ago her son had shown me that rabbit running about and I had cuddled it!

When I got home that afternoon I heard Mother talking to a woman friend of hers in the kitchen. I went in to meet her.

'Is this your English daughter-in-law then?' she asked.

'Yes, this is Muriel.'

I shook hands with the woman, who was gaunt and sour faced. She didn't smile, in the same way that the doctor hadn't smiled.

I decided to go up to my room and leave them to it. I paused in the hallway to take off my coat and couldn't fail to hear the woman's next words to Mother.

'I thought you were going to write to the Queen of England to stop it?'

'I did. But she did nothing, as you can see.'

I shot upstairs with tears in my eyes and went straight into Mother's room to get that damn letter. Furious and trembling, I stood there with it in my hands, fully intending to tear up the wretched thing. But I couldn't. It was Mother's. There would be hell to pay if she found it missing when she wanted to show it to someone. I put it back in her drawer and went to my room sobbing.

Werner found me there when he came home.

'Whatever is it, *liebling?*'

'Your mother again.'

'What? Tell me.'

'She's been gossiping to a friend of hers about that damn letter from the Queen.'

'Forget it, Muriel. You know we've had it all out with her.'

'I know, but the bad feeling goes on, Wern.'

'I'm so sorry.' He put his arm round me and kissed me gently. 'Look, why don't you have a day out in Frankfurt tomorrow? You could come with me on the train in the morning. Remember to take your passport document, though. You should always take that. You don't want to end

199

up being carted off to the Russian Zone!'

So the next day I travelled on the train to Frankfurt with Werner. He went to work and I went window shopping. The shops were beginning to look better stocked and I really enjoyed looking around. Or was it that it felt so good to be away from that house for the day?

When I went underground to the toilets at the station, before catching the train home, I heard two girls talking near me.

'We shall have to sell it or we can't pay our rail fare!'

'Let's ask her.'

'Would you like to buy this little clock? It's a musical clock,' one of them asked me.

I looked at it. It was quite a pretty little clock and I loved musical trinkets.

'How much do you want for it?'

'Four marks.'

It seemed very reasonable so I bought it. I felt quite good about it, realising I had helped the girls to buy their tickets, or so I thought ...

On the train, on the way home, it crossed my mind to listen to the tune the clock played. But the carriage was packed with people and I felt embarrassed to play it in front of them all. I would play it when I got home, I decided.

As soon as I got into the kitchen I put the clock on the table and switched on the tune.

I heard Mother charging down the stairs, two at a time.

'Turn that thing off!' she screamed as she came into the kitchen.

I was so shocked, I turned it off at once.

'Whatever is the matter?'

'That's a Fascist song!'

She swept the clock off the table and took it upstairs. At that moment I was totally unaware of the implications of having a clock that played a Fascist tune. I went up to my room to change, feeling very subdued.

A little later I heard the front door open and Werner come in, and I heard Mother running downstairs and telling him about the clock before he had even had time to take his coat off.

When he came in our room he was laughing. He came over to me and hugged me.

'What have you been up to now, my darling?'

'I don't know. Please tell me what's wrong with that clock. I don't understand why Mother is so angry.'

'All Fascist songs are banned, *liebling*. If you were caught playing that musical clock you would be thrown into prison!'

'Oh my goodness! Thank heavens I didn't switch it on on the train coming home!'

'Yes, thank heavens you didn't! Come on, I'll show you what we are going to do with that clock.'

He led me by the hand into Mother's room, picked up the clock and took it out into the garden. With Father's five-pound hammer he smashed that clock to smithereens.

'I'll buy you something else, *liebling*.'

'Something musical?'

'If you insist.' He took me in his arms again, 'I love you more and more every day, Mrs. Palmer. Do you still love me?'

'Of course, you know I always will.'

'And soon there may be three of us, eh?'

'Maybe!'

My period was three days late. Werner obviously knew this. He was keeping as close a check on my dates as I was.

That Sunday we all went to church, as we usually did. And, as usual, I prayed that things would improve for Wern and I. My prayers always included a special plea for a place of our own.

As we walked back home I felt an unwelcome, familiar sensation. My heart sank. Sure enough, when I got home I found my period had started. Werner noticed my unhappy face as I came downstairs.

'Anything wrong?'

'Not really. I've started my period.'

'Never mind. There's always next month.'

The following week Werner bought me a lovely manicure set that was also a musical box. It played a Viennese waltz.

201

When I came back from visiting Aunt Fena one afternoon that week, Mother told me an English lady with a baby had come to see me, hoping to make friends. My heart leapt. I didn't know any English people at all and the prospect of making such a friend filled me with hope.

'Oh, did you get her address?'

'Yes, she lives in Hofime and is married to an American.'

The next day I went to visit Mrs. Rutha. She welcomed me warmly. It was so good to talk to another English woman. She was quite a lot older than me and had two other children as well as the baby. She was plump and happy and a little old-fashioned in her dress. We arranged that I would go every Tuesday afternoon to talk to her and play with the baby. She became like a mother to me. I could talk to her about all the things I couldn't talk to Werner's family about. I held nothing back about how difficult I was finding it living in Germany, and not having a place of our own.

'Would you like to go back to England, dear?'

'Yes.'

There. It was out! I had said it! And from that moment on I realised that was what I really wanted to do. I knew I couldn't make it in Germany.

'I suppose it wouldn't be quite so bad if Wern and I had a place of our own, but it seems to be impossible.'

'Would you like me to ask my husband if he can help to find you somewhere?'

'Oh, yes please.'

'Leave it with me. I don't promise anything but at least he can try.'

Mr. Rutha tried very hard for us but it really was quite impossible to find accommodation. He had no luck at all.

After a few months Werner got his teaching post. He became even happier now he was doing the job he had trained for and I became more and more depressed, feeling an utter misfit in Germany, despised and abused by so many and having no home I could call my own.

I suggested to Werner that now he might be able to get us a schoolhouse.

'Huh!' he laughed. 'Everyone wants a schoolhouse. All they get is a schoolroom.'

There seemed no hope at all and I was so close to utter despair.

'Why don't you try and get a job, dear?' Mrs. Rutha advised me.

'There really isn't anything I could do round here, being English.'

'Oh, yes, there is. I know an American family who would like an English daytime nanny for their three boys. How would you feel about doing something like that? They'd pay quite well. All they really want is someone to speak English to the children all the time.'

'Well, I like children. It sounds wonderful!'

'Shall I fix you up an interview with them?'

'Yes, please.'

That evening I asked Werner if he would mind if I took a little job and told him about the one Mrs. Rutha had mentioned.

'If it would make you happy, *liebling*, you do it. You have been so down lately.'

I went to the interview a few days later. The three little boys seemed quite angelic when I was introduced to them. I was told there would be no housework involved, just preparing a snack for the boys' lunch and generally caring for them the rest of the day. There was a German girl also employed by the family, who was responsible for all the housework.

When I was asked if I would like to take the job, I said 'Yes' without hesitation.

Originally the hours were to be 8.00 a.m. until 4.00 p.m. but the reality of the job proved to be totally different to what I had been led to believe.

After just one week I had discovered that the boys were not angels but demons. The German girl just did a bit of hoovering and dusting and spent the rest of her time with her Italian boyfriend. My work pile increased every day with the lady of the house asking me ... 'You wouldn't mind doing the washing for me today would you? ... oh, and the ironing ... oh, and could you possibly cook the evening meal as well? ...'

By the end of two weeks I found myself working solidly from 8.00

a.m. until 8.00 p.m. and getting home utterly shattered in the evenings.

'Muriel, you are looking so tired,' Werner said to me. 'I should pack that job in.'

So I handed in my notice. The job had done nothing for me at all, except earn me a little money with which I bought some nice blue material to have a suit made.

By Christmas Werner had earned enough money from his teaching job for us to go on holiday.

We travelled by train and then coach to the ski resort of Mittenwalde. We were to spend three magical weeks here at the Post Hotel. For me that three weeks was like something out of a fairy tale.

The first night we were shown into our room with shuttered windows looking out on the snow-clad mountains. There was a pot-bellied stove roaring away to warm the room.

'It's the custom to wash with the ice-cold water outside,' Werner told me. 'I suppose it's no good asking you to join me?'

'No!'

'All right, *liebling*, I'll have a jug of hot water sent up for you!'

We went to bed early and left the shutters open so that we could look out on the mountains.

'Well, what do you think of it, *liebling*?'

'Oh, Wern, it's beautiful, it really is.'

By morning our room was bitterly cold. The stove had gone out and we had left the window open all night, but we were awoken by a chambermaid bringing us a steaming coffee pot and bread rolls. She stoked the stove into life again and in no time at all the room was beautifully warm.

After breakfast Werner took me to the hire shop to get me kitted out with skis and boots. He was an excellent skier himself and had brought his own skis with him.

'We'll hire your skis for the first two or three holidays,' he told me, 'then if you like the sport we'll buy you your own kit.'

I spent all morning on the nursery slopes, where a few toddlers showed me what to do. Meanwhile, Werner went off to the forest to ski.

I met a few American wives who were also trying out skiing for the first time. We had a lot of laughs and I really enjoyed myself. I knew this was a sport I was going to love. When Werner joined me just before lunch I wondered where the time had gone.

'What, back already?'

'You must be enjoying it then?'

'Yes, I love it!'

He spent about half an hour showing me a few finer points and then we went back to the hotel for lunch.

After a few days Werner told me I was picking it up really well.

It was so wonderful being in that beautiful place in the fresh mountain air. Here, Germans, English and Americans mixed without any hostility whatsoever. For me it was like being in heaven.

On New Year's Eve there was a party at our hotel. We danced until three in the morning and joined in the singing and the thigh slapping. I had never had such a good time in all my life.

Too soon the holiday came to an end. On our last night Werner took me in his arms and kissed me.

'Hasn't it been wonderful, *liebling*?'

'It's been the loveliest time of my life, Wern.'

'Here, I have a present for you.'

He gave me a little box and I opened it to discover a gorgeous silver bracelet.

'Oh, Wern!'

'That's for you to remember the lovely time we had here,' he told me.

'What a shame it's over so quickly!'

'Time waits for no man, Muriel.'

Going home after that holiday I felt fit to face anything. That feeling disappeared as soon as I arrived home. All the unhappiness of the last few months started all over again for me. Again my days seemed endlessly tedious. The tension was still there in the house between Mother and me. There seemed to be no escape.

About once a month I went to talk in English to the boys at a local school. Werner had arranged this for me and I did enjoy that. But, as I say, it was only one afternoon a month.

I decided to write a long letter to Joan. I told her how things were much worse for me here than they had been in England, how we had tried, unsuccessfully, for a baby, how I had taken the nanny job which had turned out to be no good ...

A few weeks later I got a letter back from her. She had no children either ... she was sorry things were so bad in Germany ... would we like to try to get to America, where she felt things would be much better for us?

Her letter gave me real hope. From what she had said it seemed Werner and I would be far better accepted as a couple in America. When he came home that night I put the idea to him.

'How would you feel about going to America to live, Wern? Joan says we'd get on really well over there.'

'No, I don't want to go to America. This is my country and we're staying here.'

Suddenly I broke down.

'No, we're not. I'm going home. I can't stand it here any longer. You've seen all the disdainful looks I get all the time. You know I keep getting all that verbal abuse. I just can't take any more, Werner!'

He took me in his arms as I sobbed.

'You just have to ignore them, *liebling*, you know that.'

'Yes, but I can't.'

'It won't be many years before the war is forgotten.'

'Years! I can't take this for years, Wern! And I can't live in this house any longer. Can't you realise, if we were on our own in England or America it would be so much better for us?'

'*Liebling*, you know I love you. Please don't let this come between us.'

After that outburst I spent a lot of time crying alone in my room. And praying in church ... please, God, even a single room of our own somewhere! But no escape came.

I wrote a letter back to Joan telling her it was hopeless, Werner wouldn't go to America.

The next day I decided to go to Frankfurt, just to get out and to post the letter to Joan.

I set off early in the morning to catch the train. When I got to Frankfurt I was just standing outside the station, wondering which way to go first, when two German policemen rushed up and grabbed me by either arm.

'Come on. You're from the Russian Zone,' one said.

'Get her into the truck,' said the other.

'No! No! I'm English!'

'Huh, they all say that.'

'But I am.'

They dragged me over to a waiting truck which was full of other people they had rounded up to send back to the Russian Zone.

In utter horror I realised I had come out without my passport document. I had no proof I was English!

Out of the corner of my eye I saw an American officer standing a few yards away. I shouted out to him in English: 'Help me, help me! I'm English! They say I'm from the Russian Zone!'

The American officer jumped over and stopped the German police just as they were about to load me into the truck.

'She's not German, she has no accent,' he told them.

By now I was in tears. The three of them marched me over to a prefabricated office and made me sit down.

'Where are your papers?' the American officer asked me.

'I forgot to bring them with me.'

'That's the worst thing you can do!'

'I know.'

'Is there anyone who can identify you?'

'My husband knows who I am.'

'Naturally!'

'He's German. We live at Kriftel. He's a teacher.'

'Which school does he teach at?'

I told him.

'That's a long way out.'

'Oh, please help me!'

'We'll have to get someone from the British Consulate to sort this out.'

A Miss Smith came over from the British Consulate. She questioned me for ages and finally they were all agreed that I was English. After a good old ticking off for coming out without my documents, Miss Smith told me I was free to go. The American very kindly gave me a mug of coffee and then walked me to the platform to catch my train back to Kriftel. Joan's letter was still in my handbag. I would have to post it in Kriftel after all.

I was still in floods of tears when I went into the house.

'What's the matter?' Mother asked.

I told her.

'You silly girl! You should know better than to go out without your documents. When will you ever learn?'

Her tone cut deeply into me.

'She didn't do it on purpose,' Father said, putting his arm round me.

He was so kind. He always supported me and I was very grateful. I badly needed an ally after the terrible day I had had.

When Werner came home of course, his mother told him what had happened. I then got a ticking off from him as well. But I knew his stern words came from his deep concern and love for me. They were not the words of bitter aggravation I had heard from his mother.

CHAPTER 18

As the months turned into almost two years of living in Germany, my constant underlying unhappiness remained. But I found certain events made me oscillate from the deepest despair to moments of real delight. Strangely, my few moments of happiness were always immediately followed by my darkest days. At times I would think back to our life in England and realise this phenomenon had a pattern to it. It had been the same ever since we had first met. One of our happiest times, when we were courting, had been that lovely sunny day by the river in the park in Derby, the day Werner had met Mum for the first time. Everything had been so perfect, so beautiful ... and then, that night, he had been caught and I was thrown into the first real deep despair of my life.

Our longest interlude of happiness had been in our orchard home. Because we had been alone together, we were able to rise above the problems of life ... the shortage of money ... the verbal abuse. And then that had been followed by another period of depression for me ... my long journey to Germany ... my five weeks without Werner again ...

My happiness at Werner's homecoming had been swiftly followed by an agonising ordeal with the unsmiling doctor. Yes, there was definitely a pattern. My moments of real happiness were always when Wern and I were alone together. If only we could get a place of our own. If only we could go to America or back to England ... but I knew Werner would never leave Germany now.

He did try to arrange days for us to be alone together. He would take me out for a day at weekends whenever he could.

'Let's go to the wine festival in the French Zone tomorrow,' he said one Friday night.

So the next day we set off on our bikes and crossed the Rhine on the army 'ducks'. We planned to go to the wine festival and then on to visit one of his aunts who lived in the French Zone.

It was a very hot day and I soon got thirsty with the cycling. So, at the festival, Werner sat me under a tree and got us a glass of wine each. I drank mine straight down.

'Hey, you aren't supposed to drink it that quickly!'

'But I'm so thirsty.'

'Well, that won't quench your thirst. You don't want another, do you?'

'Yes, please.'

We had two more glasses of wine each and ate a few plums Werner had bought. Then it was time to go on to his aunt's. Werner stood up and picked up his bike.

'Come on, *liebling*.'

I stood up and promptly flopped down again. My legs were like jelly!

'Oh, Wern, I couldn't possibly get on my bike, I can't even stand up!'

'Oh, darling!' Werner laughed. 'you'd better lie down and have a sleep for half an hour.'

'Yes, I think I had better.'

I slept for over an hour and when I woke up it was to see Werner's lovely smiling face watching me. He took me in his arms and kissed me.

'*Mein liebling*, are you feeling better now?'

'Yes, I'm O.K. now.'

We cycled off to his aunt's house and spent a couple of hours there listening to his cousin's records. The last one she put on was 'Sleepy Lagoon'.

'I wish that was us on a tropical island,' I whispered to Wern.

'Whatever will be will be,' he said.

I knew then that he was having doubts about whether we were going to make it together. He knew I wanted us to leave Germany for anywhere else. I knew he would never leave. In that moment we both knew I was slipping away from him.

In the following weeks I spent even more hours crying in my room and praying in the church. I began to think our relationship had been doomed from the start. How strange it was that I had prayed to God to help us, that I had longed for a baby and yet it had been when actually coming home from church that day that I had discovered I wasn't pregnant after all. Had that been God's will? Were we not meant to be together? Why was it that two people who loved each other so much were not permitted to live happily together? Why was all the world against us? Was it just because he was German and I was English? After hours and hours of tears and prayers, I could come up with no other reason.

One night Werner came home later than usual and found me sobbing in our room.

'I'm sorry I'm late, *liebling*, but I went to the mayor's office again to see if there was any chance of us getting accommodation. But there was nothing.'

'Wern, are you still certain you won't try America or go back to England?'

'You know the answer to that. Look, there is nothing more I can do, or you.'

But I knew there was something I could do. I could go back to England. I couldn't stand it in Germany any longer. But would Werner follow me if I went? I decided to ask Mrs. Rutha for help and went to see her the next day.

'Of course I'll help you, dear. I'll lend you the money for your fare.'

'If you could just lend me the money for the ferry crossing, I have some possessions I can sell to raise the money for my rail ticket.'

'Whatever you like, dear. I can see what it is doing to you here in Germany and I want to help you.'

'But please don't say anything to Werner about it, will you?'

'No, course not.'

Still Werner tried his best to lift me out of my depression.

'Come on, tomorrow is Saturday, we will put on our walking boots and go climbing in the mountains,' he told me.

211

We went. The fresh air was wonderful. For a day it was like being in a different world, alone with Werner and all the warmth he radiated. But then we had to go back home and I was back in that dark cave of unhappiness from which I could never escape, except for those brief interludes.

Father understood how I felt but, like poor Werner, he was powerless to do anything about the situation.

Then Werner said he was taking me out for the evening.

'I want only the best for you, my darling. Tonight we are going to the opera and then on to the best restaurant in Frankfurt.'

I wore my black evening dress and my pearls. The opera, the music, everything was beautiful. For another brief moment my unhappiness was submerged.

During the interval a man sitting five or six seats from us wanted to pass us to go to the Gents' or something. I stood up to let him pass but as Werner stood the man sort of fell into him, apologised and went on his way.

'Don't get too comfortable,' Werner told me as I sat down again. 'He'll be back in a minute.'

But the man never came back. We forgot all about him and enjoyed the rest of the opera.

Afterwards we went to the restaurant. It was a strange combination of white walls and beams and crystal chandeliers, with cosy nooks for couples to sit at tables. The atmosphere was very, very special. Having already been put in a romantic mood by the opera music, the place seemed just perfect for rounding off the evening.

Werner looked at the wine list and ordered a bottle while I watched three musicians who were playing Viennese waltzes. The waiter brought hors d'oeuvres with the wine and we picked at them as we drank and enjoyed the music.

'Well, what would you like to eat, *liebling*?'

'Oh, Wern, I couldn't eat. I'm too full up with the evening!'

'Me too. I'll order another bottle of wine then.'

'Oh, I couldn't drink any more.'

212

'It's all right. I've ordered a taxi home. You don't have to walk anywhere.'

So we had another bottle of wine and all my unhappiness was totally forgotten. There was nothing in the world except Wern, myself and the music.

When we got up to go, Werner felt in his top pocket for his wallet to pay our bill. A troubled look crossed his face.

'My wallet's gone! I had it. I remember putting it in my pocket before we came out.'

'Yes, I saw you put it in.'

'Oh, my God! It must have been that man who pushed past me in the opera house. He must have taken it!'

'Of course! That's why he didn't come back.'

'How stupid of me not to realise!'

I opened my bag.

'It's all right, I've got some money. We can pay the bill with this.'

Werner looked in surprise at the money I handed him.

'You shouldn't carry that much money around with you, *liebling.* Don't worry, I'll pay you back tomorrow.'

Unbeknown to Werner, I had already sold a few of my possessions. I had begun to get the money together for my journey back to England and kept some of it in my handbag.

The stolen wallet didn't really mar the evening. We had had too wonderful a time to let that spoil it. Our problem had never been to do with money. It had always been to do with what no amount of money in the world could buy ... acceptance by the rest of the world as an ordinary couple, not a German man with an English woman.

And then came the downer after the happy interlude ...

'This weekend we're all going beech-nut collecting in the forest,' Werner told me.

Mother, Father, Werner and I set off at half past six in the morning. We took an old mac each for kneeling on. When we arrived at the forest, the first thing I noticed was the lovely sweet-fresh smell of pines and beech trees. There were many other people already collecting nuts. I had imagined we would be there for perhaps an hour or so, scooping up great handfuls of the shiny brown nuts. The reality was not as I had expected at all. The four of us were on our hands and knees until six o'clock in the evening, scrabbling around to find the nuts which were very few and far between. You didn't speak at all. All day long you looked and concentrated. By the end of the day my back and knees were aching badly and my fingers and torn nails were grim and encrusted.

When we got home we weighed our hoard. I had collected six ounces. The others had managed to muster just over half a pound each.

The next day we set off early in the morning again. Again we spent all day on our hands and knees. Sometime in the afternoon I saw Werner look across to his father. He spoke for the first time since we had started rummaging: 'There's a wild boar, I can smell it!'

Then he looked at me. 'If it charges, Muriel, you have to run. But don't run in a straight line, you have to zig-zag.'

After that I could hardly look for beech nuts anymore. I was too busy looking out for the boar. Thankfully it never showed itself.

That night I was too exhausted even to eat. I just slumped on my bed and thought: 'What a bloody life this is!'

But I said nothing to Werner. Mother and I took the nuts to exchange for highly prized cooking oil. The four of us had worked for two days to gather enough nuts to exchange for just three-quarters of a pint of oil!

It was not long after that that Father dyed a blanket for a man who owned a potato field. In payment, the man said we could go and glean in his field after the potato pickers had been in.

Father thought this was grand, but Mother didn't seem all that happy about it.

'They'll have had the lot before we even get there,' she said.

'No, we'll find some.' Father insisted.

And so Father, Mother and I set off to glean while Werner was teaching.

As soon as we started I realised this was going to be hard work. There was hardly a potato to find. After half an hour my back felt as if it was going to break and I still hadn't found a single potato. Father had found one and Mother had found three. They were the size of marbles!

'Don't get despondent,' Father said.

I kept at it. After an hour and a quarter I found my first marble! Father was right! There were some there to be found. But was it really worth it? That one little potato could never replace the energy I had already expended looking for it.

We spent four and a half hours in that field. Together we collected just under three pounds of marble-sized potatoes.

When I got home I felt very rough and went to lie down on my bed. Mother went off to the hairdressers and I could hear Father whistling in his shed. They were used to this way of life, but I wasn't. I knew I couldn't go on like this. My knees ached, my back ached. I felt a wreck, too exhausted even to eat and yet I was so hungry.

Again Werner found me sobbing when he came home.

'Now what's the matter with you?'

'Werner, I wish we could go back to England. I have no proper diet here. I'm always damned hungry. And getting these spuds today was just the last straw. I can't take any more!'

'You didn't have to go. They're used to it. They could have done it without you.'

'What, and have Mother looking at me reproachfully for the rest of the week? That would be even worse!'

'Muriel, I don't know what is happening to you lately. And I'll tell you something else. I don't ever want to hear about you running from the Jews at the caves again!'

I couldn't believe I was hearing him. How had he found out?

'Please don't tell Mother you know or she'll think I told you she took me.'

But Werner stormed downstairs, leaving our bedroom door open. I heard every word he said to Mother. I heard her crying. I dreaded facing her again because I knew she would blame me for telling him.

As it happened, she didn't. When we were alone in the kitchen later, she told me it must have been the other woman we went with who had told Werner. But she also said: 'I told you you shouldn't have come with me!'

It seemed I never did anything right. I couldn't eat my meal of potato soup that night and went up to my room. I lay on the bed sobbing. Werner came in after his supper.

'Don't be so upset, darling.'

I said nothing. There was nothing more I could say.

'You know we can't get a room or anything. Look, we'll go skiing again next Christmas if you behave.'

'Don't talk to me as if I were a child.'

'Well, don't act like one, crying all the time. You have to grow up. You have to be much tougher than you are!'

Those words cut deeply into me. Werner had never spoken to me so sharply before. But I knew he was right. To face up to life in Germany I did have to be much tougher. The trouble was, to be like that just wasn't in my nature. I knew it and Werner knew it too, and there was nothing either of us could do about it.

Werner was made of tougher stuff than me. I remembered how well he had managed in England. The abuse had not cut deeply into him. He just let it bounce off. And he had always made friends wherever he went. I hadn't made any real friends here, not like my mates I'd left behind in England, who had always given me so much support.

Why couldn't Werner see we would be better off in England? He was so much more adaptable than me.

As the days wore on I was so unhappy I could hardly eat. I could feel Werner and Father watching me with concern, and as I became more hungry so I became ever more depressed. It was a vicious circle and I could find no way out.

I knew what I had to do. I sold the rest of my possessions and went to see Mrs. Rutha. She said she would buy my ticket to England. I could go in about three weeks' time.

Then I went to see the parish priest.

'Do you love Werner?' he asked.

'Yes, I love him with all my heart, but I'm not tough enough to take any more of this life in Germany.'

'But Werner stood it in England. It is your duty to be strong here, for his sake. I can't say things will get better for you. But maybe in a few years' time ...'

I knew I couldn't even take a few more weeks of it, let alone a few more years.

The next few nights I lay in bed tossing and turning, hardly able to sleep at all. Werner would turn to me and say: 'Are you all right?'

'Yes.'

'What's the matter?'

'I just can't sleep.'

Once I said to him: 'Werner, are you sure you won't reconsider about going back to England?'

'No.'

He must have heard me crying.

'Look, I'll think about it, *liebling* ...'

But the next morning he told me he had thought about it and decided it would be stupid to leave the very good teaching job he had here. I was heartbroken.

That day I went to pick up my ticket from Mrs. Rutha.

CHAPTER 19

'Would you like to telephone your friend, Joan?' Mrs. Rutha asked me when I got to her house.

She could see how upset I was about it all and she knew, from what I had told her before, that Joan was my best mate and had always given me a lot of support.

'Oh, do you think I could? I'll pay for the call.'

I knew the phone call to America would be expensive but I was in the money, having sold my possessions, and it would be well worth it to talk to Joan.

So we booked the call for nine o'clock the following morning.

I got to Mrs. Rutha's house before half past eight and we sat with a cup of tea, waiting for the call to come through.

When the phone rang I shot out of the chair to answer it. The operator told me she had Joan on the line for me.

'Hello! Joan, is that you?'

'Yes. Hi, Mu!'

It was wonderful to hear her happy voice.

'So what are you up to, you little clinker?' she asked me.

'I'm going back to England, Joan. I'm heartbroken about leaving Wern but I can't stand it here in Germany any longer.'

'Tex and I knew it would be difficult for you. Oh, I'm ever so sorry it hasn't worked out, Mu. Look, why don't you come over to us?'

'No, I don't think so.'

'Of course! You're hoping Werner will follow you to England?'

'No, I don't think he will. He has such a good job here, he'd be foolish to leave it.'

'He'd be even more foolish to lose you. You two love each other so much. No, he'll follow you all right, Mu.'

'I wish I had your confidence, Joan.'

'He will, you'll see.'

'Look, here I am talking all about me. What about you? What are you up to? Are you happy, Joan?'

'Oh yes. We're just going to move to Pennsylvania. Tex is even fatter than he ever was before. Fat and happy, you could say! We have discovered I can't have children so we're going to adopt. We're adopting a girl and a boy together.'

'Oh, that's lovely, Joan.'

'You aren't pregnant are you, Mu?'

'No. It's not for want of trying. I think it must be because I don't get enough to eat here. Either that or fate!'

'Oh, Mu. I wish you all the luck in the world back in England. Don't worry, I know Werner will follow you. Keep in touch, won't you?'

'Of course. I'll send you my address when I get settled. It's been so good talking to you, Joan. Goodbye!'

'Goodbye, love.'

When Werner got home from school that evening, I asked him if we could go out for the evening to the inn at Hofime.

'I want to talk but I don't want that judge or his wife listening over my shoulder as they always seem to do ... and then repeat what they hear about our private lives to your mother.'

'All right, darling, let's go.'

We walked to the inn, holding hands. When we got there Werner ordered the drinks and we went to sit in a quiet corner.

'It's no good, is it, Wern?'

'No.'

He looked at me straight in the eyes and I saw his deep sorrow and helplessness there. Then he looked into his drink. This was going to be the conversation neither of us had ever wanted to have. He looked up at me again as I went on.

'If we could have gone to another country, or lived on our own here,

219

it might have worked. But everyone seems dead against us.'

'Yes ... well what do you propose doing? I love you. You know that. And I don't want to lose you, but I don't want to beg you to stay if you are going to be unhappy for the rest of your life.'

'I don't want to get divorced, Werner, but I will go back to England and get a job.'

'All right, darling. Forgive me if I don't follow you. At one time I would have followed you to the end of the earth. But I have to be practical. I have a very good profession here. In England there is nothing I could do.'

'And will you forgive me?'

'You know I would always forgive you, *liebling*.'

On the walk home we talked about our courting days and our life in the orchard – as if we both wanted to live in the past.

'Oh, Wern, I'm sure we would have made it if we had stayed in England.'

'No, *liebling*, they were against me there.'

The next day we told Mother and Father that I was leaving. I could see Father was terribly upset about it. Mother said she was very sorry. That was all.

Two weeks later both Father and Mother were in tears as I said goodbye in the kitchen.

For my return journey I just had a small suitcase and my handbag. I had telephoned Mum to say I was coming and she had said she would meet me at the station in London.

Werner took me to Frankfurt station to catch my train at 11.00 p.m. I felt my heart was going to break and was choking back the tears all the way there. We sat on a bench on the platform. Werner had his arm round me as we waited for the train. We didn't speak a word.

How would I survive without him beside me? We were so in love. But the world kept telling us we should be enemies. How could we survive together against such odds?

And then I was on the train. Werner had stowed my case in the luggage rack above my seat.

'I won't say goodbye, Wern, only *au revoir.*'

He swept me into his arms and held me tighter than he had ever done before.

'I can't help it, Muriel. I love you so much!'

He jumped off the train just before it began pulling off. I watched him disappear down the platform until he was just a dot. As I sat down in my seat all I was sure of was how much I loved Wern and how much he loved me. As to the future? Well, that lay in the laps of the gods. There was nothing more I could do to save our marriage. To me it looked as if the world had won. I thought back to that first day I had met Werner in the depot. What was it I had said to Joan? ... 'I like the look of that interpreter' ... and what had she replied? ... 'You'd better stop that thought right there before you get into trouble!' Yes, right from the very beginning it had been obvious to the rest of the world that this was a love affair which should never have started. And yet ...

I drifted into sleep. On the return journey I had no fears about anyone stealing anything from my luggage. I had little enough of it. All the money I had was safe in an inside pocket of the coat I was wearing. I slept on and off for most of the sixteen-hour journey to the Hook of Holland.

Mum was there to meet me as I stepped off the train in London. She seemed very pleased to see me. She gave me a big hug and kissed me. I was pleased to see her too, but I remembered she was part of that world which said Werner and I shouldn't be together. She had never given me any real support, like Joan and Audrey had.

'Why isn't Werner with you?' she asked me in rather a suspicious tone.

'Well, I'm not going to pretend and lie to her anymore,' I thought. 'From now on I'm going to be absolutely straight with her.'

'I'll tell you when we get on the train to Derby, Mum.'

When we were comfortably installed in our seats I thought, here goes: 'I'm coming home for good, Mum!'

'What about Werner?'

'He might come and he might not.'

'My God! You aren't pregnant, are you? What about our neighbours?

221

They've been through the war, you know!'

How typical of Mum, I thought sadly, to be more concerned about what the neighbours might think than what was happening to Werner and I.

'Oh, Mum! What about Werner and me? In a way we're casualties of that war.'

With that she said no more. I think she did feel for me, but for a woman of her high moral and religious principles she obviously found herself in somewhat of a dilemma. Well, Mum needn't worry. I wanted to be independent. I wouldn't be an embarrassment to her. The very next day I would look for a job and a flat.

When we got home I said I was too tired to sit talking, I just wanted to go straight to bed. Peggy had got married and no longer lived at home, so there was no-one else to greet me.

As soon as I got in my room I saw the window – the window I had climbed through so often late at night, when Wern and I were courting. And now I had lost him!

I couldn't take any more. I flopped on my bed in floods of tears and cried until about three in the morning, when I finally fell asleep.

I slept until ten o'clock. When I awoke I knew what I had to do. Thank heavens I had something to do or I think I would have just faded away with a broken heart.

I went downstairs for breakfast.

'Mum, I'm going out to get a paper and look for a job and flat. I won't unpack. There's no point, so please don't unpack for me.'

'How do you know you're not pregnant?'

'Because I had a period last week! And it's nothing to do with you or the neighbours!'

'Don't get uppity with me!'

I went down to the café in the Strand and sat drinking a coffee while I waited for the paper boy to come along. As soon as I saw him I rushed out and bought a paper. I walked briskly towards home and then decided to go and sit in the arboretum to read it. I scanned the columns and found a flat for rent. The deposit was £30. Where could I get that amount of money? I couldn't ask Mum. I didn't want to be beholden to anyone. I did have some German marks to change. That would give me about £20. I was determined to give Mum some money, perhaps £5, so somehow I would have to find at least another £15. Well, I had a few more possessions I could sell. I didn't want to part with them but I had no choice.

I went home and had lunch with Mum and then I went out to the phone box. I didn't want her to hear me arranging about the flat.

The man on the phone told me it was a two-roomed flat above a shop. It was furnished and had a gas stove and a toilet. Would I like to go and see it that afternoon?

I went straight down. The flat didn't look all that good and it had an unpleasant smell, but I thought I could paint it up and wallpaper it. At least it would be a place of my own. The rent was 25s. 0d. per week.

'I'll take it,' I said. 'Look, I have to go to the bank,' I lied. 'Will you take this £10 now and I'll bring you the rest tomorrow, plus the first week's rent?'

'Good enough. You can move in as soon as you like after tomorrow.'

'I've got a flat, Mum!' I shouted as I took my coat off in the hall.

'Goodness, that was quick! Most people can't get them! Army blokes returning from abroad find they have to stay with their in-laws, you know ... and that's not such a bad thing,' she said, wiping her hands on her pinny as she came out of the kitchen.

Oh, wasn't it! Well, I knew what living with in-laws was like, but I didn't say anything.

I spent an hour or so gathering together all the things I thought I could sell, then I took them up to a secondhand shop I knew of on the Normanton Road.

'Good afternoon,' I said to the man behind the counter. 'I wonder if you would like to sort through this box to see if there is anything you could sell? I've been clearing out some of my clutter.'

'Yes, I'll have a look. Won't take long.'

'Well, I have another errand to run. Do you mind if I leave it with you

223

for half an hour or so and I'll call back later?'

'If you like.'

I went out and bought the evening paper and took it to a café, where I sat down with a coffee to scan the columns again.

There, I saw a vacancy for an usherette/cashier at the Alex Cinema. Well, I could do that! I knew I could. Without even finishing my coffee I rushed out of the café and shot along to the cinema. There, I was shown straight away to the manager's office.

'I've just seen you have a vacancy for an usherette/cashier.'

'That's correct. Do you want to apply?'

'Yes.'

'Do you have any experience?'

'As a cashier, yes. I'm good with figures. As an usherette, no, but I'm sure I'd pick it up quickly.'

'Yes, I'm sure you would. Let's just see how you are with mental arithmetic. Would you mind doing these few sums for me?'

He handed me a sheet of paper with some sums printed on it. They were very easy and I did them in no time at all and handed the paper back to him.

'Very good, my dear! The salary is £3 15s .0d. per week. Can you start tomorrow?'

'Yes, I certainly can!'

So now I had the means of being independent! I rushed back to the shop in Normanton Road, just before it closed. The man said he would pay me £18 for all my things. He paid me with a crisp £10 note, a dirty £5 note and three filthy £1 notes!

The next day I took the money to my new landlord.

'You can move in as soon as you like,' he told me.

Mum was amazed at how quickly I had found a job and a flat. I would have been too, if I'd had time to stop and think about it.

I booked a taxi and moved into the flat the same day. Then I spent a few hours cleaning it out with disinfectant. When I took the mattress off the bed to clean the springs underneath, I discovered it was badly soiled. So that was the unpleasant smell I had noticed!

I went and asked the landlord to come and look at the mattress.

'Oh dear, that is bad,' he said. 'I'll get you a new one.'

Actually he got me another secondhand one, but it looked clean. To be on the safe side I disinfected it all over and stood it by the gas fire to air while I slept on the floor for a couple of nights.

During that first month I managed to buy some cheap cream-coloured paint with my wages and spent my days painting up the flat, before going to work in the evenings. Because the paint was cheap it took ages to dry, but the place was already looking nicer.

I wrote to Joan to send her my address and tell her about the new life I was making for myself. I wanted to write to Werner but thought I would wait to see if he would write to me first.

The second month I bought some cream wallpaper. I had never wallpapered in my life before but I was determined to give it a go.

And it was during that second month that I received a letter from Werner. It had been redirected from Mum's. Why had she redirected it, instead of bringing it round to me straight away? I couldn't understand. I tore it open and read:

'Darling, I shall be arriving any day. I have your address. Your mother sent it to me. Werner.'

I suppose I must have always known he would come. That must have been what motivated that determination in me to set up a place of our own to live, so that if he did come we could be on our own. Have a real chance! I was ecstatic! I went and told my boss my Dutch husband was coming home. Could I have a couple of days off work?

'As long as you don't make a habit of it every time he comes home,' he said.

'Oh no! He's coming home for good!'

I spent all day until 8.00 p.m. wallpapering the bedroom. I wanted it to look nice for when Werner arrived. The wallpaper seemed to be going up beautifully but when I had finished I noticed there were gaps between the edges. I daubed my brush with paste and pasted over the gaps to make the edges stick better. That would be all right!

I went to bed that night feeling very satisfied. Two hours later I was woken by a bang on the door. I stumbled out of bed wondering who on earth it could be.

It was Wern! He had arrived by taxi.

'Oh, my darling,' he said as he took me in his arms.

We held each other for ages. It was as if neither of us could believe we were together again, as if we couldn't let go for fear of losing each other again, but eventually we went inside and I made us a drink.

'I've been papering the bedroom today, Wern. It'll be nice to wake up to tomorrow.'

'You are a wonder, Muriel. It's so good to see you looking so happy.'

'Well, of course I'm happy ... now you're here! I've got a little job as an usherette/cashier at the cinema. We can be completely independent now, Wern. Oh, I just know everything will work out for us now you are here, darling.'

'It will if I can get a job.'

'Oh, you will. I know you will. Thank you so much for coming, Wern!'

'Well, how do you think I could live without you, *mein liebling*? I think you knew I would follow you?'

'Not really. I wasn't sure. Joan was. But I ... well I was beginning to feel our relationship had been doomed from the start.

'I know, that's what I was beginning to think.'

'But now we can start a new life. Everything will be fine.'

'As I said. It will if I can get a job teaching.'

There was no need for any more words. We went to bed.

Some time later I woke up to discover Werner laughing.

'What is it?'

'Look at your wallpaper!'

I looked. There were terrible strips where I had tried to join it. The whole room looked like a disaster area!

'Oh no!'

He kissed me and then broke off, laughing.

'Don't worry, *liebling*. I'll do it again tomorrow. And I'll do the living room as well.'

Werner and I were happy again. In those first few days we revisited all our old haunts. He bought me flowers for our table. It seemed everything was going to be all right now for us.

'Tomorrow I'm going down to the labour exchange to find a job,' he told me.

'Well, don't forget to tell them you're Dutch.'

'Oh, *liebling*, why must we lie all the time?'

'You know we have to, Wern. I was lucky to get this flat. If I had told the landlord my husband was German I would never have got it. It's the same with jobs. You know how it is.'

'But I hate all this lying.'

The next day Werner came back from the labour exchange very disheartened.

'There are no teaching jobs at all. And I had to register as a German. There was no avoiding it.'

After a few days a friend of mine told me a man at the council offices was looking for language teachers. I told Werner about it.

'It's no good, *liebling*, they won't employ a German.'

'Yes, they will. I know they will.'

'How do you know?'

'Because I know the man,' I lied.

Somehow I had to get him down to the council offices. He had to give it a try.

So we went. While we waited in the reception area I went in to see the man.

'Would you be interested in a teacher who speaks fluent German and French?'

'We certainly would! Why, do you?'

'No, but my husband does. He's waiting outside.'

The man went out and asked Werner to come in.

'What nationality are you?' was his first question.

'German.'

'Oh, I'm sorry, sir. We can't employ Germans. You must understand the position. It really is quite impossible. Maybe in three or four years'

227

time ...'

'It's all right. I quite understand,' Werner said. 'Come on, Muriel, let's go home.'

After a few weeks I could see how unhappy Werner was becoming. He would sit in the cinema where I worked, watching the same film over and over again. He couldn't get a job. He had no money of his own. It was truly terrible for him. And then, at last, he was given a position in an I.C.I. laboratory. There he was very good at his job and passed all his exams with honours. For a few months things began to look better. He wasn't teaching but at least he had a job. But gradually he began to realise other, less able, people were getting promotion and he wasn't. They were English! A friend told him it was the same with the Irish. They could never expect to get promotion. Again Werner began to get disheartened. Finally he became despondent. He reached that rock bottom level I had reached in Germany. I understood exactly how he felt.

After weeks of not seeing that smile on his face that I loved so much, I knew it was time for a serious talk.

I postponed it for days, remembering the last 'serious talk' we had had in the inn in Hofime that had resulted in our parting ...

But one day Wern came home from work and had nothing to say. He sat at the table and ate the meal I had prepared, without a word.

I couldn't bear it any longer, I had to say something to break the ice. We couldn't go on like this. The problem had to be discussed.

'Oh, Wern, if only we could be missionaries somewhere on the other side of the world, where our nationalities really didn't matter!'

'*Liebling*, you can see how I am. I know you understand how I feel. Please, please come back to Germany with me, will you?'

'I couldn't go through all that again, Wern. Now you must understand how I felt there.'

'Darling, I always understood.'

'What are we going to do, Wern?'

'*Liebling*, all I ever wanted was to make a good life for us together, to give you all the things you deserve. I have always wanted only the very best things in life for you. The only place there is any possibility of me being able to provide for you like that is in Germany, where I can earn a good living as a teacher. I have to go back, Muriel.'

'Oh, Wern, I could never go back!'

He came over to me and pulled me up out of the chair and into his arms. First he kissed me. Then he held me gently. Then he spoke.

'Tomorrow I will give in my notice at work and arrange my passage back to Germany.'

I couldn't speak. All I knew was that I could never follow him there as he had followed me to England. From the way he was holding me, like a butterfly he was afraid of crushing the life out of, I knew he knew that too.

I suppose I must have felt the same way he felt when I told him I was coming back to England. When you really love someone, you can't bear to see them unhappy. I didn't want him to go, as he hadn't wanted me to go then. But I couldn't beg him to stay and watch him continuing in his misery day after day, as he hadn't begged me to stay in Germany, knowing how unhappy I was there.

One morning I woke up and felt for Werner beside me. He wasn't there. In a panic I remembered this was the day he was going back to Germany! Sounds in the other room told me he was making a pot of tea. I got dressed and went to join him.

We didn't look at each other. We didn't talk. I sat down at the table and Werner poured the tea for us. We drank it in silence.

When I had finished mine I looked into his eyes for the first time that morning. They were full of tears, and when he saw me looking at him the tears began to spill.

At that I felt my own eyes filling up.

'Please, Werner, don't say goodbye to me. I just couldn't bear it. I'm going to go out shopping now. Please just go while I'm out.'

'I can't leave you like that!'

'Please, Wern, do it for me. I'm heartbroken.'

He looked away from me.

'All right, my darling.'

229

I grabbed my coat and bag and went out without looking at Werner again.

For two hours I wandered around the shops, hardly aware of what few little items I was buying. All that time I was in a daze ...

When I got back to the flat there was no sound to be heard. Had Werner gone? I checked the bedroom. He wasn't there. I checked all the drawers. Yes, all his things had gone ...

I remembered his face as I had last seen it, with the tears spilling from his eyes: that lovely face I knew I would never see again.

Some time later I received a little card from him. It read:

'Muriel, to love and be loved
is the greatest joy on earth.
Yours always, Werner.'

THE END